The Longer The Fall

By

Aviva Gat

The
Longer
The
Fall

Prologue

"She'll be the first female president."

"And to think the first female president will be a Republican!"

"We've been waiting for someone like her."

"She's our Obama, our very own Rockstar politician."

"She's too pretty to go all the way."

"And too perfect. No one's life is that perfect. Just look at her husband and kids. Don't they just make you jealous?"

The members of the crowd couldn't stop themselves from commenting during the applause. They were in awe, in full admiration. Some allowed themselves to wonder if she were too good to be true, but most shook their heads and smiled while thinking about how history was being made right there in front of their eyes. There was no question about it, Madeline Thomas had something special about her. A star quality. A twinkle in her eye that quieted all your nerves and made you believe. Even the most ardent skeptics couldn't ignore it. Even they would have followed her wherever she went.

But of course the higher you are, the longer the fall. And Madeline was still climbing higher and higher, straight to the top. And she could have made it there. She could have made it all the way into the history books. She had lived her life with her eyes at the peak, knowing that every step that didn't bring her closer was a wasted stride. Every move was carefully calculated to help her achieve her ambitions. Except... except one. A misstep, a falter. If you closed your eyes you may have missed it. Or it's possible it never happened at all. The misstep could have been fabricated by the forces trying to bring her down. Because there were many forces against her. People jealous of her image, people who resented a woman of her ambition and promising future.

The problem is, ironically, that when there are so many eyes on you, the truth is harder to see. And once people think they see something, it's almost impossible to convince them otherwise.

Chapter 1

Madeline stepped into the wings gracefully after finishing her speech. The roar of the crowd followed her, possibly getting louder as she disappeared from their view.

"Madeline, that was wonderful, just perfect, you nailed it," Jane said, holding her bluetooth at her ear as though she were afraid it might fall out. "Now we have exactly 27 minutes to get to midtown where you are meeting with the Israeli ambassador. We need to hurry."

"Thank you, Jane," Madeline responded calmly, obviously not feeling the urgency her chief of staff was trying to transmit. "What about staying to mingle for a few moments? I'd like to talk to the students."

"The students?" Jane's could not have been more surprised had Madeline suggested they ride an elephant downtown to their next stop.

"Well, this is Columbia University, isn't it? There must have been some students in the auditorium. When I used to go here, the CRNC would always meet up after these kinds of events to discuss our thoughts. We always appreciated it when the speaker would come say hello. Surely the CRNC reserved one of the classrooms here."

"We don't have time for the College Republican National Club!"

"We should," Madeline responded. "They're the new generation of voters."

"Madeline, we can't keep the ambassador waiting," Jane said while forcefully putting her hand on Madeline's back to guide her out. "You remember, Mr. Zahavi, so impatient. It's imperative we're on his good side." She leaned in a little closer and continued in a whisper. "People don't become presidents without support of the Israelis."

Madeline smiled at Jane, giving a look that Jane immediately understood. It was the look that meant Madeline had made up her mind and while she respected Jane's hard work and difficult planning, Madeline's desires trumped all. "It will just be a few minutes," Madeline said, making her way from the wings into the halls of the auditorium building. Spectators filing out of the auditorium already filled the walkways. Madeline smiled at each one, causing jaws to drop and conversations to silence as the spectators gleamed in her presence.

Lucky for Jane, none of the spectators approached Madeline, allowing the senator to easily weave her way through the parting sea of people as she headed down the hall lined by empty classrooms. Madeline peered inside each room, absorbing the echo of debates, lectures and heated discussions that surely had taken place just hours ago. In one of the classrooms at the end of the hall, the echo was less faint. In fact, it wasn't an echo at all. Rather it was the enthusiastic speech of

4

inspired students, who still carried ideals and believed the world could be changed.

Madeline went straight to that classroom. The noises reminded her of her own days as the president of the CRNC. Of the time when her own eyes were filled with ideals. It was then that Madeline knew she would be a politician. She would join a corrupted system, she knew, but her ideals were stronger than most, and she believed changing the system would have to come from the inside. Twenty years later, she still held her ideals tight, although now behind layers of thick skin and transactions that she knew were necessary on the path to change.

Walking into the classroom was like walking into the past. Madeline could see her own college colleagues standing and recounting the evening. There were the students whose hearts stirred with desire to do something, who were ready to become disciples. On the other side were the skeptics, the ones who said the speech was too idealistic and change like that could never happen—not in a hundred years at least. Even the skeptics had ideals, they just weren't strong enough to pursue them through adversity.

"Well, what did you think?" Madeline said as she made her way into the room. The heated debate that had already been kindled, quieted momentarily.

"We're behind the New Republican movement!" a young blonde woman said. "I think it's exactly what this country needs. There isn't a party for people with our beliefs, and the Republican Party will surely die out if it doesn't change with the times."

"I'm sure there are enough bigots in the country to keep supporting the Republican Party," a young man with a crew cut said. Surely he was one of the skeptics. "We would need all the young people of this country to unite behind the New Republican movement in order for it to take over."

"Our generation must ensure those bigots aren't taking over our party," said another young man. "The New Republicans will make the Republican Party the party for young people again. We'll stop being the party associated with old white men."

Madeline smiled as the students volleyed their views back and forth. These students were the reason her movement had gained traction, the only chance for the New Republicans to survive.

"I'm so sorry, Mrs. Thomas, we didn't offer you anything to drink," another young woman stepped forward offering Madeline a paper cup.

"Oh, we don't have time for a drink," Jane yelled from the doorway. "We really should get going. Thank you so much for your support!"

"Thank you," Madeline said to the girl who offered her the cup. "What do you all think about the SAVER Bill that I am proposing?"

"It's very controversial," the first woman who had spoken up declared. "But I think it's exactly what this country needs right now."

"I agree this country needs to change on this issue," said the skeptic. "But you can't legislate away racism."

During Madeline's speech that night she had introduced a new bill that she was sure she could push through congress: the Sensitivity and Volunteering to End Racism Bill. On paper, it was a bill that Republicans and Democrats could support: it didn't increase government regulations and it proposed a solution to one of the country's biggest issues right now. Although politics was much more than about what was on paper. Madeline knew she would have to fight tooth and nail to get the support the bill needed. Under the SAVER Bill, police department that applied for federal grant money would need to undergo racial sensitivity training and complete 100 hours a month of volunteering in uniform in schools where the students were mostly minorities. Madeline believed that if police officers and minority students got to know each other in a classroom setting, then some of the animosity between these two groups could be settled.

"Well something has to be done about it," said the young woman who had given Madeline the water. "We can't just sit back when the country is rioting every time a minority is killed by a police officer. I think it is a very brave bill to propose."

Brave was right. Madeline had spoken to a few of her colleagues in the Senate about the bill. Many were afraid to support something so

7

controversial. Senators with vast support from the police unions knew this could harm their reelection; while others believed police departments needed more funding, not more hurdles to getting the limited funding they were already receiving. But Madeline wasn't worried about police support. She had spent months thinking about what she could do as a Senator to help resolve this conflict. She believed in her solution and she believed she could make others see the benefits of it too.

"Very brave, indeed," Jane said. She had entered from the doorway and had her hand on Madeline's shoulder. "We really must be going! Thank you again for your support!"

This time, Madeline gave Jane a quick nod before turning back to the students. "Thank you all for your support. It truly means a lot to me. I wouldn't be able to do what I do without the support of students like you." After shaking a few hands and smiling for several pictures, Madeline allowed herself to be led out by Jane. The two women almost sprinted through the halls to the back entrance of the building where Madeline's Lincoln was waiting to take them downtown to the meeting with the Israeli ambassador.

"Brandon called during the speech," Jane said once the car had begun moving.

"Why didn't you tell me?" Madeline responded, grabbing her personal cell phone from the pouch that Jane carried for her.

"I'm telling you now. It was something about Noah, I think his school called again," Jane said. Madeline had already dialed Brandon's number. As important as her politics were, a call from her husband took top priority.

"Madeline," Brandon said when he answered the phone. "How was the speech at Columbia?"

"Fine," Madeline responded. "Jane said something happened with Noah? His school?" She could hear Brandon sigh that she imagined went along with him brushing his hand through his thick brown hair.

"He got in a fight again," Brandon said. "Mr. Kendrick called. Molly picked him up."

"Oh, he is at home?"

"He's been suspended again."

"He needs to be in school," Madeline responded angrily. "They can't just suspend him every time something happens."

"I think they don't know what else to do with him."

"I'll talk to him when I get home," Madeline said curtly. "Are you still at work?"

"Yes, I told Molly I would try to make it home for dinner today, but it is going to be tough. We have that big release coming up and I expected things to be in better shape by now."

"I understand."

"When are you coming home?"

"We're meeting the Israeli ambassador now and then we'll fly back to California. I'll be home late tonight. But I'll have breakfast with the kids."

"All right, love you," Brandon said. Madeline repeated his sentiment before hanging up the phone.

"Now, regarding the meeting with Mr. Zahavi," Jane started as soon as the phone was away from Madeline's ear. "He wants to discuss you visiting Israel with your family."

"We're going to a meeting to discuss me going on vacation?"

"It's not a vacation," Jane responded. "It means the Israelis believe you to be influential and they want to create strong ties with you."

"I'm a first-time Senator from California," Madeline said. "I'm hardly influential in Middle Eastern politics."

"They believe you will be," Jane said. "And if you want to be, it's also good to have their support."

Jane began listing possible discussion topics for the meeting with the Israeli ambassador as their car weaved through the crowded streets of Manhattan. Madeline was listening with one ear while she looked out the window, recognizing the streets she used to run down when she lived in Manhattan. She starred closely at the brownstones, studying the ones with beautifully trimmed rose bushes and shrubbery out front. The perfect shape of the greenery made Madeline smile, putting old memories into her head. But she couldn't let herself get lost in those memories. They were from so long ago. Before she had made any mark on this world. Before she had so much to lose.

Chapter 2

A full three hours of sleep in her own bed was enough to leave Madeline feeling refreshed. She'd slept on the plane the previous night after her meeting with Mr. Zahavi, but that sleep was just about bodily needs. The three hours in her own bed, next to Brandon's rhythmically breathing body, refreshed her mentally. When she woke up, though, Brandon was gone. He had been going to the office early those days. He said the few hours before the employees came gave him some time to get his real work done.

She walked downstairs to the kitchen, where Molly, their nanny, was already flipping pancakes. "Good morning, Mrs. Thomas," Molly said. She never called her Madeline, no matter how many times Madeline invited her to.

"Good morning, Molly," Madeline responded while grabbing herself a cup of coffee from the pot that Molly had already brewed. "Are the boys up?"

"They'll be down in a few moments," Molly said. "Noah didn't want to get up, saying he didn't need to if he wasn't going to school, but I made him understand that suspension is not vacation."

Madeline smiled at Molly. She wasn't just a nanny; she was a member of the Thomas family. She'd been with them part time since Noah was born 10 years ago. She moved in full time when Adam came two years later.

"Mommy!" a chorus rung out when the boys came hurdling into the kitchen. Noah and Adam ran to hug Madeline just as Molly placed two pancakes on each of their plates on the table that was already set with cut fresh fruit, syrup, and glasses of orange juice.

"How was New York?" Adam asked. "Can we go with you next time?"

"It was a busy trip," Madeline said, kissing her sons on their foreheads. "We'll all go together one day when I'll be there for more than 24 hours." The boys each sat at their spots at the table and began to eat their breakfast. Madeline also helped herself to a plate of Molly's delicious pancakes. She made it a point to eat with her boys as often as she could, even though that was usually just a few times a week.

She spent her weeks flying back and forth between Washington DC and California. When she was elected, she and Brandon had discussed moving to the DC, but together they decided that it would be too difficult on the family. The boys had friends and were studying in a good private school that would prepare them for the Ivy League educations they were destined for. Brandon's company was doing well and needed its CEO at the office full-time. They agreed to discuss their location in the future should Madeline get elected a second term.

As they ate, Adam told Madeline about how they were learning about the California Gold Rush in school. "Do you think there is still gold in the water here?" he asked his mother. "Or did they already find all of it? Maybe we can go look for some on the weekend!" On Madeline's other side, Noah sat quietly, eating his pancakes and rolling his eyes at his younger brother's excitement.

"All right, boys, it's time to get in the car," Molly said. "You too, Noah, even though you aren't going to school, you're coming along for the ride." Noah let out a big sigh and rolled his eyes for the tenth time that morning.

"You know what Molly," Madeline said. "Noah can stay here with me this morning. We'll hang out until you get back."

"I'll be doing a grocery store run and a few other errands before I get home," Molly said. "It might be a couple hours."

"That's fine, I'll tell Jane I'm busy this morning."

"Oh, I don't think Jane will appreciate that," Molly said with a chuckle.

"She'll be fine," Madeline smiled back. She knew she needed to talk to Noah, he needed his mother to listen to him, to support him, maybe even scold him for his recent behavior. After Molly left, Madeline sat quietly at the kitchen table with Noah. She suddenly remembered how he looked as a baby, so fragile, his pale skin almost translucent in the light. He had such an innocent smile, one that melted Madeline's heart even after a sleepless night. She wondered what happened to that boy. How he turned into someone who got into fights in school, someone who made other children afraid and other mothers judge Madeline relentlessly. *It's because she's never around*, the other mothers said. *It's what happens when you're raised by a nanny.* Madeline was sure she had heard the other mothers saying these things at school functions, but Brandon insisted it was all in her head. *You need to stop judging yourself*, he always told her. *You're an amazing mother, and you're setting a great example for the boys.* Of course, Madeline wanted to believe him, but it simply couldn't be true. If it were true, why had Noah been labeled as he had? Why had his actions led to him receiving that label? Madeline had a hard time even thinking of that word, the word the other mothers called her son. It made her cringe, made her feel like a failure, made her angry at Noah. Noah, the Bully.

"Do you want to tell me what happened yesterday?"

"It was nothing," Noah said. "Can I go back to my room?"

"Mr. Kendrick didn't think it was nothing," Madeline responded. "How about we go out for ice cream?"

"Mom, we just had breakfast."

"So what? If I buy you ice cream, you won't eat it?"

Noah let a smile escape his lips. Madeline motioned him to follow her and they walked together to the driveway where Madeline's car was waiting. Noah jumped in the front seat and Madeline entered the driver side. She liked driving. It gave her a sense of control that she always missed when sitting in the backseat being chauffeured around while she worked. When she drove, she had a clear view of what was ahead. She could choose which routes to take, and she sometimes preferred the longer ones if it brought her past a park she used to bring the boys to, or the old restaurant where Brandon had proposed. She could drive by the restaurant now if she wanted, on the way to Noah's favorite ice cream store. It would only add five minutes to the drive, but it would bring hours of calmness to Madeline, reminding her of why she loved her husband.

"Buckle up," Madeline reminded her son before she reversed out of the driveway. Noah sat silently looking out the window as she drove. Madeline weaved through the streets of their Southern California neighborhood. She turned left when it would have been faster to go straight so she could pass the restaurant she wanted to remember. It was a small Italian place run by an immigrant family from Tuscany. Madeline remembered the wine cabinets that lined the walls and the smell of crispy cheese that always wafted through the dining area. The restaurant had closed many years ago. Today it was a pizza parlor, a much more casual setting where teenagers came in bathing suits after the beach to grab a slice. Although there were still remnants of authenticity corked into the walls. Surely no one but Madeline recognized those.

"Mom, you're going the wrong way," Noah whined when Madeline turned. "It's straight and then a right."

"Of course, sweetie," Madeline responded. "My mistake."

"It's a good thing you have a driver when you're working," Noah said. "Otherwise you'd probably get lost all the time and miss all your events."

Madeline laughed. "You're right." A few minutes later they pulled into the parking lot where the ice cream store stood. The storefront was dark and empty.

"It's closed!" Noah whined. "Mom, you wasted our time."

Madeline looked at the storefront. She should have checked, she thought. What kind of ice cream store is open so early? But next door was a small coffee shop that was alive with business. Women in sports attire were entering and exiting with paper cups and brown bags.

"Let's go in there," Madeline motioned to Noah. "I'm sure they have desserts."

Noah agreed begrudgingly, and followed his mother into the coffee store. Sure enough at the counter was a glass case full of cakes and pastries that immediately drew Noah in. He approached it and placed his hands on the glass as he studied his options.

Madeline ordered herself a second coffee and the cheesecake slice Noah had requested. "It's not ice cream, but I guess it's OK," Noah had said to

17

Madeline regarding his choice. *Poor boy,* Madeline thought to herself sarcastically. *What a difficult life he has! Being forced to give up ice cream for cheesecake!* Sometimes she wished her boys grew up differently. With a few more hardships. Not too many that they struggled in school or went to bed hungry. Just enough struggles that they would be able to understand the privileges they had.

Madeline took her coffee and Noah's cheesecake to an empty table in the coffee shop. Once they were sitting down and Noah had eaten enough of the cake that the sugar would have already changed his mood, Madeline decided to bring up the topic from earlier.

"Do you want to tell me what happened at school yesterday?"

"Nothing happened," Noah said, forking another bite into his mouth. "It was nothing, everyone is just making such a big deal."

"Why do you think everyone made it a big deal?"

"Because Jamie cried," Noah said. "He's such a baby."

"What made Jamie cry?"

Noah shrugged and continued eating silently.

"Did you say something to him before he cried?"

"I told him to stop being a baby."

"Why did you say that?"

"Because he was being a baby!"

"Madeline Thomas?" Madeline was just about to ask Noah another question when their conversation was interrupted by a blonde woman wearing leggings and a down vest carrying a tray of four coffees. "I'm sorry to bother you."

"No problem, yes, how can I help you?" Madeline immediately put on her politician smile and looked at the woman as though she were sure she would say something profound.

"I just wanted to say I really admire you," the woman said. "I saw parts of your speech on the news last night. I think your proposal is very smart. It will help get minority communities to respect the police more. Education is the key to reduce the altercations that have been happening."

"Thank you," Madeline responded, keeping her politician face on. "I do feel very strongly that my proposal can bring understanding to both sides of the issue."

"Yes, definitely," the woman said. "Once the blacks start respecting the police, things won't be so problematic."

"And when the police respect the communities they are supposed to protect," Madeline added, saying it in such a way that made the woman feel that it was her own idea as well.

"Of course! Of course!" the woman said. "Well I don't want to bother you. But I just wanted to tell you how much I'm rooting for you! You are an inspiration to all women. Can I get a picture?"

"Thank you, of course," Madeline responded and stood up to lean into the woman as she held out her camera to take a selfie. After the camera clicked, the woman hugged Madeline and went on her way.

"Do black people not respect police?" Noah blurted out.

"What?"

"That's what the woman said, isn't it?"

"Well there are two sides to every story," Madeline responded.

"The police are the good guys," Noah said.

"They are supposed to be good guys," Madeline said. "But sometimes they are not." Madeline looked around the coffee shop before turning back to Noah. "Can you tell why you called Jamie a baby?"

"He sucks at basketball and I didn't want him on my team. So I told him he couldn't play. And he cried."

"Do you think that what you said could have hurt his feelings?"

"There are two sides to every story," Noah responded, repeating his mother's words from just moments ago. Noah put the last bite of his cheesecake in his mouth and stood up from the table. "Can we go home now?"

Just then Madeline's cellphone rang. Her phone was never on silent and never out of reach. You never know when someone important might be calling or when you would receive news that could change everything. Madeline reached into her purse and pulled out her phone, seeing that it was Jane on the line.

"Good morning, Jane," Madeline answered.

"Madeline, good morning," Jane responded. "When are you coming to the office? We need to discuss your response to Senator Shuker's abortion bill. His chief called this morning and Shuker wants to meet with you on it."

"I don't support his bill," Madeline cut in.

"Well he wants you too, maybe it can be leverage for him to support the SAVER Bill. He doesn't support your bill either."

"I can't support any bill that adds restrictions to abortions."

"We need to discuss it. Also we're scheduling a meeting with the head of the FOP," Jane said. Surely Madeline's new SAVER Bill would receive backlash from the Fraternal Order of Police union. But Madeline needed to meet with the FOP leadership. She could explain to them why she needed their support. "Where are you?"

"I'll be in soon," Madeline responded as she stood up and walked with Noah back to her car. She drove the shortest way home, skipping a longer route that would have taken her passed a small park with perfectly pruned shrubbery that reminded her of a place she used to spend time at in New York.

They arrived back home before Molly. Madeline parked in the driveway, noticing that the mail had been delivered while they were out.

As Noah ran up to the front door, Madeline went down to the mailbox, emptying the contents. She shuffled through the mail as she walked to the house. There was the usual junk mail – the mailers from different stores, the notices that she had been pre-approved for new credit cards. But stuck in the middle of all the junk was a large envelope addressed directly to Madeline. The envelope looked unassuming, like something ordinary, rather than something that was about to change her entire life. But that's how these things always start; unexpectedly, during the most mundane activities such as checking your mail.

Madeline opened the front door of her house, letting Noah shoot inside. She then dropped the junk mail in their recycle bin and took her letter to the kitchen. If only she had known then that she was opening Pandora's box. That once the letter was opened, there would be no turning back.

Chapter 3

"Lauren, I need to speak with Brandon right away," Madeline said to his secretary when she answered the phone.

"He's in a board meeting right now, they just started," Lauren responded. "You know these things can take hours, especially with all the changes happening at CyTech. I can slip him a message that you called."

"He'll want to know," Madeline urged Lauren. "It's urgent. I need him to come home as soon as he can."

"I'll pass the message along," Lauren responded.

When big things happened in Madeline's life, Brandon was the first person she consulted. They made decisions together; it was one of the most important things in their partnership, one of the things that made their marriage work.

When they first met, it was as though they were destined to be together, betrothed by their elders, brought together by forces greater than themselves. Some could say it was almost an arranged marriage, if that sort of thing still happened. Madeline remembered the first time she heard the name Brandon Thomas. She had just been elected Chairman of the New York Young Republican National Federation. She had become involved in the youth organization after graduating from Columbia where she had been president of the College Republican National Committee Club. It was only logical that she would continue her support of the party in the YRNF. Three years out of college and she had won her first election to be the organization's New York Chairman.

One of the first orders of business as Chairman was a congratulatory dinner with the local GOP leaders. During what was most definitely the most expensive meal she had ever eaten up to that point in her life, she listened to stories from her elders discussing the different conventions to attend and the behind-the-scenes fun in which she would eventually partake. They told her stories of doing keg stands with George W. at the White House and about the affairs between senators that surely helped them pass the most controversial bills. Madeline joked around with the table of older, white men, who had all remained respectively flirty throughout the night. Then out of nowhere, one of the men said, "You know who Madeline has to meet?" The question was addressed more to the table than to Madeline herself. The table quieted and looked at the man who had asked the question. "Brandon Thomas!" His exclamation was met with enthusiastic confirmations all around. *How did I not think of that? What a great idea! How is it possible you haven't met yet!? They must meet as soon as possible! You two would just get along perfectly! Should I call his parents? Get him on a flight over here now?* Madeline had tried to ask who Brandon

Thomas was and why it suddenly seemed imperative that she meet him. All she got was that he was her counterpart in California, leading the YRNF on the country's other coast. Surely Madeline had many counterparts she should meet. In fact there were at least 49 other state chairmen for the YRNF, but none of the others were mentioned. The only important one was Brandon, leading a YRNF chapter in one of the country's most democratic states. After that dinner, Brandon did not take a flight straight over to New York to meet Madeline, but his name kept popping up wherever Madeline would go.

At a fundraiser to help New York Republicans running for Congress—a lost cause that still received wide support mostly due to Madeline's planning of an extravagant event—someone mentioned that her idea for tax reform reminded them very much of what Brandon Thomas had told them at a different event earlier that year. *And Brandon Thomas certainly understands tax reform, he recently founded that new software company that will revolutionize the way corporations secure their financials. Such a smart young man!* At a networking event for young Republicans on Wall Street, someone mentioned drinking wine at the Thomas vineyard with young Brandon. *He's so articulate and ambitious, much like yourself!* The following year, when Madeline had shown up without a date to the YRNF Christmas party, someone had asked her why she still hadn't met Brandon Thomas. *You two would be an unstoppable force! A power*

25

couple that could accomplish even the impossible. She nodded politely, not mentioning that she wasn't looking for the other half of her power couple.

At that point, Madeline had begun getting sick of the name Brandon Thomas. Everyone seemed to know who he was and everyone had something good to say about him. If she didn't know better, she would have thought he was a prophet from above, rather than the California Chairman of the YRNF. Whenever his name was mentioned, she just smiled and tried to stop her eyes from rolling before quickly changing the conversation.

That all changed when she finally met Brandon Thomas. The next year at the National Convention of Young Republicans she came face to face with the spirit who had seemed to follow her everywhere over the last couple of years. It happened at the opening cocktail hour, when many of the convention guests were still arriving, but those with stamina and ambition were already there, working the floor. She saw Brandon Thomas across the room and knew it was him without ever having seen a picture. He was tall, with broad open shoulders that looked inviting and strong. His lips were permanently curved up, as though his natural expression included a warm smile. His brown hair was perfect styled, parted on the side and brushed back. He held a glass in his right hand, which he periodically brought to his lips, taking the tiniest sips, to give the illusion that he was drinking while he nursed the same cocktail throughout the night. Madeline recognized this trick, as it was something she too would do at these events. No one likes to mingle with someone who doesn't drink, but in the presence of people who could make or crush her career, Madeline would never get drunk.

Brandon had caught her staring at him and his already curved lips arched a little more. As he walked over to her, Madeline took a fake sip of her own drink—a gin and tonic that was already watered down from the melted ice.

"Brandon Thomas," he introduced himself, sticking his hand out to shake Madeline's. "I don't believe we've met."

"Madeline Clark," she responded, giving his hand a firm shake.

"You're Madeline Clark?" He gasped. "I expected a halo, or some sort of aura to be surrounding you." He moved his head around as though looking for something.

"On me? I could have said the same thing about you, based on what everybody seems to be saying."

"I'm actually surprised you're a real person," he continued. "I was beginning to think you were just a legend, or Wonder Woman."

"Who says I'm not?" Madeline joked, taking another fake sip of her drink.

"True, it is definitely still possible, or maybe even probable that you are Wonder Woman," Brandon said.

During the rest of the convention, Madeline and Brandon were inseparable. They sat next to each during different lectures and speeches, discussing the speakers' merits and what they would do differently. During social hours, they mingled near each other, often sharing a look when one was caught in an unbearable conversation. When they stood near each other, they often received comments from other convention attendees. *You two look marvelous together. I can't believe this is the first time you've met! The Republican dream team!* Madeline reveled in the attention. She loved feeling like a part of something bigger than herself and she loved that people saw her as such a force to be reckoned with.

When the convention ended, they headed to the airport to return to their respective coasts. After passing through security Brandon waited with Madeline at her gate because her flight would take off first. There hadn't been a lull in their conversation throughout the trip and their conversation continued animatedly until it was time for Madeline to board.

"Come to California," Brandon said as they stood face to face. It wasn't a question. It's debatable whether it was even a suggestion. It was more a statement, something that surely was inevitable in Madeline's path. Madeline smiled in response and then Brandon kissed her.

It was their first kiss. There weren't fireworks or butterflies in Madeline's stomach, but it was a good kiss. A solid kiss that sealed their partnership much like the way two children might prick their finger to mix their blood for an oath of undying friendship. Then Madeline got on her plane to New York. She spent the entire trip reminiscing over the weekend and daydreaming about what a future with Brandon could be like. His parents and family were long time GOP supporters, who donated significant amounts and had the ears of Washington DC in their cell phones. Brandon himself was no less impressive, having founded his own software company with a couple friends after finishing his Master's in Business Administration from Stanford five years ago. The company's software was now considered a 'must-have' for corporations all over the world, allowing them to manage financial data securely. Brandon was no doubt the driving force behind the company's success and had been named one of the top 30 under 30 by every business and political media outlet that Madeline had ever heard of.

The next month she and Brandon spoke daily on the phone. They often spent hours talking, until Madeline—whose time zone was three hours later than Brandon's—ultimately announced that she needed to get at least some sleep before she had to get up in the morning for her own job working as a project manager at a large business consulting firm. When the month ended, she had successfully negotiated a transfer to her company's Southern California office and had gracefully given up her beloved position as the Chairman of the New York Young Republican National Federation. She had every confidence

29

that her vice Chairman would be able to step up and complete her duties as well as she had. While the other members of the YRNF chapter were sad to see her go—they declared that no one else shared her enthusiasm and her ability to solve problems before they arose—they understood why she was leaving. They could see that she and Brandon *belonged* together. She belonged with Brandon much more than she could ever belong in New York.

And that was that. She gave up her Midtown apartment and packed what she could carry on a plane. The rest of her things were shipped to Southern California where they would arrive at her new home with Brandon. Brandon met her at the airport with the largest bouquet Madeline had ever seen and then he drove her to his apartment, where he had already cleared out half of his closet. He told Madeline to feel free to change any of the design in the apartment, even suggesting that they go furniture shopping together to find a new bed, couch, dining table and whatever else to make sure the apartment didn't feel like Brandon's. It was no longer Brandon's apartment; it was *their* apartment.

Madeline didn't need to replace all of the furniture. She agreed they should get a new bed, one in which she wouldn't feel like she was on a roller coaster every time Brandon rolled over at night. She also added several houseplants, abstract paintings on the walls, and replaced a few light fixtures. Even before making her changes, Madeline was impressed with Brandon's good taste. The apartment already was well designed, but with her changes it felt like home.

Madeline quickly fell into place in her new life. She became close with Brandon's parents, who welcomed her into their home and family debates. His father held a PhD in economics and served as a political consultant to the last four presidents and his mother was a top oncologist who was specially sought out by the country's wealthiest sick. Family dinners often revolved around debates on the country's healthcare or economic state. Madeline felt at home debating with the Thomases and they appreciated her perspective and obvious passion for policy.

Madeline also fit right into Brandon's social circle. Many of his friends were also members of the YRNF and they too had heard of Madeline before she had moved to join their chapter. She quickly became a leader in the organization and bonded with other women in their circle. Life with Brandon appeared perfect to all who looked in on them. They were both ambitious, intelligent people who were obviously destined to do great things. On a personal level, they were both good-looking, friendly, and appeared like they fit together perfectly. No one could say a bad word about them.

It wasn't long before Brandon proposed. They were out to dinner celebrating Madeline's recent promotion to director at her consulting firm. Brandon ordered the Italian restaurant's most expensive bottle of champagne and when the waiter brought the glasses, Madeline's had a shiny diamond ring inside. Brandon had secretly invited their friends for an engagement party in the private room at the back of the restaurant. Once Madeline slipped on the ring, they joined the group that was already celebrating their future union.

Madeline was thinking about that time while she waited at home with the letter in her hand. Life was so simple back then. She and Brandon were ready to conquer the world and everyone believed they could do it. Years went by and Madeline still believed she could do it, but here in her hands was the first threat to her ambitions. Someone was trying to stop her from achieving, stop her from reaching the top.

Her phone suddenly buzzed and she looked over to see a text from Brandon. *Got your message. Cut the board meeting short. Home in 15.*

Brandon was nothing if not reliable and dedicated to her success as much as to his. They would solve this new dilemma together, just as they had solved all previous ones. On her own, Madeline wasn't sure what could be done. But with Brandon, the other half of her dream team, she believed this was just an obstacle. A hurdle she could jump without looking back. There was no way something so trivial could ruin everything.

Chapter 4

Madeline was still sitting at the kitchen table with the letter in her hand when Brandon walked in the front door. His face was white, and lines of worry ran down from his eyes to his cheeks.

"Madeline? Is everything all right? What happened?" he started saying even before he entered the kitchen where he knew Madeline would be sitting. That's where she sat when pondering difficult subjects. That was where she sat when she first decided to run for senate in California six years ago. That was a dire decision, one that wasn't borne from idealistic enthusiasm and inspired optimism. When she made the decision, she knew her chances were slim—after all, a republican had not won a senatorial seat in California in more than 20 years. She knew that most likely she was running a losing campaign, but she felt driven to do it anyway, knowing she was running her family through the biggest obstacle they would ever meet. She knew running would throw a few stones through her solid relationship with Brandon and she knew it would build the foundation for the wall between her and her sons. But sitting in the kitchen, at her spot across from the window, she decided to do it anyway. Her heart was heavy when she decided to run, but it was something she had to do. For herself, and for her country.

"We need to talk," Madeline said, sitting in her same spot across from the window. "You should probably sit down." Brandon did as he was told and waited patiently for Madeline to gently unfold the letter and place it and the enclosed picture down on the table.

"I'm being blackmailed," Madeline began.

"Blackmailed?" Brandon let a smile break through his lips. "That's it? I was worried it was something serious. I thought something happened to you or, I don't even know. Lauren had me so worried when she came into the board meeting to deliver your message."

Of course Brandon wasn't worried. The two of them had always discussed the importance of ensuring there were no skeletons in their closet, no fodder for hungry journalists or opponents trying to bring them down. How could somebody possibly blackmail them if there was nothing to hide?

"What are they saying? And what do they want?" Brandon asked, looking down at the typed letter that Madeline had placed on the table.

"They want $1 million," Madeline responded. "Otherwise they will release proof to the media that I cheated on you."

"That you cheated?" Brandon almost laughed. Their marriage was the envy of everyone they knew. Magazines had even written profiles on them about what a perfect couple they were, how they lifted each other up, provided unending support for each other's ambitions, and held hands like teenagers first discovering love. "Don't they realize that no one would believe them?"

Brandon then grabbed the picture that had been wrapped in the letter. It showed Madeline walking into the entrance of the Langham Hotel in New York City. The Fifth Avenue hotel was where Madeline always stayed on her visits to New York. It was centrally located and accommodating for the security and entourage that Madeline had been forced to travel with since entering the world of politics.

Madeline recognized when the picture was taken by the red suit she was wearing. It was two years ago. She was in New York giving a speech to The WISH List. Standing for Women In the Senate and House, the organization helped pro-choice women in both political parties get elected to national office. The WISH List had greatly helped Madeline six years ago when she first started her senate campaign and she had supported them after her win, championing their cause and helping to mentor other women that the WISH List assisted. She knew her association with them was controversial within her own party. Most of her colleagues were not pro-choice, and if they were, they tended to keep their mouths shut about it. But not Madeline. She believed there was room in her party for others of her belief and that if the party didn't evolve with the times, they would become obsolete. In fact, during that speech she gave to The WISH List two years ago, she championed the slogan "It's our party too," calling other young female republicans to come forward to fight for their beliefs.

Madeline remembered how energized she had felt after that speech. Women on both sides of the political spectrum applauded her. Some republican women even admitted that she had inspired them to come forward. In the picture of her, walking into the Langham just hours after that speech, were two other people: the hotel doorman, easily recognizable from his black and red uniform; and a tall African American man wearing a short sleeved blue plaid shirt passing by on the sidewalk. In the picture, Madeline's head was turned toward the doorman and the two of them held obvious eye contact.

After studying the picture for a few moments, Brandon looked up to Madeline. "Are they saying you slept with the doorman?" From his expression, Brandon obviously saw this as hilarious, absurd. For a moment, a glint of worry passed his face. Madeline thought she saw it, but any expression from him was gone before she could acknowledge it.

"I'm not sure exactly what they are alleging with this picture," Madeline responded. She too saw the absurdity of this image, but she took everything seriously that could endanger her upcoming reelection campaign.

"So what is the plan?" Brandon asked. "Have you talked to Jane? Obviously we're not paying anything to this lunatic."

Madeline picked up her phone to call Jane and explain the situation. The blackmailer wanted the money before Madeline's campaign launch event, which was exactly one month out. At that event, Madeline was to officially launch her reelection campaign for her second senate term. She had invited all her biggest donors, the leaders of her supporting political action committees, some congressional colleagues, state legislators and of course all the local and national media. She could only imagine what would happen should the conversation at that event turn from her campaign to an alleged cheating scandal. Whether or not the allegations were true wouldn't matter. All that would matter was that someone suggested it and from there, all journalists would be scrounging for evidence. Her supporters would doubt the image of morality that she had worked so hard to build. Donors would wonder if their money would be better spent elsewhere. If Madeline wanted to be reelected, there was no way she could allow this allegation to be released. Not before her reelection launch. Not ever.

Thoughts continued to swirl in Madeline's head after she hung up with Jane. Of course, Jane understood all the same things that Madeline did. That if these allegations came to light, truth took a back seat. People love scandal more than they love what's right. Scandals never disappear; they ruin careers, whether or not they are based on truth. Jane had told Madeline and Brandon to stay put, not to speak to anyone else about the letter.

The FBI would be on their way to their house soon to begin their investigation.

Madeline and Brandon sat quietly as they waited. Eventually Brandon stood up and brewed a new pot of coffee, making enough for the team of FBI agents that would arrive soon. When the aroma of coffee filled the air and the coffee machine sighed its signal that it had finished, Brandon poured two cups and brought them to the table. Moments later the doorbell rang and Brandon went to answer. He returned to the kitchen followed by Jane and three agents in dark suits carrying briefcases.

"Can you believe the nerve of this person?" Jane bellowed as she came in. "I mean, if you're going to allege something, it should at least be believable!" Jane sat down at the kitchen table, as did the three FBI agents, two men and one woman, who all introduced themselves. Agent Murray, Agent Hart and Agent Jones were all part of the FBI's special investigations team specializing in political blackmail. Apparently it was something all politicians deal with, usually multiple times, and they were California's specialists in finding the blackmailer. They just recently closed a case for another California politician who was being blackmailed for allegedly taking bribes to support recent legislation. They couldn't reveal the name of the politician, but it was someone very prominent that surely could have had their career toppled had this team not found the blackmailer. The agents said whether the allegations were true or not was not their concern. Of course, if they were true, as they often were, it usually made it easier to find the blackmailer because they would know who was privy to the information.

"Apparently being friendly and greeting a doorman is now cheating!" Brandon exclaimed back to Jane's outburst as he retrieved coffee for all of their visitors.

"The first question we have is whether you have any enemies," Agent Murray started. "Is there anyone who comes to mind who might hate you? Want to end your career? Want revenge on you?"

"Wow, well that would make quite a long list," Jane yelled. "Madeline is a republican senator in California who supports abortion and gay rights! She has more enemies than she can count! Democrats hate her because she took a California senate seat that they usually can count on! Republicans hate her because she doesn't just blindly vote for what they tell her to! Just last week Madeline voted against Senator Collins' bill that added new chapters to the tax code. She was the only republican to vote against it! A few didn't vote and that of course shows they were against it, but Madeline was the only one with guts! Senator Collins was really angry with Madeline. What did he say? *It takes some nerve for a freshman senator to defy party lines.* Could he be behind this?"

"It's possible," Agent Hart responded. "We'll pursue all leads. Is there anyone else?"

"Like I said, Madeline has many enemies in Washington. A lot of people would benefit from her losing her seat," Jane continued.

"Anyone with a personal vendetta?" Agent Jones, the woman investigator, said. "If they are asking for money, it seems to me that it would be less likely to be a political opponent. A political opponent might ask Madeline to vacate her seat or vote a certain way."

"Wouldn't that make it too obvious who they were?" Jane retorted. "It the blackmailer *said vote for bill 1234 or else*, well, then obviously the blackmailer is whoever is trying to pass that bill."

Madeline thought deeply, but she had no names to offer the FBI agents. She was always nice to everyone, tried hard to be respectful, not too offensive to political opponents. She was always professional, never attacking an opponent's personal life or family, sticking solely to politics, to what really mattered to her.

"What about you, Mr. Thomas?" Agent Murray turned to Brandon. "Do you have any enemies? Someone who could be doing this to Madeline to get to you?"

Brandon pursed his lips as though giving this question deep thought, before shaking his head. "We live like politicians, people in the spotlight all the time. We're careful not to make enemies."

The officers stayed for hours, continuing to ask questions that Madeline and Brandon couldn't answer. *Is there someone who may believe that you cheated? Have either of you ever had a stalker or an admirer? Did Madeline remember this doorman that she greeted as she entered the hotel? Had the doorman entered her room at the Langham?*

When the agents finally realized they wouldn't be getting any helpful information by sitting there in the kitchen drinking coffee that had long since gone cold, they stood up to leave. They took the letter and the picture with them and promised to keep the Thomas' apprised of their investigation. They would be travelling to New York to interview all the employees who had worked at the Langham two years ago when the picture was taken. They would investigate anyone who might be running against Madeline for her senate seat. They would even set up surveillance in the Thomas' very private neighborhood to ensure they weren't being watched, nor that were any of their neighbors were showing an unusual interest in them or the investigation.

"We don't have much time," Jane urged the agents as they headed out the door. "You need to find the guy before the reelection campaign launch next month. We can't have this clouding the event or the campaign. It will be hard enough to prove Madeline's success last time wasn't just a fluke. We need to make sure she wins again."

The agents nodded politely and assured Jane that this case would be their top priority until it was solved. They needn't worry, they needn't do anything differently except keep their eyes open for any suspicious activities. By the time the agents got in their car and drove away, it was getting dark. Jane stood at their doorway unsure of her place in this new reality.

"Maybe we jumped the ball on announcing the SAVER Bill," Jane said. "It's too controversial right now, with everything going on. And of course with the upcoming election." Her statement was met with silence from the couple, who was standing in the doorway with their arms around each other's backs. Brandon was rubbing Madeline's shoulder in the calming way he did when he sensed that Madeline was stressed. Madeline focused on the sensation while smiling to her chief of staff.

"The bill is important," Madeline responded. "Especially now. Maybe I'm getting new enemies because of it. But I think the public, the voters, like it. I think they see the benefit and they will support me because if it."

"I just hope they get the chance to show you support come Election Day," Jane responded with a sigh. "I'm sure the agents know what they are doing."

"I'm sure they do," Brandon concluded, inching back into the house. Jane understood the signal and said goodbye, forcing Madeline to promise that tomorrow she would be back to work so they could start lobbying for the SAVER Bill. She had phone calls scheduled with senators who were likely allies on the bill and she would need to fly back to Washington this week for in person meetings with others who would need a little more incentive to support her. Brandon kissed Madeline's forehead as Jane finally left. Then he gently closed the door.

Chapter 5

"You are not going to believe what I heard last night," Jane whispered to Madeline after the plane had reached cruising altitude. The two of them were sitting first class on a red eye to Washington DC. Madeline was tired, ready to close her eyes for the six-hour flight when Jane started talking.

It had been a long day, made even longer by the fact that Madeline had barely been able to sleep the night before. After receiving the letter and spending the day with the FBI agents, Madeline couldn't stop the wheels in her head from turning. That evening, after the children went to bed and Molly the nanny retired to her apartment, Brandon had opened a bottle of wine trying to ease the tension that had filled the air. They sipped the wine silently on the couch together, trying to have a normal conversation. *How was your day?* Madeline tried to ask, hoping Brandon would have something to tell her. Maybe something about work, about his board meeting, but Brandon just smiled and responded *Not as rough as yours*. Then they spoke about the children and Madeline told Brandon about her morning with Noah at the coffee shop. That conversation seemed to lift his spirits and with that, they corked their wine and went to bed. Madeline had spent the night tossing and turning until light shone through their window and she could get up. She tiptoed downstairs to their home gym, where she ran on their treadmill for an hour before going back upstairs to shower and head to the office, all before Brandon and the children were awake.

At the office, Madeline had immediately started making phone calls. She liked getting up and starting her day early, Brandon even joked with her that she lived on "East Coast time" when in California. It was convenient for her, meaning that at 6:00 am, when most people on the West Coast were still in bed, Madeline could be in meetings with her colleagues on the East Coast where it was already 9:00 am. She had spoken with three other senators who supported the SAVER Bill all before Jane had arrived at the office. Jane's arrival was like a hurricane, disrupting the calming morning that Madeline had had. But the disruption was necessary, as no one was a better chief of staff than Jane. She could juggle events, crises, constituents, and Madeline's schedule with her two hands and not one thing would fall to the floor.

Madeline had then spent the day in strategy sessions with her team who had analyzed the chances and the necessary moves to pass the SAVER Bill. She had lunch with a group of CEOs who supported her and spent the afternoon reviewing and redlining speeches that she believed should have been in better shape by the time they reached her office. After a quick trip home to have dinner with Brandon and the kids, she was picked up by a car taking her to the airport

45

for her red eye to Washington where she would finish the week.

"What did you hear last night?" Madeline responded to Jane who was looking at her like a child with a secret ready to burst out.

Jane looked around the first-class cabin. It was mostly empty as most business and first-class passengers seemed to avoid redeyes. Madeline preferred them, they seemed the most efficient use of her time, ensuring she didn't waste any working hours. Jane leaned in closer to Madeline before parting her lips.

"Someone is vetting you for Vice President," Jane whispered, the words leaving her lips like bubbles floating into the air.

"What? Who?"

"I'm not sure yet," Jane responded. "I have to do some asking around."

"Then how do you know?"

"Someone is polling about you," Jane said. "My neighbor's grandma, she always gets those telemarketer calls where they ask surveys about all kinds of things and she answers. Most people who answer the surveys are the elderly, you know, because who else wants to waste time talking to a stranger? Anyway, she got a survey about different politicians and whether she would vote for them. They asked about you, Mark Raymond, Kent Fein, and Jim Holloway. Mark and Kent and Jim have all been open about their interest in running for president in the next election. That means someone is trying to find out which candidates people like and which could help them win. Someone either thinks you might run for president and thinks you're competition or they think you could help them win if you are on their ticket. I'm not sure anyone would expect you to run for president. I mean, you're a 38-year-old first term female senator. You'd be one of the youngest candidates yet! So that means someone thinks you are a potential vice."

Madeline's heart rippled with the thought of running for vice president. She had always hoped that being a senator was just a step for her, a way for her to prove her worth as she moved on to a bigger platform where she could effectuate bigger change. She had always known she was meant to leave her mark on this world, that she could make the country better, the world better. Being vice president would give her more opportunities to do that.

"So now what?" Madeline asked Jane, her eyes closing but her ears still very much awake.

"Well, I'm going to find out who it is," Jane responded. "We're going to do whatever we can to make sure you are chosen as a running mate. I mean, whoever it is, you will up their chances to win hugely. For one, you're a woman, so many women would vote for you just because. Two, you're young and beautiful. And let's not underestimate the importance of looks in politics. No one can forget the 1960 presidential election. Kennedy won on looks alone! And on top of all that, you're moderate, even liberal if I am allowed

47

to use the 'L' word to describe a republican. You'll get all the undecideds and even central democrats on your side. Wow, the more I talk, the more I'm convinced you should be president. Why waste you being the vice of some old white man?"

"All in good time," Madeline said with a smile. It was too early for her to think about the presidency. She needed a few more years, a few more accomplishments to ensure her candidacy was a shoo-in. She wouldn't run unless she knew she could win. If she ran and lost, that was the end. Losers never turn into winners. She needed to wait until she was sure she was a winner.

"I wonder if it is Joe Hamlin who was vetting you, or Ben Townsend," Jane continued rambling on. "When Ben was out in the last primaries he swore to run again..." Eventually Madeline dozed even with Jane's train of thought chugging through her ears.

But sleep did not provide Madeline with an escape. In her dream she found herself in a hotel room. She wasn't alone and she could feel herself aching to be touched by the man in the room with her. In her mind, she knew the man was Brandon, but he didn't look like Brandon. He did in some ways, but not in others. There was something different about him. She let the man kiss her passionately and push her back onto the bed where they gripped each other's clothes. She felt herself wanting this man more and more, this man who was Brandon, but also wasn't. When her desire couldn't be stronger, she pushed the man over onto his back and slipped on top of him. Relief fled through her with every thrust as she and the man devoured each other grasping at each other's skin, pulling each other close. When they finished, Madeline snuggled into the man's arms and felt calm. She hadn't cheated, this man was Brandon on some level, even though the sex didn't feel like it was with Brandon.

Madeline was jolted awake suddenly as the plane hit the ground. She followed Jane off the plane to the tarmac where a car was waiting to take them to the Capitol. Madeline was silent, even as Jane spoke about their plans for the trip. She would be needed on the senate floor, there would be a vote on a budget earmark that had already passed in the House of Representatives. Lunch was planned with the Liberty Caucus, a group of other moderate republican senators, and she would be greeting a school group that was visiting Washington from California.

Madeline was shaken from her dream. Over the last years, she hadn't considered herself much of a sexual person. Of course she had sex, enjoyed it, even wanted it sometimes, but the desire she had in her dream was a desire she hadn't felt in a long time. Not since... well, not since mothering two children while trying to pursue her own ambitions in her career. But that was normal, right?

"Yoo-hoo, are you there, Madeline?" Jane said. Their car was stopped in front of the Capitol and Jane was standing on the sidewalk waiting for

Madeline to get out. "We've got to go, they're already giving speeches on the senate floor. You promised Senator Copper you would be there."

Madeline shook herself out of her mind and jumped out of the car. Focus, she told herself. You need to stay focused.

Chapter 6

After a few long days in Washington, Madeline returned home to California. She came back late that Friday night, after the kids had already gone to sleep. But Brandon hadn't. When Madeline walked in the door he was sitting with his laptop on the couch, feet up, his reading glasses halfway down his nose and one hand cupping his chin. Madeline loved seeing Brandon with his reading glasses in this thinking pose. It made him look sophisticated, like if he thought hard enough he could solve every problem, from how to fix a broken hair dryer to ensuring peace in the Middle East. He didn't look up when Madeline walked in the living room. Instead he dropped the hand from his chin and started typing away on the keyboard. Madeline watched him for a moment, before approaching the couch and gently moving his legs so she could sit down next to him.

"One sec," Brandon said without looking up. His fingers continued to type at a speed that surely could have been record breaking. "There," he concluded pressing hard on the last key before looking up at Madeline. "Just going through the quarterly reports."

A few months ago, Brandon's company CyTech had gone public. It was a huge step for the company and was considered a huge success. Within hours the stock price had doubled and since then it had been steadily rising. Being the

51

CEO of a public company, however, was much more work than running a private company. If Brandon hadn't been busy enough before the IPO, he now had to deal with investors, boards and constant reporting to the SEC. "Anything interesting?" Madeline asked, peeking over to the screen.

"Brick wall," Brandon joked as he closed his laptop. He was right, they were obligated to keep certain parts of their professional lives separate so as to avoid allegations of insider trading and other influences that could be less than ethical. "How was DC? Missed you." Brandon turned his body so that he was sitting next to Madeline and kissed her on the lips. Madeline's mind wandered back to the dream she had on the flight a few days before. She kissed her husband back, turning the kiss that would have been a short peck into a longer embrace. She caught his bottom lip and slipped her tongue into his mouth. Brandon immediately reacted and shifted his body further so that he could wrap his arms around Madeline's upper back. He mirrored her movements with his lips and he let out a little moan. "Madeline," he said. "I really missed you."

Madeline began to kiss her husband harder and she slipped her hands under the ratty t-shirt he was wearing. Brandon moved his hands down by her waist and started touching her all over. He pushed into her, closing the small gap that was still between their bodies. As they kissed, Madeline waited for the desire she had felt in her dream to come. She wanted to feel young again, excited, full of the anticipation between young lovers.

"Let's go to the bedroom," Brandon offered, slowly standing up as they continued to kiss. They walked up their stairs together, Brandon behind her with his arms wrapped around her waist, still kissing her around her neck. When they got to the bedroom, he quietly closed the door, careful not to wake the boys, and pulled his shirt over his head. Madeline looked at his body. It hadn't changed much in the 13 years they had been together. He wasn't athletic, or fit, but his body was tight and hadn't gained the pudge that many of their peers had started to carry around. "Take off your clothes."

Madeline was still wearing the same clothes she had worn to the Senate hearings that day. A navy-blue skirt suit with a white blouse. She started unbuttoning the blouse and hung it up in her closet as Brandon watched her. His eyes made her slightly uncomfortable even though he had seen her naked countless times. But this time felt different, he looked at her like a teenager about to lose his virginity, or a hungry wolf who had cornered his prey. She then unzipped her skirt and pulled down her stockings, just as Brandon embraced her. He continued to kiss her hard and Madeline kissed him back, still waiting for the desire, the passion, to come. They lay down on the bed and Brandon's hand wandered down on her. Then, he got on top of her and began making love to her. "You're so beautiful," he said. "I can't believe I am so lucky to have such an amazing wife."

Madeline smiled and continued moving in their rhythm and kissing her husband. When she was tired of having sex, she told him she was about to orgasm and then a few moments later let out a small whimper, a sigh and held Brandon tight in her. She knew he would believe she came and that by itself would make him come seconds later. When he finished he rolled next to her. "Oh my God," he said. "That was amazing. How was it for you?"

"Great," Madeline responded, giving him an assuring smile. Inside she was disappointed in herself. Why didn't her body surge with desire for her husband? Her husband who was so perfect, so good looking, and treated her so well? Why didn't his touch make her feel electricity?

Unfortunately, this lack of desire wasn't new for Madeline. As she lay curled in Brandon's arms she thought about the first time they had sex. It was right after she moved to California to be with him. The first few nights she spent in his—their—apartment, the two of them stayed up all night talking. They kissed passionately, and even rolled around in the bed together, but they took it slow physically. After almost a week, when Madeline was dying to take the relationship to the next step—and she was sure that Brandon was too—they finally did it.

When it started, Madeline was full of desire, full of wanting Brandon to touch her everywhere, to have him deep inside her. But once it started, Madeline's body quickly recoiled. Brandon moved in his own rhythm, completely out of sync with Madeline. He seemed oblivious to movements and Madeline quickly felt like sex was a battle between each of them trying to get what they want, rather than the two of them trying to reach something together. When it was over, she told herself it was normal, not everyone has great sex from the beginning, that she could teach him to meet her desires, that sex would improve with time. This was definitely not symbolic of anything else in their relationship, she assured herself.

The second time they had sex was much like the first and Madeline again was left feeling disappointed and unsatisfied. She faked her satisfaction to end it quicker and pretended that everything in their relationship was perfect. Because, for the most part, it was. Wasn't it? Besides the sex, everything with Brandon was perfect. He was a gentleman, he was ambitious, thoughtful, intelligent. He was everything Madeline had ever wanted in a man, except for when they were naked. But that wasn't a big deal, was it? No relationship was perfect. Madeline decided this was a problem she could live with and one that would surely improve over the years.

She was right. Over the years it did improve. She learned to tell Brandon what she liked and what she didn't like, even when it had confused him since, in his mind, she had been orgasming from the things she didn't like for years. She trained him on how to touch her, how to move

55

with her and how to sense her feelings. Brandon was eager to please and took direction well. He did exactly what she said and was proud of himself when Madeline actually did orgasm with him. But even so, even with Brandon completely changing the way he made love, Madeline still didn't feel a burning desire for him. She sometimes enjoyed sex, sometimes wanted it, but she hadn't longed for Brandon as she had for others in her past. But that wasn't important, she told herself. Because passion fades with time anyway. It's better to be married to someone who has everything else than to marry someone for passion.

Over the years, their sexual relationship morphed as does all couples'. During the years when their children were babies it was difficult and sometimes nonexistent. They were often too tired and seemed to always have one son crying, awake from nightmares or snuggling with them in their bed. As their children got older and stopped waking them up, Madeline decided it was time for them to manage their sex life as they managed all other aspects of their lives. They should have sex once a week, she decided. It would be quiet, simple married-people-sex, the kind that ensured their sex life never completely disappeared and Brandon would not be incentivized to stray. It was the kind of sex life where both of them could rationalize that that was what sex was like for people approaching forty while managing busy careers and two children. There would be no dry spells, no reasons to fight about not having sex and they could both feel good about the fact that they still had sex, even after 13 years together.

"Second time this week!" Brandon said with a big smile as he drew circles on Madeline's shoulder with his fingers. "Guess you really missed me too with everything going on." Madeline smiled at her husband, who appeared satisfied with their sexual relationship throughout the years, except during the young baby period.

"What can I say?" Madeline smiled back at him, giving his masculinity a huge boost. "It's been a long week." It truly had been. Madeline thought back to the blackmail, the rumors of her being vetted for a vice presidency run, the whirlwind days in DC. She was ready for a quiet weekend at home with her family. One without politics, or appearances. Where she could just enjoy being a woman, mother, and wife to a truly wonderful man, even if he wasn't the best in bed.

Chapter 7

• — • —◆— • —•

"What about a picnic in the park? Or a trip to the zoo?" Brandon suggested to Madeline the next morning when they were still in bed. Madeline was wearing her pink plaid pajamas, which she had put on the previous night after the necessary twenty minutes of post-sex naked snuggling. Brandon had also put on a pair of boxers— sleeping naked was something for carefree young lovers, not parents of two children who could easily surprise them with an early morning visit.

"Picnic," Madeline responded after taking a moment to think about her choices. "I feel like I just spent the last three days in the zoo."

Brandon laughed. "It was that bad, huh?"

"I'm not sure I'd say bad, but it's definitely a jungle," Madeline responded, thinking about the hours in senate hearings, the meetings, the networking events that filled her days in DC. She'd rather not think about them now, she decided, pushing everything to the back of her mind. It could all wait until Monday.

Suddenly they heard a scream and then a loud crash coming from downstairs. Madeline and Brandon both jumped up and looked at each other. "Sounds like we're also living in the jungle here," Brandon remarked. "Must be the boys making breakfast. I'll get up and join them. You take your time." Brandon kissed Madeline's cheek and then leaped out of bed into their master bathroom to brush his teeth. With one hand on his toothbrush, he used his other hand to brush his hair and splash a little water on his face. Then, exactly two minutes later, he dried his face and threw on a shirt as he left the master bedroom, closing the door behind him.

Super dad, thought Madeline, smiling to herself. She was sitting up in their bed and she remained still for a few more moments. She treasured having a few minutes to herself whenever she could get it, even if she could hear Brandon and the boys yelling downstairs. There was more banging, the sounds of stomping feet, whining voices and laughter, but Madeline tried to tune it out for a few minutes.

She pulled herself out of bed and into the bathroom where she caught her eyes in the mirror. She had deep green eyes that Jane was constantly trying to complement with her outfit choices for Madeline. Her wavy brown hair, which she pulled back in a ponytail when she slept, was messy and falling around her ears. Frizz lined her forehead, which was greasy and creased with lines from too many photo opportunities in front of strong flashes. Lines also surrounded her thin pink lips and crept out from her eyes. She put her hands on her face to trace them, the maze on her face. This maze would never be seen outside of her home. For any appearances where there would be cameras, she had her make up professionally done, covering her pores, wrinkles and making her skin look even better than it had in her 20s.

On the day-to-day, she made up her face herself, following detailed instructions from her makeup artist, to ensure she was never candidly caught on camera. One bad picture and that would be the first people would see when they Googled her name.

First, she released her ponytail, letting her messy hair loose to graze her shoulders. Then she combed it back into a neat ponytail at the nape of her neck. Then she brushed her teeth and washed her face, following with her routine of anti-wrinkle creams and moisturizers that she had been assured were necessary for her career's success. She laughed when thinking about her image consultant's seriousness about this matter. Would they ever say something like that to a man? That he needed to rub six different creams on his face throughout the day if he ever wanted to even think about the White House? Of course not. Men could get away with sun spots, wrinkles, white hair—for a man these were signs of wisdom; but for a woman, signs of obsolescence. Madeline understood she was playing in a man's game and she had to work extra hard to succeed. She would do what she needed, go the extra mile, rub the creams on her face.

Still in her pajamas, Madeline made their bed and left the master bedroom. From the hall, the sounds of giggles and clanking in the kitchen were louder. She made her way downstairs to the kitchen, where Brandon was standing in front of the stove with pancakes sizzling in the pan in front of him. There was orange juice spilled on the counter and the boys were already snacking on Cheerios as they waited for Brandon to finish cooking.

"Maybe it's time we tell Molly to stay on the weekends," Brandon said with a smile. Molly was usually only with them during the week, unless they had a specific reason they needed her on the weekend. Mostly Madeline and Brandon tried to be full-time parents on the weekend. They wanted their kids to feel like they were a normal family, but it was hard sometimes. Sometimes Madeline traveled on weekends or had to attend different events. Sometimes Brandon had to work on reports or projects that hadn't been finished during the week. Molly helped them those weekends. But when their weekends weren't an extension of the workweek, when Madeline and Brandon slipped into full-time parents, they put in the same effort they did in their careers, trying to excel in parenting as though it were just as competitive as political elections or the technology industry. They always wanted to be the best, no matter what it took.

Madeline immediately started wiping down the orange juice on the counter. Then she poured glasses for the four of them and took out plates and syrup for the pancakes. When Brandon finished cooking, he brought a steaming plate to the table and the boys abandoned their Cheerios for the hot pancakes. They ate as a family, the boys telling them about their week. Adam had learned how to play basketball at school and had now decided that when he grew up he would be a professional basketball player. He'd been practicing all week during recess and lunch at school! Noah, on the other hand, had been home with Molly, finishing up his suspension. Molly had forced him to clean his room, help organize the living room and dust the bookshelves. She hadn't even let him turn on the TV once, not even once! They ran errands or cleaned, Noah complained. Even being at school was better than being stuck home with Molly, he admitted reluctantly. Madeline was happy that Noah hadn't enjoyed his suspension. She hoped it meant he would avoid further punishments at school, but she decided not to bring up the subject of the recent bullying incident, especially not in front of Adam who didn't seem aware of his older brother's behavioral issues.

After breakfast the boys brought their dishes to the sink and disappeared to get dressed and steal a few moments of television while Madeline and Brandon prepared for their picnic. Madeline washed dishes while Brandon packed a basket with bread, cheese, fruit, crackers and other items they had in the house that would make for good picnic food. When they finished, they got dressed and finally got the boys into the car.

They drove to a nearby park where there was a playground with big slides and plenty of things to climb. Brandon lay down a blanket on the grass where they could watch the boys play. Once the boys were running on the playground, Madeline and Brandon sat down on the blanket and opened a bottle of sparkling water. Madeline leaned into Brandon's shoulder as she sipped her drink.

"Madeline Thomas!" Someone said from behind them. The voice had the hint of a snicker filled with satisfaction as though it said *I caught you*. "Look at you just lounging around!"

Madeline and Brandon turned their heads to see a woman in dark jeans and a t-shirt standing above them with her hands on her hips. "Even senators get some time off," Brandon responded with a polite smile.

"Senators maybe, but not mothers," the woman replied. She had a smug smile on her face, still holding the *I caught you* look. Madeline was used to people looking at her this way. For every person who admired her, there were at least three who hated her—for being a republican (she was from California after all), for not being a good enough mother, or for the most absurd reason of all, for being a woman. This woman, no doubt, fell into the second category.

"That's why we're here spending Saturday with our boys in the park," Brandon again responded politely. "Can we help you with anything?"

"Oh, yes I can see how much time you spend with your boys," the woman said. "You don't know who I am, do you, Madeline?" The woman addressed Madeline as though it wasn't Brandon who had been speaking to her. Madeline pushed herself off of Brandon to sit up a little straighter.

"I'm sorry, you're right, I don't know who you are," Madeline now took control of the conversation. She needed to appease this woman, make her feel important. Then, she could even turn her into a supporter if she felt like she had the Senator's ear. "Would you mind introducing yourself?"

"I'm Mrs. Albertson," She responded, as though that should ring a bell for Madeline. Madeline's brain started filing through the folders in her mind for Albertson. This woman hated her for her mothering, and believed Madeline should know who she was. That made it simple enough for Madeline's brain to zero in on the right folder right away.

"Jamie's mother," Madeline said. She stood up to face this woman eye-to-eye, although Madeline was a few inches taller than her. This extra height helped her in these situations, people were forced to look up to her, which subconsciously had a desired effect. "Hi there, so nice to meet you." Madeline extended her hand to shake Mrs. Albertson's.

Mrs. Albertson returned the gesture, shaking Madeline's hand. The first step toward turning from hating Madeline to supporting her. "You would have known who I was already if you had been to Parent's Night at Highland."

"You're right, I felt awful that I missed it," Madeline responded, still shaking the woman's hand. "Brandon was there though, did you have a chance to speak with him?" Madeline motioned to her husband, still lying on the blanket.

"I wanted to speak to you," Mrs. Albertson said. "Your son is bullying mine." She said this as though she were revealing a devastating secret to Madeline. "You would know that if you were around more."

"I am aware of the situation and we're working on it," Madeline responded. "I apologize for Noah's actions."

"What are you doing about it?" the woman asked, crossing her arms in front of her chest. "You know this is a very *serious* issue and it can't be taken lightly. Maybe in your line of work bullying is used to get what you want, but in school it is a *serious* problem. I'm not sure what you are teaching your boys, but..."

"I assure you, we take this very *seriously*," Madeline responded, mirroring the woman's stress on the word serious. "I don't condone bullying in my job or at home."

"I hope that's true. Jamie is a very sensitive boy and he was very hurt by Noah. If it happens again, we're going to have to take further actions," the woman said, seemingly content with her threat. "You know, my brother-in-law is a lawyer and he is also very committed to ensuring this doesn't happen again." The woman nodded her head as though her motions said more than her words.

"We understand completely," Madeline responded. "Thank you for voicing your concern to us." Madeline nodded and turned to sit back down on the blanket, signaling to the woman that the conversation was over. The woman didn't seem to understand that her ambush had been squashed and that her reprimanding of Madeline was over.

"Is Noah here? At the park? I'm not sure that is a good way for Noah to spend his suspension," the woman said, her tone becoming more judgmental than passive aggressive. "Playing in the park is not the kind of punishment that will teach him to stop bullying."

"Don't worry, ma'am," Brandon said, putting his arm around Madeline, who was again leaning on his shoulder. "We are perfectly capable of making our own parenting decisions."

The woman raised her eyebrows and smirked. "Well, if I were you—"

"You're not," Brandon said, cutting the conversation short. "Thanks for your input, but we don't really need your help with our children."

"Maybe if you were around more—"

"Thanks again, but we're done here," Brandon again cut her off. "Have a great day."

The woman opened her mouth, either in shock or to continue spewing her unwanted advice, but no words came out. Instead, she turned around, muttering under her breath and looking up at the playground where Noah and Adam were climbing through the jungle gym.

"Don't worry, you're a great mom," Brandon said, kissing the top of her head. "Even if you bully everyone into doing what you want."

Madeline laughed and took a drink of her sparkling water. She watched her boys laughing and running around and listened to Brandon's breathing behind her. Even without further interruptions, with just a picnic and a sunny sky above them, Madeline couldn't relax. Her mind was still racing, connecting the incidents of the last week, trying to find meaning in them all, find how to fix things. She kept a smile on her face, trying to enjoy the day off with her family. But even with the cloudless sky, the warm air, the breeze, her happy family, something was nagging her. Holding her back from enjoying the moment.

Chapter 8

"I wish we had something more substantial to tell you," Agent Murray said. It had been almost a week since Madeline had received the blackmail letter. A week during which the letter hung over her like a cloud casting a shadow on everything she did.

"Can you tell me again exactly what you have been doing in this investigation?" Madeline asked, sitting across from the three agents in her kitchen.

Earlier that morning, Agent Murray, who seemed to be the team leader had called Jane. It was just a friendly call to tell her there was no news and that they were still working on the case. When Jane called to update Madeline, Madeline insisted the agents come to meet face-to-face. "No news" was not good news. It meant time was running out before her campaign relaunch event, before the blackmailer promised to publish whatever evidence he or she allegedly had about Madeline's alleged infidelity. With the clock ticking, Madeline needed to see the agents to understand whether they were taking this as seriously as necessary, or whether her career would start spiraling down the drain in just a few weeks.

"We spent two days in New York last week interviewing employees at the Langham," Agent Murray said. "Mr. Chase was very cooperative, as were the other employees we interviewed."

"Mr. Chase?" Madeline asked.

"The doorman in the picture," Agent Murray responded, recalling the picture of Madeline walking into the hotel in her red suit where she greeted the doorman. "He's still a doorman there, although he now usually works early morning shifts. He said he used to work in the evenings two years ago when the picture was taken. He spoke about you very fondly, saying you were one of the few important guests they have at the Langham who actually said hello to him. He said most guests look right through him, not even noticing him opening the door, nor responding to his greetings of 'Good morning' or 'Good evening.' He said he appreciates your visits and hopes to see you again soon. He couldn't recall anyone suspicious around the hotel that could have taken the photograph or followed you."

"What about the other man in the picture?" Brandon asked. "The African American one."

"Mr. Chase didn't recognize him. He said he was likely just someone walking down the street who got caught in the picture. We have no more leads on him. Other hotel employees all said the same things."

"And what about the letter? Any clues from that?"

"The letter and picture have been in forensics all week," said Agent Hart. "The letter was typed on standard paper that could have been purchased anywhere and printed on any standard printer. The letter was mailed through the post office from a drop box near the Langham..."

"That's a clue isn't it?" Brandon jumped in.

The agents all looked at each other. "It tells us the blackmailer, or someone working on their behalf, was near the Langham on the day the letter was mailed. That could narrow it down to, let's say, at least a million people," Agent Hart responded.

"What about fingerprints?" Brandon asked.

"The letter itself had no fingerprints," Agent Hart responded. "The envelope was covered in fingerprints, but most were not legible, but this is standard for anything that has passed through the post office. All the different mail handlers touching it during sorting, it isn't worth it for us to follow that unless we believe that someone at the post office is the perpetrator and I don't think that is the case."

"Regarding the picture, based on the angle it appears to be taken from the security footage from the convenience store across the street's security camera," Agent Murray offered. "The footage from that time period is gone, but we spoke with the store's owners and employees and none of them seemed to even know who you are."

"Don't you have any other ideas? You're the FBI, this is supposed to be your expertise right? Political blackmail?" Brandon's voice sounded strained and angry.

"We are following our protocol and I am sure something will come up," Agent Jones said.

"We're still conducting interviews with all of Madeline's past competitors and their staff members, as well as anyone rumored to be running against her in the next election. We're also looking at other political adversaries that Ms. Randall mentioned." Agent Jones nodded toward Jane who was also sitting at the table, typing on her phone.

"I gave them a long list," Jane responded, without looking up from her phone. "From Senator Coldwall, who has already come out against the SAVER Bill to Senator Hill, who you accidentally wore the same outfit as during that photo op at the UN a few months back. Senator Hill does seem like the kind to hold a grudge for something silly."

"So if you're interviewing everyone who disagrees with me politically and all their staff members, that, well, that's a long list of interviewees," Madeline said after holding her tongue while Brandon interrogated the agents. "Let's say you conduct ten interviews a day, and that's generous, right?" The agents looked to one another, nodding their heads in agreement. "Alright, seven a day, it will take you months."

"Well we're starting with people who are more likely to have a motive to hurt your political career," Agent Jones reasoned. "Senator Hill and her staff are very low priority. We're focusing on potential opponents. People who could be hurt by your success, or have something to gain from you losing office or political clout."

There were many who didn't want to see Madeline succeed. Democrats who wanted her seat back on their side. Republicans who called her a liberal, like it was a dirty word. Senators who had wide support from police unions and were receiving flack now that her SAVER Bill was being talked about on every news program.

"What do we do if you don't catch the person by my reelection campaign launch in a few weeks?" Madeline asked, trying to analyze the worst-case scenarios that were playing out in her head.

"Well, we expect to find the person by then," Agent Murray stated. "However, if not, then we'll have to see what happens. This could be an empty threat to get money. Especially since you have been faithful to your husband and therefore whatever proof this person may have is fake or doesn't hold water. Like the picture from the Langham, it doesn't prove anything. The second possible scenario is that they release something to the public. If this happens, it will actually be quite easy to track them since they will have to be in contact with someone to get 'proof' out there. Should this happen, we'll be able to catch them easily."

Catching them won't be the issue then, Madeline thought to herself. At that point, it wouldn't matter who was behind this. All that would matter was that everyone would be talking about this scandal. No one would remember Madeline as the champion of the SAVER Bill or the promising young senator who could make it to the top. Her name would be scarred forever by this smear campaign. If she were lucky, she wouldn't have to resign. If she were lucky, she could maybe even get another term in the Senate. But that would be all. Her career would have peaked before she knew it and it would be downhill from there, with no possibility of climbing back up.

Madeline thanked the agents, saying she didn't want to waste any more of their time while they had so much to do. After they left, Brandon kissed Madeline on the forehead and headed out for work, leaving Jane and Madeline sitting together in the kitchen.

"Shall we get going?" Jane asked, still typing on her phone. "We have a meeting with the Penhursts who are sponsoring the reelection campaign launch party. They wanted to have coffee this morning to talk about our vision for the event. Just ten minutes."

Madeline nodded and followed Jane out the door. She had a great vision for the reelection campaign launch party. She wanted the party to focus on inclusivity and the New Republican Movement. She wanted to convince police chiefs to attend and show their support. She wanted to portray to everyone that a vote for her was a vote for taking America in a new direction. But she feared the event would go differently. Instead of lauding her for being a visionary, she would be chastised for ruining her family, for not upholding the family values that she so cherished, even if other mothers from her children's school couldn't see it. The wheels in her head were already turning, how she could get ahead of this, make sure the world was on her side even if she were under attack.

Chapter 9

Madeline sat in her local office waiting for the regional leader of the Fraternal Order of Police. Since she had announced the SAVER Bill, the police organization had been actively speaking out against her proposed policy. They said it wasted valuable police time, forcing officers to spend time volunteering instead of protecting citizens, and that the stations were already underfunded as it was; they didn't need any more obstacles to receiving the funding they needed to keep America safe.

Madeline had read every news article, press release, and blog post on the Internet that quoted members of the FOP and other police organizations discussing her bill. In fact, she had a dedicated staff member whose entire job it was to comb the Internet for anything related to Madeline or her politics. This staff member started her job at midnight every night, compiling everything that had been written the previous day and catching all the new articles published in the early hours before newspapers would hit the stands. She had alerts set up on her computer for Madeline's name, her opponents' names, and more than 100 keywords relating to Madeline's policies, and past political actions. After reviewing all the alerts, the staff member started reading the major newspapers, blogs, commentary sites, to see if anything was missed. By 5:00 am, she had bookmarked, printed, hole-punched and organized every article by importance, filling at least one 3-inch binder every morning. There was an entire system for organizing the articles. Many were repetitive and these took lesser priorities. Some were absent of facts, and these were organized by their likelihood of gaining traction. The highest priority articles were those that quoted Madeline, or revealed something new about a colleague, adversary, or policy that could affect Madeline's work. The Binder, as it became known, was dropped off at Madeline's house every morning by 5:30 am. Each morning, this staff member held the binder close to her as she left the office and drove to Madeline's house. She had a key to the back door, where she would quietly let herself in and place The Binder on the kitchen table, ensuring it was secure from anyone who might be interested in learning about what Madeline was interested in. Then, she would let herself out, lock the door, and be relieved of her job until the following evening.

Madeline flipped through The Binder every morning, reading all the headlines and as many articles as she could. She couldn't read everything, it would take her the entire day, but that's what her staff was for. Every article placed in The Binder was also distributed to at least one of her staff members. Articles about Madeline's personal life, family and looks were distributed to her image consultant. Articles about specific policies were distributed to the staff member with that expertise. Jane, of course, also received a binder the size of Madeline's and she too read whatever she could in the early morning hours.

That morning there had been several articles quoting different police chiefs and members of the FOP about Madeline's SAVER Bill. Nothing new had been said, but Madeline reviewed these articles closely in advance of her morning meeting with the regional leader of the FOP. She was ready to personally hear all of his arguments about the SAVER Bill and she had her own arguments in response, which she was sure would convince the police leader to at least consider changing his mind. Would it waste police officers' valuable time? Certainly in the beginning. But this was a small sacrifice to save time and lives in the future. Madeline rehearsed her talking points in her head. Imagine, she would tell him, that each of your police officers spent two hours a week volunteering in a school largely filled with minority students. Because that's all it would be, really, two hours. If you have 20 police officer in your department, that means each one needs to complete 5 hours a month volunteering and you easily get the 100 hours a month. In fact, that's nothing, barely any time, if you think about it. It's less than the amount of time officers spent in meetings every week, or writing up reports about their shifts.

In those two hours, the officers could play basketball with students. They could help them with homework, eat lunch together. In fact, it would be fun for the police officers! They could join students during physical education classes, or recess. It would be like a break for them. During this time, they'd get to joke around with the students, get to know them, talk to them about their families and friends, they could even commiserate with the students about how annoying their teachers were. Maybe give them advice about crushes they had.

Now, these students, who grew up spending a couple of hours a week shooting hoops with Officer Steve or Officer Bill—who of course is wearing his uniform while volunteering—maybe they have a different perception of police officers. Officer Steve and Officer Bill are their friends. They may suck at shooting hoops, but they are fun to beat! On the other hand, Officer Steve and Officer Bill now have relationships with these students. They know what they like to eat for lunch and what bothers them at school. Maybe they even feel affection for them, and have been able to provide them some advice that had proven helpful.

Let's now imagine, that these students are getting older. One of them is driving late at night with a broken taillight and is pulled over. It's not Officer Steve or Officer Bill who pulls them over— that would be too much of a coincidence—but this officer also volunteered at a different school. This officer comes up to the window and is reminded of a student he mentored earlier that day or week, or maybe years before. The man pulled over is reminded of a time Officer Steve almost made a basket. The two men speak to each other cordially and respectfully, and the traffic stop is completed according to procedure. The driver gets a warning to fix his taillight and the police officer bids him good night. The two continue on their way, and no one thinks twice about this routine event. It made no difference to the officer that the driver was African American, and the driver had no preconceptions that the officer was evil.

Of course, this is optimistic. Maybe you think I am naïve for thinking this could happen, but can we agree this is a very possible scenario? Maybe even a probable one? If this traffic stop ends this way, weren't those two hours a week worth it for the officer?

At this point in the conversation, the FOP regional leader would have to agree. Two hours—ones that could even be an enjoyable break for the officer—could lead to years of cordiality, respect and understanding. Yes, maybe you're looking at the short term, but let's focus on the long term, because this is a long-term solution—something politicians rarely seem to think about. Long term, the effects will be life changing, even lifesaving. Doesn't that make it worthwhile?

To address the FOP's second concern, that it added more obstacles for them to receive funding, Madeline would ensure them that the process for applying for federal grants won't be much different. Yes, the application will be different, but police stations are already filling out these applications and filing reports for the grants. So what if the applications and reports have changed?

Yes, there was no disagreeing with these arguments, Madeline thought. She just needed the FOP regional director in her office so she could convince him. Her eyes drifted to the clock on her wall, on which an American flag was painted on the face under thick brass hands. 10:11 am. The FOP regional director was late.

Suddenly, Jane burst into the office holding her phone to her ear. "Madeline!" she screamed. "We have to go! Evacuate! Now! Up! Let's go!"

Madeline didn't take a moment to think. Her instincts took over, she jumped from her desk following Jane out her office door, through their lobby and down the stairs—they couldn't take the elevator, Jane insisted!—out of the tall office building where her office was housed. The staircase was full of a stream of people all running, pushing each other, screaming as they rushed down.

Madeline stayed behind Jane, seeing the rest of her office staff members dispersing through the stairway as they all rushed down. "What's going on?" Madeline yelled to Jane, hoping she would hear.

"A bomb!" someone else in the staircase yelled. The exclamation was met with further screaming, a wave of fear rolling down the crowded staircase like a heatwave. Madeline looked at Jane who was yelling into her phone. Jane caught her eye.

"This building received a bomb threat," she said into Madeline's ear, pulling Madeline close.

Madeline nodded and continued down the stairs. She had many more questions, but this stairwell was not the place to ask. Once they reached the bottom and spread through the lobby's bottleneck entrance, Madeline and her staff gathered around in a circle in a park across the street, far enough away from the perimeter being set up by the police who had already arrived.

"What else do we know about the bomb threat?" Madeline asked.

"I'm on the phone with my contact at the police station," Jane said, the phone still at her ear. "They received an anonymous call at 9:53 this morning saying that a bomb was placed somewhere in this building. The call was made from a cell phone that was found in a trashcan a couple blocks away. The police are searching for the caller and in the meantime they are evacuating the building to check for bombs. The bomb squad is on the way. They aren't sure if it was just a threat or if it is real. They're already checking surveillance of the building and all nearby cameras."

Madeline looked at her staff members who, she was sure, were all thinking the same thing. She also had the same thought and let it out in the open. "Do we think it has something to do with us?" All of the staff members must have believed it was possible Madeline was the target of the bomb threat because of the SAVER Bill. There were so many against it, some opponents could even be crazy enough to try to stop it with force.

Was someone trying to stop her from meeting with the FOP regional director? Why was he late for the meeting? But there were other questions running in Madeline's head. Was this connected to the blackmail letter she received the previous week? Was someone trying to take her down from several different angles?

Jane shrugged and nodded at the same time. "I would guess, but we don't know anything yet."

"I suggest everyone go home," Madeline said to her staff. "You can all work from home today, and we'll be in contact regarding tomorrow." Her staff members nodded and dispersed, leaving Madeline and Jane together.

"We should talk to the agents," Madeline said. "This may be connected to the letter."

Jane nodded and raised her finger signaling that her contact on the phone had returned and was talking. "They think it was an empty threat, that it was nothing," Jane said. "They're of course still doing a full sweep of the building." Jane hung up the phone and looked to Madeline. "Yes, I'll talk to Agent Murray. And Officer Austin from the FOP. We'll reschedule that meeting, but it's strange, no? He's late, there's a bomb threat? There are easier ways to cancel!" Jane let out a fake sounding laugh.

Madeline smiled. It was fishy. Even more so that the police were so sure it was an empty threat without doing much investigation. There were a few other meetings scheduled for that day, Jane said she'd try to reschedule or change their locations, but in the meanwhile they could work from Madeline's kitchen. On the drive, Jane called the FOP offices for Officer Austin. They answered quickly and Jane was put through to the officer's direct line. It rang and rang with no answer.

"I guess he was already on the way," Jane said, putting her hand over the phone. Then, when the voicemail tone clicked, she immediately changed her tone. "Hi, Officer Austin! This is Jane Randall from Madeline Thomas' office. So sorry for the inconvenience! Madeline needs to reschedule your meeting. I so hope you aren't already at the building. If you are, you'll see it was closed off for a bomb threat! Maybe you could even give us more insight about the incident! OK, well, please do get back to me! Thanks so much!"

Chapter 10

Madeline sat with her eyes closed as the plane landed in California. She wished the flight were a little longer, maybe they could get stuck on the tarmac for a while waiting for a gate to open up. Maybe she could just stay there, sitting in the large first-class seat with an eye mask on for a few more minutes. Maybe they wouldn't notice her when they were cleaning the plane, she really did need just a few more minutes.

But to her dismay, her on-time flight pulled up to the gate and the flight attendants quickly opened the doors for the rest of the eager passengers to deplane. Madeline stayed seated, letting everyone else pass her by. She'd deplane later she said, she wasn't in a hurry. Well, she was, but a few more minutes couldn't hurt.

She had spent the last 48 hours in Washington DC. After the bomb threat at her California office, she and Jane had started working at her kitchen table. Then they got a call about an emergency session in Congress that Madeline just couldn't miss. Senator Shuker was calling for a vote on his bill that granted additional autonomy to insurance providers to choose which procedures could be covered. This bill, of course, became a battle ground for abortion rights, with pro-choice supporters railing that this bill could allow insurance providers to decide not to cover abortions, specifically medically necessary abortions. Madeline was right at the middle of this debate, as one of the few republican senators who openly opposed the bill. It meant that every time this bill was discussed, Madeline received hundreds of press calls for comment and was requested by her democratic colleagues to attend all hearings and speaking engagements. This time, a group of senators were planning to filibuster the bill—meaning they would be giving speeches on the Senate floor against it until Senator Shuker decided not to pursue a vote. It was a process that could take days, weeks even, which Madeline didn't have. But she agreed to come support the filibuster, to throw in her own two cents while the filibustering democrats took bathroom breaks.

She spent 48 hours on the hill, sitting through hearings, giving a few short speeches, talking to press out in the hallways, and occasionally changing her outfit and washing her face when Jane forced her to. She hadn't slept, hadn't visited her Washington DC studio where she often slept during the week. She would have, if she hadn't needed to get back to California urgently that Friday.

Yes, she felt guilty for leaving—the filibuster had not yet ended and exhausted senators were still jabbering on the Senate floor trying to block the vote demanded by a tired and cranky Senator Shuker—but Madeline also had other priorities. So she gave a few last press comments and squeezed a few hands in support before she took a car to the airport, leaving Jane to field any calls or colleagues who would be angry at her absence.

Now, she had slept five hours on the plane, but it was not enough to recover from the 48-hour marathon session. But she didn't have a choice, she would stop quickly at home to change her clothes, apply her face creams and freshen her makeup so she could make it to Noah's and Adam's school for Career Day. For the last four years, Brandon had attended Career Day, giving talks to both boys' classes about being the CEO of a highly successful software company. He would sit with the other parents, listening to each of them talk about their careers as real estate investors, engineers, doctors, and C-level executives and then the children would talk about their own aspirations for when they grow up. The parents would all finish by patting each other on the back for what great role models they were and then they would eat lunch with their children in the school's pristine cafeteria which served— special for career day—a buffet that would have been more than adequate at a five-star hotel.

Madeline remembered last year's Career Day. She had been in Washington working on a bill for tax reforms and hadn't been able to attend. That evening, Brandon spent an hour on the phone with her, detailing the other parents' pretentious speeches, as each one believed their profession was Godsent, that society just couldn't function without people like them! Especially the real estate agents! They weren't just selling houses, they were helping people live their dream! They were providing an unequivocal service! No mention of what people paid for these services, they were invaluable! Of course every parent at Career Day was highly successful, even the stay-at-home-moms who talked about their life choices, the most profound of them all. Brandon didn't argue that these moms made valuable contributions to their families, their work was necessary in raising their families and supporting their husbands who worked long hours and generated enough income to pay the exorbitant cost of Highland Academy—one of the top private schools around.

This year, Madeline had promised she would attend Career Day. Not only had the school been asking (they had never had a politician at Career Day before, unless you counted Mrs. Baker who had served one term on the City Council), but also because of what Adam had said in his class on the previous year's Career Day. He had stood up in front of the classroom and said he was going to be a Majority Whip when he grew up. The other seven-year-olds in his second-grade class all laughed at him. They were laughing too hard to hear when Adam tried to explain the significance of this position—the person in charge of garnering enough votes to pass a bill—which was also the third highest-ranking position in the Senate. For the rest of the year, students made fun of Adam, calling him Major Whip and pretending to flick a whip every time he walked by. Madeline had wanted to cry when Brandon told her this story—both from pride that Adam wanted to follow her footsteps into the Senate, but also from sadness that the spoiled children in her son's class didn't understand what it meant to be a politician. This year, Madeline would talk about being a senator at Career Day. She would tell them that being Majority Whip was no joke—it was a worthy aspiration, even for someone with Madeline's own pedigree. She would also show the other parents— in particular the stay-at-home-moms—who judged her for her career choice, lamented her parenting and clucked their tongues whenever she was near.

Not to mention, attending Career Day made a great photo opportunity for Madeline. Jane had quietly leaked Madeline's participation to the local press, who would send photographers and reporters who would add to Madeline's press portfolio of articles calling her the woman who had it all. This type of press was exactly what Madeline needed right now. It gave people a good feeling about her, and was a great way to prep the public for her reelection campaign launch. It also couldn't hurt to garner more positive press, especially with Madeline's hanging fear that doom was imminent. That her blackmailer would never be caught and her career would be ruined. Maybe if that happened, someone would remember that she came to Career Day and that her reputation, after being dragged through the mud, would still have one positive attribute. Would that be too much to ask for?

Madeline felt a tap on her shoulder. She lifted her eye mask to see a smiling flight attendant grinning at her. "Mrs. Thomas, are you all right?" the woman asked her. All the flight attendants knew her by name. That was the kind of service received in first class, as well as an occupational hazard for Madeline who flew cross-country weekly.

Madeline nodded and stood up, realizing that the plane was empty of other passengers. She grabbed her purse, thanked the flight attendants who were all standing at the front with abnormally happy faces, and exited the plane toward the car that would be waiting for her. She arrived home to see the boys sitting in the kitchen eating eggs that Molly had cooked for them.

"You made it!" Adam screamed when he saw her.

"Of course I did! I promised I would!" Madeline tried to match his enthusiasm.

"Yeah, but still!" Adam said, the enthusiasm still shooting out of his ears. The comment stung, but Madeline tried not to flinch. She hugged her boys and ran upstairs for a quick shower so she could take the boys to school.

She walked into the master bedroom and could immediately smell Brandon's aftershave. Steam from the shower was seeping through the bathroom door, which she opened to see Brandon standing in front of the mirror with his towel around his waist.

"Hey babe!" he said with the same enthusiasm as his son. He came to hug Madeline, wrapping his naked and still slightly wet body around Madeline's suit. She hugged him back quickly before peeling off her dirty clothes to jump in the shower. "Woah there, I didn't think there would be time for a quickie this morning!" Brandon smiled, placing his strong hands around her waist.

"Sorry, I'm in a hurry," Madeline responded, giving her husband a quick kiss and jumping in the shower.

"I know, I figured," Brandon said, grabbing his toothbrush. "Just thought I'd try." Madeline showered and Brandon finished brushing his teeth. He left her in the bathroom to finish getting ready. She quickly rinsed herself and stepped out of the shower, drying herself off, lotioning her body and face, and going through her intense facial regimen. "See you this evening?" Brandon peeked his head back in the bathroom door. This time, his body was covered in a blue button-down shirt and he had a tie hanging over his shoulders.

"Yup," she responded, pecking him on the lips. "Have a good day." Brandon disappeared from the bathroom and Madeline finished her makeup, blew dry her hair and put on a fresh suit. She put on a navy-blue skirt suit and pinned an American flag to her lapel—the ultimate Senator uniform. She was back downstairs in fifteen minutes, to see the boys waiting for her by the front door.

"Mom! We're going to be late!" Adam yelled. Noah stood next to his younger brother with his arms folded in front of his chest. So much apathy for a ten-year-old, Madeline thought. How did he already learn to care so little?

"I offered to take them," Molly said, as though apologizing to Madeline. "I told them you could meet them at school, but Adam insisted..."

"It's fine, Molly," Madeline responded, giving Molly a thankful shoulder squeeze. Then she turned to the boys. "You ready?"

She drove them to school, where, sure enough, there were already several photographers and reporters hanging around the entrance. She parked the car and the cameras instantly started clicking as she and the boys started walking into the school. She put on her big senator smile and placed her arms on her boys' shoulders, gently greeting the cameras without giving them too much acknowledgement. She walked the boys to their classrooms, first dropping off Adam and then going with Noah to his, where she would be talking first. When she walked in, the teacher handed her a nametag with her name and occupation on it.

"Well, well Madeline! Was that circus outside planned just for you?" It was Mrs. Albertson, the woman who they had run into at the park the previous week. The mother of Jamie who had been the victim of Noah's bullying—Madeline's brain immediately started outlining the facts about this woman.

"Mrs. Albertson, so nice to see you," Madeline responded, as Noah took his seat and she found a place at the front of the classroom with the other parents. "What did you say your first name was?"

"Bonnie," she responded. "But I prefer Mrs. Albertson. What a treat that you joined us this year! Although I am sure everyone misses Brandon! He's such a great addition to our parents' group."

Madeline smiled. "How's Mr. Albertson? Has he had the privilege of attending Career Day?"

Bonnie scrunched her face together as though Madeline's question was endearing. "Oh, Pete would just love to come, but you know, surgeries just can't wait! He's needed at the clinic all the time."

"Of course," Madeline responded with a smile. Pete Albertson was a well-known plastic surgeon. His clinic had even contacted Madeline's office several times offering discounted services for the senator. Madeline could not, nor would not ever accept his offers. Not only could they be seen as bribes, but she was also fundamentally against plastic surgery. Wasn't her cream regimen enough? Was plastic surgery also recommended to male senators?

When the bell rang, Noah's teacher introduced Career Day and thanked all the parents for joining. She then explained that each parent would get 10 minutes to talk about their career and then the students would get five minutes to ask questions. They had many parents to go through, so there would be no going over the allotted time! Madeline listened as a mother talked about her career as an accountant. Then Bonnie stepped forward to talk about her choice to give up her job in marketing to be a stay-at-home-mom. She talked about how many of the skills she learned in college and in her career were so important in what she did at home every day. As she spoke, Madeline couldn't help but notice most of the parents in the room were women. There were two fathers waiting to speak, one wearing a green polo—Mark, Engineer—and the other in a suit—Dan, Lawyer. She also looked at Noah, sitting in the back of the classroom, studying his hands. She worried about him, his engagement at school. Whether his behavioral issues were her fault as Bonnie less than subtly believed.

After Bonnie spoke, Madeline was offered the front of the room. She began by talking about why she became senator, how she wanted to help people and make America a better place. She talked about her daily life, which included a lot of meetings, talking to people, giving speeches, and her favorite part: thinking about solutions to the country's problems. When her ten minutes were up, the teacher notified the students they could raise their hands to ask questions.

"Have you met the president?" a kid in the front row asked.

"I have," Madeline responded. "A very honorable man."

"Do you want to be president?" a kid in the back asked. Madeline could hear Bonnie tsk her tongue.

"It's not about whether I want to be or not, it's about whether the citizens think I can help them in that position. I would love the honor if it's possible."

"Can a woman even be president?" a girl called out without being called on. "My dad says that would be a disaster!"

"Gemma!" the teacher snapped. "Raise your hand!"

"Of course a woman can be president," Madeline responded, ignoring the teacher's outburst. "It just hasn't happened yet."

"Why not?" the girl questioned, again without raising her hand.

"Gemma! It's someone else's turn!" the teacher yelled out.

"There are many reasons, but it's much more difficult for women," Madeline responded.

"Couldn't you pass a law that it has to be a woman every other time?" Another girl called out.

"Ava!" the teacher screamed. "Raise your hand!"

"That would be a great idea," Madeline said with a smile. "I will look into that."

"I think we're out of time and the students are forgetting to behave!" the teacher said. "Mark, I think it's your turn. Tell us what it's like being an engineer! So fascinating!"

Madeline thanked the students for listening and left the classroom. She walked through the halls to Adam's class where another mother was standing up talking about being an interior decorator. This time, when Madeline was called to speak, she gave a similar talk about being a senator. When it was time for questions, all the hands shot up. She called on a small boy in the middle of the classroom.

"My dad said you're ruining our country," the boy said in a soft voice that seemed incongruent with his words. "Isn't your job to fix things instead of making them worse?"

Madeline was used to hearing from people who were against her politically, but not used to hearing these things from sweet eight-year-olds in glasses. The question took her aback a moment and she placed an armored smile on her face. "My goal is always to fix things, but some people have different opinions on how to fix things. Your dad probably has different opinions than I do."

"My dad says you're a bitch and you're going to get what's coming for you," the boy said in his sweet little voice.

"Clark!" the teacher called out. "Language! Mrs. Thomas I am so sorry!"

"It's fine," Madeline responded. "Clark, I'd be happy to talk to your father. You can tell him I'd love to hear his opinions about how I could be better at fixing things." The boy nodded and Madeline answered a few more questions before stepping back to the edge of the classroom to listen to the Director of Creative at an advertising agency begin his talk.

Chapter 11

"Sorry about the confusion last time," Officer Austin said as he stepped into Madeline's office. "Things get so hectic sometimes."

"I can only imagine," Madeline responded as she stood up to offer her hand. Officer Austin gave it a quick shake and then dropped into the chair across from Madeline's giant wooden desk. It hadn't been easy rescheduling with the regional director of the Fraternal Order of Police. In fact, it had been rather difficult and Jane had started believing that Officer Austin was avoiding a meeting. After all, he rarely answered his phone—shouldn't police officers be better about that?—and he always seemed to be busy—how did he have so much time to complain to the press about Madeline's SAVER Bill? But finally, Jane was able to get a meeting on the books. Even more surprising, was that Officer Austin showed up for the meeting. "And it was a good thing our last meeting was postponed," Madeline continued, choosing the word 'postponed' very carefully, rather than mentioning that Officer Austin had stood her up.

"Yes, what a strange situation," Officer Austin commented. "Probably some kids pulling a stupid prank. They seem to do that a lot these days, especially at schools. Every time there is a big test, we get tons of anonymous bomb threats coming through."

"Yes, but you can usually find out who called in the threat in those situations, can't you?" Madeline questioned.

"Oh yes, that's usually pretty easy," Officer Austin responded. "Our squad is great at that."

"But not so great that they found out who called in the threat for this building." Madeline softened her tone to not sound accusatory or condescending. This was an important skill for a woman speaking with a man who believed he had all the power.

"Well, I guess they are still looking into it." Officer Austin raised his arms as though to say he didn't know. Madeline wasn't sure if he really didn't know. Something about this situation was suspicious, but she needed to focus on the real reason she was meeting Officer Austin.

Madeline quickly changed the subject. "I really appreciate that you are able to take the time to meet with me about this important issue."

"Of course," Officer Austin said. "I want to help, I can see you really need it. Although I don't understand why you didn't talk to us before you proposed the bill. We could have told you how unrealistic it is and what a waste of your time it is to pursue it. It will never pass."

"I'd like to discuss your concerns and I think if I can explain it properly, you might actually change your mind," Madeline responded, using every technique she knew for being a convincing speaker. She was ready to address every concern Officer Austin had detailed in multiple interviews for different newspaper. Her arguments had been running through her head all morning and they were ready to be let loose and attack every counterargument.

"It's not necessary," Officer Austin replied. "I'm here as a courtesy, but the FOP won't be supporting this bill. In fact, we're actively fighting against it. We're actually fighting pretty hard to ensure this never sees the light of day." His tone became sinister and deep. "In fact, I think it would be best for you if you'd just drop it altogether."

"Officer Austin, I'm sure we can come to some sort of arrangement on this," Madeline responded. "There must be a way to align our interests."

"Our interests are not even close." Officer Austin's voice was starting to sound a bit hostile. "You know nothing about what you're saying. This bill would be a disaster, you're a dis—"

Officer Austin was cut off short when Jane popped her head in the room.

"Madeline, so sorry to interrupt! Officer Austin, I apologize, I do!" She said, her cheeks flushed as they often did when she felt embarrassed. Jane wasn't good at being in the spotlight, that's why she was such a great chief of staff. "Madeline, there's an emergency at home, Brandon called, he wants you to come home."

"Did he say what it's about?" Madeline's heart began racing. Was it Noah? Was he in trouble again? Was it Adam? Being bullied still for his comment about being the Majority Whip?

Jane shook her head. "He just said, come home."

Madeline nodded and turned to Officer Austin. "Well I thank you for your courtesy in coming. I'm sorry I couldn't change your mind." She was slightly glad she wouldn't be wasting any time talking to Officer Austin who surely would never support her. She shook the officer's hand and excused herself, allowing Jane to show the man out of the office.

"So sorry about this inconvenience!" she heard Jane saying. "I'll talk to your secretary to reschedule again and I promise there won't be any more hiccups!"

"It's not necessary," Officer Austin replied, just as Madeline was out the office door.

In the car, Madeline called Brandon's cellphone. She couldn't wait the fifteen-minute drive to know what was the emergency.

"Madeline? Where are you?" Brandon said without any greeting when he answered the phone.

"I'm driving, I was just worried. Is everyone OK? What happened?"

"Everyone is OK, just come home."

"I am, but can you tell me what's going on?"

"I can't. I have to show you." The conversation ended abruptly with a click and Madeline continued driving, her heart pounding and her blood boiling.

Madeline pulled into the driveway, half expecting to see police cars or black vehicles parked out front. But there were none. Nothing unusual outside the house, nothing that could clue her in to what this emergency was. She quickly parked the car and walked inside. Brandon was sitting in his usual spot at the kitchen table, fingering the edge of one of the crocheted placemats in front of him. She squeezed his shoulders as she walked past him to sit in her spot.

On the table was a ripped open envelop with the edge of a picture hanging out. Next to it, was a cassette tape, the kind people used to listen to before CDs or MP3 players took over. "What's this?" Madeline asked, picking up the envelope. She was afraid to look inside because she instantly knew what this was. It had been two weeks since they first received the letter of blackmail. With the FBI failing to do their job, and her reelection launch coming up in just a few short weeks, there was only one thing this could be. The blackmailer would be applying pressure. They hadn't followed the blackmailer's directions and sent money. For all the blackmailer knew, they had completely ignored the requests.

Madeline held the envelope in her hands. Brandon had undoubtedly already looked at the picture inside. She could tell from the distress on his face. She tried to read his expression, it was one of fear, guilt, defeat. He sat quietly, his eyes on the envelope in Madeline's hands, ignoring her question. Madeline's fingers trembled, but she forced herself to pull the picture out. It was startling, she had never seen herself so exposed.

The picture showed Madeline from the waist up lying on her back, naked with her breasts exposed. Her body was arched, her chin pointed up and her eyes were closed. She wasn't sleeping, that was obvious from her agape mouth and the way her arms were bent around her body; one up to her head pushing on the headboard behind her and the other reaching down, below the edge of the picture. The sheets she was lying on were a creamy white and the dark wooden headboard behind her was not the one in the Thomas' master bedroom. Words escaped her, she couldn't ask what this picture was or how it was taken. She had no questions because she knew there were no answers. All she could do was look at Brandon, who was still avoiding her eyeline.

"It must be photoshopped," Brandon said quietly. "It can't be real." He said it like a challenge, and Madeline felt compelled to nod in agreement.

Surely anyone with basic knowledge of photoshop could easily put her head on a naked woman's body and make the picture look real. They could easily search through the millions of pictures and videos of her online and find some facial expression that could be distorted to look this way. But there was one thing in the picture that caught Madeline's eye. Right at the bottom of the picture, before it cut off, right below Madeline's bellybutton, there was a faint line. A scar from her Cesarean section from when Adam was born. When she went into labor with him, the umbilical cord was wrapped around his neck and doctors decided to perform an emergency c-section to deliver him. Madeline remembered that day, the fear she felt, the anxiety. She didn't care if they cut her in half, so long as the baby was safe. At first, she hated that scar, a reminder of the trauma of that day. But years later, the scar didn't matter, it was just another part of her body, like her arm or her ear.

If someone had photoshopped the picture, they would have had to know about Madeline's scar. With enough research, that wouldn't have been too difficult. She had spoken about her c-section in interviews and the blackmailer could have easily added the scar to make the picture more realistic.

"What's on the tape?" Madeline asked.

Brandon shrugged. "I haven't listened to it. Do we even have a tape player?"

Madeline got up and walked to the home office she and Brandon had made for themselves when they moved in. They had designed an office with a large desk, big enough for a computer and extra monitor, and huge bookshelves and drawers for storage. However, over the years it became clear that they didn't like working in the office. Madeline mostly worked from the kitchen and Brandon often worked on the couch. Working in the office, for both of them, felt like being banished. They only did it if they were in the way.

Over the years, the office became more of a storage room. Madeline was sure there was a tape player somewhere in there. She walked inside and started fumbling through one of the drawers until she saw a Walkman, covered in dust. She picked it up and brought it to the kitchen. She tried to turn it on, but it didn't work.

"What kind of person sends a tape?" Brandon asked, his tone angry and bitter. "Wouldn't they know people can't play these anymore?"

Madeline understood that tapes were the most secure option for a blackmailer. CDs and MP3s could be traced. Data stored could be interpreted and tracked back to where the files were copied or what type of computer was used. Tapes had no such options, being from the pre-smart technology age.

Madeline walked to the refrigerator where batteries were stored in the door. She switched the batteries in the old Walkman and then again tried to turn it on. It started clicking to life. She put the tape inside and pressed play, her mind screaming, afraid of what she could hear.

At first there was a crackle. Then a man's voice. "Maddy, Maddy, I missed you so much." Then silence. Brandon and Madeline didn't say a word. They kept listening, as the tape crackled on.

"Is that it?" Brandon said. "This is fake, no one calls you Maddy." Madeline hated being called Maddy. It made her feel like a little girl, a child. Even Brandon called her by her full name.

Suddenly the crackle on the tape turned back into the man's voice. "I missed your smell, your voice. Most of all I missed kissing your little strawberry." The voice turned back to crackle.

Brandon's mouth dropped open. "Somebody has been spying on us!" Brandon threw his hands up to his head and he stood up. He started pacing around the kitchen. "Madeline. Our kids, someone is watching us...how do they? Do you think our house is bugged?"

To anyone else, the tape's last sentence may not have made sense, but it made perfect sense to Brandon. In between Madeline's thighs, just inches from her panty line, Madeline had a tiny birthmark. It was shaped like a triangle, but on one side little lines popped out, like the stem of a strawberry. Madeline called the birthmark her strawberry, and Brandon had delighted in that the first time he saw it. It was like a little secret between the two of them. When they were younger and newly together, Brandon would always joke about her sweet strawberry smell down below and how tasty it was. Now, it felt like their secret had been violated.

Brandon stopped the Walkman, which was still crackling. "We need to talk to the FBI," Brandon said. "They are not doing their job! This is totally unacceptable!"

Madeline took a deep breath, still absorbing the voice she just heard. "Maybe we need to pay."

"What? You're joking right?"

104

"This is our family's safety we're talking about," she said. "If someone has such intimate knowledge of our lives, we don't know what else they know. They could be dangerous. We need to do whatever to protect ourselves."

"Is that what this is about?" Brandon asked. "Protecting ourselves? It's not about your fears about reelection? You'd rather be blackmailed into paying than risk your reelection?"

"Brandon..."

"Seriously, Madeline, if we give in now, they could blackmail us again for more. Who knows what else they have! And who's to say that if you pay they won't publish this stuff anyway!" Brandon was still pacing, his arms now swinging back and forth. "I'm calling Agent Murray! They need to step up! They need to fix this. Maybe we should all stay in a hotel for a little while, in case we're being spied on."

Madeline nodded and stood up from the kitchen table. She stopped in front of Brandon, halting his pacing. "First, give me a hug," she said, opening her arms to embrace him. He fell into her, wrapping his arms around her waist.

"Did you...?" Brandon started to say, his voice trembling. "You would tell me if you did, wouldn't you? You wouldn't do this to me...after everything..."

"You know me," Madeline responded. She held Brandon tight in her arms, afraid to let go. She wanted to contain this, not just for her reelection campaign, which would be devastated by a picture and recording like this, but for Brandon. How he would suffer if their family's name were drawn through the mud like this.

She thought about other politicians, strong females, who were forced to give up their positions because of smear campaigns like these. Men cheated, sent nude pictures of themselves to underage girls, even used their positions of power to get favors from women and these men could overcome smear campaigns. Some were even reelected in the midst of these accusations. But women did not have the same privilege. A woman's reputation had to be spotless. Any stain would stop her from getting to the top. Even stains from dirt that was thrown at her from her opponents, stains that she acquired from no actions of her own.

Truth in smear campaigns was a minor detail. So minor that it could be easily overlooked or ignored. In fact, no one needed to even consider truth when there was so much mud being thrown. The truth, no matter what it was, would simply be buried under layers and layers of mud that would cake and dry up, becoming harder and harder to dig through. Truth didn't stand a chance, Madeline knew this and that was why she suddenly made up her mind.

Chapter 12

"VACATION!" Noah screamed, jumping up on the couch. Two bellboys followed them into the suite, wheeling a large cart carrying their suitcases. The FBI agents agreed that staying in a hotel while this matter was resolved was a good idea. They booked the hotel and had already done a full security sweep before escorting the family in. There would also be 24/7 surveillance and security watching the family to find out if anyone was watching them or trying to contact them.

Their house was also being watched. The FBI couldn't find any evidence of their house being bugged, of any microphones or hidden cameras. Molly, the nanny, had also been subject to a day-long interrogation and polygraph test which resulted in the conclusion that she wasn't involved in the blackmail.

After this second letter from the blackmailer, the FBI began to double down their efforts. This perpetrator was smarter than most, they observed. He was careful and able to obtain intimate knowledge without leaving any trace of footsteps. This took skill, the agents said, optimistically calling it a clue. This wasn't just anybody out for money, this was someone who had obviously been preparing for a long time. Someone with intimate knowledge of security and how investigations work. It could even be someone on the inside, someone leading the FBI astray, or someone with inner knowledge about the Thomas family. It was possible that there was a bigger conspiracy afoot, the agents postulated. Was someone from the top trying to stop Madeline from getting there?

"Can we order room service?" Adam asked, holding his hands in front of his chest. "I'm starving!"

"You bet," Brandon responded, squatting down to Adam's height. "Get me a burger." He winked at his son who was already running to the phone with the menu in his hands.

Madeline thanked the bellboys and handed them a tip. Jane and Agent Hart from the FBI were still standing in the doorway. "I suggest you lay low for the meantime," Agent Hart said. "It's probably best not to make big appearances until we resolve this."

"No appearances?" Jane laughed. "That's hardly possible! Madeline has appearances scheduled daily until the reelection campaign launch! She can't just lay low, that will destroy the campaign!"

"I'd suggest you postpone the launch party," Agent Hart replied. "We're just not sure what this person is capable of and we're trying to protect this family."

"Protect?" Jane yelled. "Postponing the event would be death for Madeline! Can you imagine what people would say? Everyone already knows about the event. If we cancel, people will say all sorts of things about Madeline! That she's flaky, not ready for reelection, she's unstable! It would destroy her career!"

Agent Hart shrugged. "My job is to keep this family safe."

"No, Detective," Madeline cut in. "Your job is to figure out who is blackmailing me and to stop this from getting out. If my career is ruined, then you didn't do your job."

"Ma'am, we're doing everything we can," Agent Hart gave a nod and excused himself. He promised to update with any new information from forensics, the department that was already examining the new picture and tape. After Brandon and Madeline had listened to it in their kitchen, they called the FBI agents. Brandon was reluctant to hand over the new evidence. It was just too intimate, too revealing. Calling it evidence made it seem mechanical, like it wasn't exposing a piece of Madeline or their marriage.

"What should we do about the reelection campaign launch event?" Jane asked Madeline. "Everything is booked and we've already been getting RSVPs. Cancelling would look really bad."

"Don't cancel yet," Madeline responded. She still had hopes that this would be resolved in time. That she would be able to launch her reelection without traipsing through the mud on her way to the podium.

"Maybe we need to step back on the SAVER Bill," Jane said. "Tone down the rhetoric. Let's pursue other things for now?"

Madeline gave a reluctant nod. The SAVER Bill was what made voters like her. People liked her ideas, they would stand behind her come election day because of her principles. But the people in power didn't like her principles as much. Maybe it was possible she had to step back if she even wanted to give the people a chance to vote for her on Election Day.

"Let's try to be less controversial for the next few weeks," Madeline responded. Jane agreed and left the hotel suite, where Brandon was just getting off the phone.

"Ordered you a Caesar Salad," he said to Madeline.

"Aren't you going to work today?" Madeline asked. Brandon hadn't taken a day off work in months. He rarely did, only for very special occasions like when Madeline was sworn in after her first Senate seat win. Or for Career Day at the boys' school.

He shook his head. "I think I'm with Noah today. VACATION!" He yelled trying to make this as fun as possible for the kids. They agreed not to tell the boys the real reason for their hotel stay. The boys believed their house was being fumigated for termites and that they were just taking a nice vacation in the meantime. Noah had stopped jumping on the couch and was already flipping through channels on the large TV in the suite's living room. Adam was busy exploring the bedrooms of the suite, "Noah and I have to share?"

he squealed with excitement as his older brother rolled his eyes.

Madeline walked to the kitchen where a coffee maker sat next to a bag of grinds. She began making coffee just as Brandon came up behind her and squeezed her shoulders. "It's going to be all right," he said quietly.

"I think we should pay," Madeline responded in a whisper.

"What? Madeline! How could you say that?"

"This can't get out."

"What is going on? Why can't you just tell me?"

Madeline shook her head. Brandon didn't understand. There was no fighting it if it came out. Her name would forever be associated with scandal, betrayal, nudity. She could never advance in politics. Whoever was vetting her for vice president would immediately drop her name from the running. If she ever wanted to advance to the White House, her opponents would constantly bring this up, no matter how hard she tried to focus the conversation on policy. "It's too risky," Madeline responded.

"How could you, of all people, say that?" Brandon asked. Their discussion in the kitchen was becoming heated, enough so that the boys were starting to glance over from the suite's living room. "Is this coming from Jane? Is she pressuring you to pay?"

"Not at all," Madeline responded. "I'm just worried about what would happen if this gets in the news. Think about the boys. Do you want them to see me naked online? Do you want their friends making fun of their mother to their faces? And what will I do? What if I have to resign?"

"Because of stupid rumors? Because of lies!? That's absurd." Brandon's voice became louder and Madeline flashed her eyes to the living room, where the boys were pretending to watch TV.

"It wouldn't be the first time it's happened," Madeline replied, hushing her tone. "Lots of people's careers are ruined by lies."

Brandon shook his head violently back and forth. "I don't understand you, Madeline. As a politician, you are so strict on your values. You never vote for something you don't believe in. You always speak up about what you think is right. That's why people love you. Because you're genuine and you have principles that you cannot be convinced to break, no matter what. But now, it's like you're ready to give up your principles because you're afraid of not being reelected. It's so unlike you, I don't get it."

"It's not unlike me." Madeline grabbed Brandon's hand. "Listen, to continue fighting for my principles, I can't let this explode. No matter what."

Brandon again started violently shaking his head, just as the doorbell rang. Noah and Adam both immediately jumped from the couch.

"Don't answer it!" Brandon yelled with slight paranoia in his voice. He pulled his hands from

Madeline's and ran to the door, peeking through the peephole.

"Room service," came a voice from the other side of the door. Brandon opened it for the bellboy who came in wheeling a table covered in a white cloth and four cloches covering their lunch. Brandon tipped the man and sat down with the boys to eat.

"You coming?" He asked Madeline who was still standing in the kitchen, next to the coffee maker that had just finished brewing.

With a deep breath, she nodded and walked to the table where her Caesar Salad was waiting. She ate silently while Brandon talked to the boys about what they were missing in school that day. The conversation was a blur to Madeline. How could she make Brandon understand? There was so much at stake. More than her principles, more than family. There were things like the SAVER Bill, like the constituents she fought for. People needed her. She couldn't let those people down. And as her trust in the FBI started to shrink, she feared she had no other options.

Chapter 13

"Mrs. Thomas, so sorry to bother you," Mr. Kendrick said on the phone. "I tried calling Mr. Thomas, but he wasn't answering."

"No problem, Mr. Kendrick," she responded politely to the principal at Highland Academy. "How can I help you?"

"There's been another incident with Noah at school," the principal said. "He's sitting with me in my office."

"What happened?"

"He pushed Jamie Albertson," Mr. Kendrick responded. "He's in the hospital."

"What? Is he all right?" Madeline felt herself getting angry with Noah. What had he done? This was exactly the kind of thing that could make it into the press if Jamie's mother Bonnie wanted to make trouble for Madeline.

"He broke his arm," the principal explained. "When Noah pushed him, he fell on one of the concrete benches in the courtyard. He'll be OK, but this is a serious issue. I'm going to have to suspend Noah again. Mrs. Albertson wants an expulsion, but I'd like to speak with you and her first. See if we can work something out. Are you available to meet this evening? In the meantime, I need you or Molly to come pick up Noah."

"No problem," Madeline responded. "I'll come. I'm on my way." Madeline hung up the phone and rushed out of her office. She waved goodbye to Jane, promising she'd come back soon. She had plenty to do at work, but first she needed to see Noah. Her insides wanted to scream at him, to shake him as hard as she could and slap his face until he understood that he couldn't bully another student. He made her so angry, an anger that only a mother can understand—one so strong and full of rage that can only be borne from feelings of love and disappointment. How could Noah do this to her? With her reelection campaign launch coming up. With the blackmail threatening to topple that. With everything else going on? But of course, she reminded herself, Noah wasn't aware of any of these things. He was just a kid, with an anger issue and two parents who didn't know how to solve it.

In the car ride Madeline called Brandon to update him that she was picking Noah up from school. He agreed they should both attend the meeting that evening with the school's principal and Mrs. Albertson. She then called Molly, to tell her she would be dropping Noah off at home. Then she pulled into the school parking lot and hightailed it to the principal's office. When she entered, she saw Noah sitting quietly in a chair, rocking slightly back-and-forth as he stared at his hands. He looked up when the door opened.

"Noah!" Madeline stated, flicking her head at him. She then looked at Mr. Kendrick, who was focused on his computer screen.

"Mrs. Thomas, thank you so much for coming it," he said too politely when he looked up at her.

"Sorry again for the bother. Will I be seeing you or Mr. Thomas this evening?"

"We'll both attend," she responded and motioned to Noah to grab his backpack and follow her out. She glared at her son silently, portraying her anger and disappointment. He needed to understand there were consequences for his actions. Maybe taking him out for dessert during his last suspension was a mistake, Madeline thought to herself. Noah followed her to the car, trailing a few paces behind. After they were inside and buckled, Madeline turned to her son.

"What is wrong with you?" she exploded. She instantly hated herself for it, but she couldn't help herself. She felt like a volcano, unable to stop itself from bursting out and spewing lava everywhere. Noah looked straight ahead, without even flinching. "Hello? Can you hear me? Noah! Do you want to explain?"

Noah shook his head. "Can we just go home?"

Madeline started the car, but her anger continued flowing from her mouth. "You can't just bully other kids! There are consequences! It affects all of us, don't you get it? You being a bully hurts me. It hurts dad, it hurts Adam! There is never any reason for it!"

Noah remained silent.

"Don't you have anything to say?"

He shook his head. Madeline let out a huge sigh.

"I just don't know what to do with you," she continued. "Maybe we'll ship you to boarding school. Would you want that?"

Noah shook his head and mumbled something under his breath.

"What? Speak up!" Madeline yelled at her son.

"It's not my fault!" Noah screamed. "Jamie started it! He always does!"

"He started it? What? He pushed himself into a concrete bench? He broke his own arm?" Noah's avoidance of blame made Madeline even angrier.

"You don't understand," Noah said, shaking his head.

"So help me understand."

"Jamie lies. He says things."

"That doesn't mean you can push him!"

Noah didn't respond.

"Well, what did he say?"

Noah again mumbled something too quiet for Madeline to hear.

"What!?" Madeline shouted.

"He called you a whore!" Noah screamed out. "He said his dad said you were a whore!"

Madeline's mouth fell open in shock. "What do you mean?"

"That's what he said! That his dad called you a whore."

"You still shouldn't have pushed him," Madeline said, although her tone had become calm as the lava of her anger flowed from Noah to Jamie. Noah shrugged and the two remained silent for the rest of the car ride. Madeline dropped Noah at home and then again called Brandon as she drove back to her office.

After she recounted to him what Noah told her, he breathed heavily into the phone for a few moments. "Do you think this is connected?" She asked him, thinking of the picture of her lying naked on the cream-colored sheets flashed in her head.

"I don't know, but I will alert Agent Murray," he responded. "Maybe it's a lead." The couple agreed to meet at the school that evening for the meeting with the Albertsons.

Madeline had a difficult time concentrating for the rest of the day. She sat in meetings with supporters, discussed her reelection campaign launch and reviewed talking points for a few upcoming engagements she couldn't cancel. The day continued as a blur and more than once Jane had to remind her exactly what they were doing or talking about at that moment. When the clock ticked closer to evening, she excused herself, and drove back to the school. When she arrived, she saw Brandon sitting in his parked car, talking on the phone. She parked next to him and got out. When he saw her, he also opened his car door, but he was still on the phone.

"I need to see an updated version tonight," he said, with his phone to his ear. "No more delays." Then he hung up and turned to Madeline. "Everyone is so incompetent," he confided and kissed his wife on the cheek. "What's our game plan in there?"

"I think we start by listening and see what they say," Madeline responded. "Once they've gotten out all they have to say, we can confront them about what Jamie said." Brandon nodded and the two continued toward the office, their fingers intertwined between them.

Inside Bonnie Albertson and her husband were already sitting across from Mr. Kendrick. "We just love running the bake sale," Bonnie was saying when the Thomases walked in.

Madeline and Brandon released a friendly greeting and sat down next to the other couple whose anger radiated around them. The four parents sat silently as Mr. Kendrick began their meeting.

"Thank you all for coming in this evening," the principal started. "As you know, it is very important that our school be a safe place for everyone and that we all get along."

"Well it is definitely not safe now!" Bonnie exclaimed. "Poor Jamie! He's in a cast! He can't play baseball for months now! This will set him back significantly! He was the first baseman, you know. Coach Roy said he has real talent and that scouts would definitely be looking for him when he finishes high school!"

"He's ten," Brandon retorted. "Plenty of time to heal before the college scouts come."

"You see?" Bonnie turned to the principal. "This is what I am talking about. The Thomases think they are above everyone, they don't care that their actions have consequences. In fact, I'm pretty sure their actions usually don't have consequences! They get away with everything!"

"What does that mean?" Brandon shot back. Madeline squeezed his hand trying to remind him of their plan to first listen. The message was not acknowledged. "Do you think that if we drop a plate it doesn't fall?"

"What?" Bonnie turned to look at Brandon and then to her husband with whom she shared a look and a laugh. "Does that have anything to do with what's going on here?"

"Please," the principal cut in. "I understand everyone is upset—"

"Upset is right," Brandon cut in again.

"You're upset?" Bonnie screeched. "Your son put mine in the hospital! How could you be upset? Your son should be expelled! Mr. Kendrick, you have to expel Noah! He is a danger to the other students! My poor Jamie! He's been bullied all year by Noah and you should have stopped it before it got this far!"

"Mrs. Albertson," Mr. Kendrick said, his voice significantly softer than Bonnie's. "Let's all try to discuss this together, rationally, as adults. Now, I noticed Mrs. Albertson and Mr. Thomas have been the only two speaking. Mr. Albertson, Mrs. Thomas, would you like to say anything?" Mr. Albertson shook his head.

"I would like to say something," Madeline spoke up. "I think this conversation has been very one sided and no one has listened to Noah's perspective on the issue."

"Noah's perspective?" Bonnie gasped. "On his bullying? Are you kidding?"

"Noah sees his actions as defensive," Madeline was careful to maintain an even tone and made eye contact with everyone in the room. "Yes, he pushed Jamie, and that was wrong, but he did it because of something Jamie said to him."

"What a lie! Mark!" Bonnie stood up and looked toward her husband. "We will not sit by and listen to this talk! We will take legal action if needed! Mark! Tell them what you told me! About how we can sue the Thomases and the school!"

"I don't believe Noah was lying," Madeline said, facing the principal. "In fact, I think Jamie was repeating something he heard at home."

"Now you are accusing us?" Bonnie said, standing in front of her chair with her hands on her hips. "This is absurd!"

"Jamie told Noah that I am a whore," Madeline said, facing the principal but her eyes were peering at Mark Albertson to gage his reaction. It was a good thing she focused her eyes on the man because if she hadn't she might have missed it. The man who seemed utterly unengaged until that moment let out a swift chuckle and shake of his head as though quite satisfied with what he heard. His expression of emotion lasted less than a second, and then his face again went blank and he looked to his wife.

"What?" Bonnie said. "Jamie would not use that language! Nor do we at home!"

Madeline quickly changed her demeanor, the same way she did in debates or other round tables with opponents. Her strategy was always to start looking like the underdog, like the quiet one that no one need fear, but once her opponents were riled up, she flipped, using their own emotions against them, making them look like petty children while she gave the final word of reason.

"Actually, I believe Mr. Albertson does," Madeline said, turning to the man to address him. "Mr. Albertson, is it possible that you told your son, or said in a way that he would hear you, that I am a whore?" The man's mouth dropped slightly and he hesitated as he looked to his wife and the principal as though one of them could signal him the right answer.

"This is ridiculous!" Bonnie yelled, throwing her hands up. "Mark, let's go. We're done here. Mr. Kendrick, if Noah isn't expelled there will be legal percussions! I hope you understand that! Madeline, Brandon, you will be hearing from my brother-in-law's firm!" Bonnie stood up and motioned to her husband to follow her out of the office. He did, with his eyes stuck to the floor as though still searching for his defense.

"Well, that didn't go as planned," Mr. Kendrick said. "I'm so very sorry."

The Thomases thanked the principal, who agreed to further look into the issue with Noah and Jamie before making any permanent decisions. Then Madeline and Brandon left the office to walk to their cars.

"You were so sharp in there! Really impressive," Brandon said, putting a hand on Madeline's shoulder. Then he whispered in her ear, "It almost turned me on." Madeline smiled and batted him away playfully.

"Almost?" She added her own banter. She excused herself to stop in the bathroom before they got to their cars, telling Brandon she would just meet him at home. No need to wait for her. They kissed and Brandon got in his car to drive away. Madeline used the bathroom, the stalls had obviously been cleaned since the school day ended but an old musky smell remained. Graffiti lined the walls where boys' names were written either with hearts or profanities next to them. When she finished, she walked to her car in the parking lot and got in.

"You are a whore," she heard suddenly as she was about to close the door. She looked up to see Mark Albertson in his own car, pulled up next to hers. Those damn electric cars were so quiet, she was startled he was so close. "I'm sure I'm not the only one who knows it." Then he drove off.

Chapter 14

"We need to go over this one more time," Agent Murray said to Madeline. They were sitting in Madeline's office with the door locked. Madeline rarely locked her office door, but this time, she was afraid someone might come in, see something they shouldn't.

"We've already went over it several times, I'm not sure I can tell you anything new," she responded to the agent. He was sitting across from her, leaning back with his legs crossed. He held a small notepad in one hand and a pen in the other. The page in front of him was blank, logically, as there really wasn't anything Madeline could tell him.

"We've been looking into Mark Albertson," Agent Murray said, a slight change of subject. "He doesn't appear to be the perpetrator according to our initial findings but we're still looking into it."

Madeline nodded, but stayed silent. Agent Murray let the silence linger for a moment before he continued talking. "Let's just go over everything once more." He pulled the picture of Madeline naked out from behind the notebook and placed it on the desk in front of Madeline. His eyes carefully avoided looking at the picture as though he were trying to preserve her honor, although Madeline was sure he had stared at it fully when not in her presence, in a purely professional way of course.

"Do you recognize this picture being taken? Do you recognize the sheets? The headboard? The situation?"

Madeline shook her head, her eyes filled with ennui. She had answered these questions before.

"Is there anyone other than Brandon who could have taken this photo?"

Brandon had never taken nude pictures of her. She would never have allowed it. Nude pictures, even taken by husbands, were fuel for scandal. All someone had to do was steal a phone, hack into a storage account and the pictures would be everywhere. Madeline again shook her head. "The photo isn't real."

"Our forensics believe it is," Agent Murray responded. "It doesn't have any of the signs of photoshop, no pixelated edges, or mismatches in the lighting. The team couldn't find any pieces of the image anywhere else online, which usually happens with photoshopped pictures. Usually the image of the body could be found on a porn or stock photo site. But this body isn't anywhere else online."

Madeline shrugged. "So what are you saying?"

"I'm saying we need more information about this photo so we can develop new leads. There are a few scenarios of how this photo could have been taken. Since it is taken from above, it is a little more complex. Often, when nude photos appear online they are from someone's phone or computer being hacked. Someone hacks the device, controls the camera, films or takes a picture, then erases the evidence from the device, OK? That's a typical scenario we see. These photos are often taken from strange angles, catching people in mirrors, or having parts of the picture covered by something else in the room. This picture is from above, making it look like someone planned on taking the picture, either by holding a phone or device above you, or by sticking a camera on the ceiling. So I ask again, is there anyone who could have taken a picture of you like this?"

"No!" Madeline responded, her annoyance simmering into anger.

"Because if there is, that's a lead, a hot lead," the agent said. "It could be the person who took the photo, or someone who has access to their phone or photo storage."

"Listen," Madeline said. "I am a US Senator and I have been living my life knowing that I am going into politics and that I plan to go far. From when I was young, I knew this was my path. That means that I have constantly thought about ensuring there are no skeletons in my closet. You will not find any pictures of me drinking, underage or not, in college. No one can honestly tell you I cut corners somewhere or took advantage of them. I never smoked, did anything illegal, and I certainly would never have naked pictures taken of me, by my husband or anyone else. That would be careless and detrimental to my life goals, you understand?"

"So you're saying this picture was taken without your knowledge?" Agent Murray responded. "That's the other option."

"If it's a fact that it wasn't photoshopped then I guess that must be the case," Madeline said.

"And you don't recognize it?"

"No, I don't recognize how I look in this picture. I can't remember every set of sheets I've slept on in the last eight years, since this was obviously taken after Adam was born. I can't remember every sexual experience I've had in that time either."

"Every sexual experience with Brandon," the agent questioned.

"With Brandon," Madeline confirmed. The conversation was starting to feel like an interrogation to Madeline. As though this blackmail was somehow her fault or that she had in some way put herself in this position. It was time for Madeline to turn this conversation around, put blame where it belonged. "Agent Murray, from this conversation and our previous ones, I understand that you and your team have made absolutely no progress in this investigation. I am not saying you're incompetent, since I am sure you have solved many cases prior to this—"

"Mrs. Thomas—" the agent cut in. But Madeline did not let him speak.

"But I'm beginning to lose confidence. It's been weeks now and it seems like I am your only suspect. I'm not sure what you suspect me of, but I haven't heard you accusing anyone but me. If necessary, I'm ready to speak with your superiors and see if another team could more adequately handle this situation."

"Ma'am—"

Again, Madeline did not let the agent speak. "As you know, my reelection campaign launch is fast approaching. That is when the perpetrator wants to release this information to the media, I shouldn't need to remind you of that. This needs to be resolved by then. There are no reasons it shouldn't be, even if we need to get a new team involved."

"Ma'am, we are doing the best we can," Agent Murray responded, this time without being cut off. "It may seem like little progress to you, but we've ruled out a lot of possibilities and have narrowed down the long list of potential leads that you provided us. In our work, checking suspects or possibilities off the list is significant. It takes a lot of legwork, interviews and analysis that our team has been conducting furiously over the last few weeks. In fact, we've been working so hard that we're pretty sure there is something big we are missing here and that's why I'm back, asking you these questions. As someone who has been doing this for twenty years, I know when there is something that someone is not saying. I know when a case follows the regular trajectory and when something is off. In this case, something is off. Someone is lying, some big piece is missing."

"And I assume it is your job to figure out who that is or what's missing, correct? Agent?"

Madeline responded, again ensuring blame was placed where it belonged.

The agent sighed. "Correct."

"I think you are focusing on the wrong thing," Madeline said, now leading the conversation. "You came in here accusing me of something because of this picture. But your focus is wrong. The focus is not why I was naked on a bed, the focus is who is using this to blackmail me."

"It's connected."

"Of course, but we've established that I don't allow naked pictures of myself. We've established that I am a married woman who likely has a sexual relationship with her husband. So you need to focus on who is blackmailing me." Madeline paused as her words sunk in. "So what are the next steps?"

The agent's tone changed. It now had less confidence and a slight hint of defeat. "I'm going to speak with Brandon after this conversation. I want to confirm his story and see if anything else has come up for him."

"Well it seems like you have a lot to do, so you might as well get to it," Madeline said, ending this inquisition. The agent raised his eyebrows and stood up from his chair, closing his notebook, which he still had not written on. As he left the office, he hesitated slightly at the door as though there was something else he wanted to say, but he remained silent. He left, but his presence still very much seemed to hover in the doorway.

Madeline sat quietly at her desk for a moment as she contemplated what she should do. She was beginning to get an itch inside her that she couldn't scratch away. As her confidence in the FBI agents continued to dwindle, she saw her options bright and clear in front of her eyes. What would happen if this scandal came out? What would happen if her name and naked picture were all over the media? If it came to that, it was only a matter of time before collateral damage began to fall. The itch inside her told her what she needed to do. She needed to make a phone call. She needed to call someone that she hadn't talked to in a very long time, someone she didn't think she would ever talk to again. Someone that she probably shouldn't talk to ever again, but at this point she wasn't sure what else to do.

Chapter 15

"Hunter Williams, how can I help you?"

"Hunter, it's Madeline." Madeline felt as though she were holding her breath as she said it, barely letting out the air needed for the sounds to come out.

"Maddy?"

"Hi."

"You make your own phone calls these days? You don't have a secretary or publicist to do it for you?"

"Hunter, please."

"What's going on? What brings me the honor of hearing from you today?"

"We need to talk." Madeline tried not to make her tone sound too dire.

"You know, that's convenient, because that's what these telephone things are for. You know the device you're probably holding to your ear right now, it's great for talking." Madeline wasn't sure if Hunter was trying to joke with her or if his sarcasm came from something more sinister. She decided to respond as though he were joking.

"Oh, really? You know I could never figure out what these things were for," she said lightly. "I'm so glad I called you so you could tell me."

"That's what I am here for, Maddy," Hunter responded. "You know I'll always tell you what you need to know."

"I know," she responded, the whimsical tone fading away. "I'm going to be in New York next week. Can we meet?"

Hunter hesitated. "I'm not sure that is a good idea."

"Why? What's the problem?"

Again Hunter was quiet, as though carefully choosing his words. "Because..." But then his tone shifted as though something had changed his mind. "Sure, just have your secretary or chief of staff or whatever you got these days call mine," he said. "It's this same number, I'll pretend I work for Hunter Williams and will look for a slot in my boss's busy schedule to fit you in."

"No secretaries," Madeline said. "Just tell me when I can come to your office."

"Aren't you worried of what people would say? A Republican Senator from California coming to the office of a Democratic city council member from Harlem?"

"It doesn't have to be a big deal, Hunter. We just need to talk. Besides if anyone asks, you're the city councilman responsible for my alma mater. It's not weird."

"OK, well, I'm usually in my city council office on Tuesdays and Thursdays. Come whenever you want."

"I'll see you on Tuesday morning," she responded before hanging up the phone.

A gush of memories flooded over her as she sat, still hearing Hunter's voice in her ear. Hearing him speak made her feel like she was being crushed, crushed by the emotions, the regrets and the decisions she'd made in her life. She believed she had made the right decisions for herself, the right decisions for someone of her ambitions, but that didn't mean she didn't have a lingering feeling of 'what if.' What if things were different? What if she had chosen differently? What if she hadn't been forced to choose between her life ambitions and young love? She could spend all day thinking of the what-ifs, but she knew that if she had to do it all again, she would make the same decisions, no matter how hard they were.

Madeline first met Hunter when she was a senior at Columbia University. She was on her way home after a long night of studying in the library. In fact, the night had been so long that it was already dawn when she arrived at her old brownstone on the edge of campus. Her parents had hated that she refused to live in the dorms. Instead, she and a girlfriend rented a small two-bedroom together two blocks away from their prestigious university. But while it was only a seven-minute walk to campus, it was a world away. It was Harlem, the neighborhood where young Caucasian females were told not to walk by themselves late at night. But Madeline saw it differently. To her, it was the neighborhood where jazz wafted out of the basement club on her corner and the smell of frying oil greeted her from the street vendor who sold hotdogs near her stoop. She never felt afraid when walking in her neighborhood. How could she be, when her neighbors were so friendly? There was Tom, the elderly retired man who often spent days sitting on a crate watching the sidewalk and smoking his pipe. There were also Dayvon and Daya, the children who lived with their single mother in the apartment under Madeline's. The kids were often sitting on the stoop outside the apartment building playing with sticks, cardboard or anything else that could be considered a toy. On hot days, Madeline would sometimes take them to the corner market to eat popsicles. Madeline loved her neighborhood and her brownstone there that had a small garden in front. Someone who didn't live in New York City wouldn't have considered it a garden. They would have considered it a small patch of dirt the size of a ping-pong table with a few shrubs and weeds somehow thriving without any water and rare sunlight that shone through when it wasn't being blocked by the surrounding buildings. When Madeline first met Hunter that early morning, just after dawn, he was planting flowers in that garden.

"Well this is certainly an upgrade," Madeline commented to him. He was wearing a dirty ripped T-shirt that said *Smith and Sons Landscaping* on the back.

"A garden to walk in and immensity to dream in," he responded. Madeline instantly recognized the quote. She had just seen the play recently and had also been struck by that line in *Les Misérables*.

"One definitely needs immensity to dream in when calling this a garden," she said about their little patch of dirt. She was struck that her landlord would have a landscaper come to beautify the dirt patch. This was the same landlord who had taken months to fix her air conditioning, suggesting she sleep with bags of ice in her bed while she waited for his technician to be available, and refused to put in a new lock on the brownstone's front door after someone jammed it. "Is Smith and Sons Landscaping doing some volunteering in beautifying the neighborhood?"

"Doing it as a favor to my uncle, your landlord, I guess," Hunter said. "Hope it makes you smile when you come and go." Madeline blushed and smiled at him, noticing his strong arms, short curly hair and deep dark skin. Then she went into the brownstone, walked up the three flights of stairs and went to sleep.

The next time she saw Hunter, she was in a friend's dorm room at school. It was a Saturday evening and they had just ordered delivery from *P's Diner*, the place with the best burgers in all of Manhattan if you asked any Columbia student. When the doorbell rang, there was Hunter in a *P's Diner* t-shirt standing with a brown bag that had grease stains soaking through the bottom corners.

"Jean Valjean," Madeline said, calling him the lead character in the play he had quoted at their last meeting. "What are you doing here?"

"Delivering burgers," he said with a smile. Madeline wasn't sure if he recognized her, she was

135

focused on his white teeth surrounded by his thick lips.

"Landscaper by day, food delivery man by night," Madeline commented as she took the burgers from him and handed him the money. She was suddenly self-conscious about the tip she and her friends had contributed for their dinner. Did it make her look like some cheap, privileged, college student?

"I try to be well-rounded," Hunter responded. "That's what you call it, right?"

Again, Madeline blushed and thanked him, as she closed the door and brought the burgers to her friends. For the next few weeks, Madeline ordered burgers whenever her college budget would allow it, but sadly, *P's Diner* apparently had multiple deliverymen and Hunter hadn't been the one to bring her orders.

The next time she saw him, she was sitting on the stairs outside of her apartment. Her lock was jammed and her key got stuck inside, leaving her locked outside of her apartment. She called her landlord, who as usual, was angry for the disturbance and had to be strong armed into helping. After a heated conversation, he promised he'd get a locksmith over to her soon. She needed to study, but her books were inside. Every minute wasted could be docking her grades that semester. She'd been waiting for more than two hours when Hunter showed up.

"Don't tell me you're a locksmith," Madeline said when she saw him.

"I'm not," he responded. "But I'm good with my hands and my uncle asked a favor. No guarantees I can fix the issue."

"Well that's promising," Madeline said with fake annoyance. Being stuck outside her apartment wasn't as frustrating anymore now that Hunter was there. Hunter fiddled with the lock, tried pulling out the key and even tried breaking into the apartment, but all attempts failed.

"I think you need a real locksmith," he said after thirty minutes of effort seemed to make the door even more stuck. "I have a friend I can call."

Madeline sighed deeply as she thought about more hours of waiting for Hunter's friend to come. Hunter called his friend who promised to come soon, and then he looked at Madeline. She must have looked like a pathetic Ivy League princess, sitting there with her backpack and books that she had just gotten from the library.

"Do you want to get something to eat while we wait?" Hunter asked. "Anything but burgers."

Of course she wanted to get something to eat. She gathered her backpack and her books, which Hunter offered to carry for her and he looked silly doing it, and the two of them walked a few blocks to a small deli that Hunter recommended. "The best chicken and waffles," he promised and he was right. The chicken was just the right amount of salty and crispy and the waffles were thick, fluffy and soaked up the maple syrup they slathered on top.

While they ate, Hunter asked her about the books she was carrying – *The Clash of Civilizations* for her International Relations course, an anthropology textbook (for one of her general education requirements which she had put off in previous terms and absolutely hated), and a copy of Ayn Rand's *Atlas Shrugged* (reading materials not prescribed by any professor).

"This book is an insult to our society," Hunter had said about the last one, holding up the beat-up paperback. Afraid that Hunter would judge her, she said it was for a class she was taking on capitalism and literature and she quickly threw the book back in her bag. She would never mention to him that she found the story fascinating and honestly believed that society could be making its way towards the downtrodden dystopia described in the novel. It would be years before she would tell anyone outside of her Republican circle about her love of the book.

Hunter said he always thought anthropology would be fascinating and Madeline joked that maybe with a different professor it would be, but truthfully she thought the subject was as dull as the professors who studied it. Madeline didn't want to talk about her classes—she thought about them enough already—but Hunter was interested in her thoughts on what she was learning. Oddly, Madeline had never thought about her courses in that way, she had only thought about them in the ways required to pass an exam or write a perfect paper. The conversation made her even more intrigued by Hunter, who seemed to defy everything a stranger might think of a tall, African American man who worked in landscaping, food delivery, and was handy enough with his hands that someone might think he could also perform the job of a locksmith.

By the time they finished, Hunter's friend was already waiting for them at the brownstone, annoyed that Hunter wasn't there when he arrived. He fixed the lock, letting Madeline into her apartment and leaving her with a feeling of disappointment that Hunter would also probably now leave.

"Everything good?" he asked standing at her doorstep. She nodded, realizing they never introduced themselves to each other.

"I'm Madeline, by the way," she said. "So you know the next time we run into each other."

"Hunter," he responded. "If you're interested, we can run into each other on Friday. My bro is performing at the Cat Club. Been there?"

Madeline shook her head. She'd never been to the Cat Club, but she'd walked by. There was always loud music, usually rap, and a line around the block. "Your bro?" she commented with a smile.

"Yeah, my little brother. He raps. The next Tupac if you ask any deaf person." Hunter responded. "I promise he's not so bad."

Madeline agreed. That Friday, Hunter met her at the stoop in front of the flowers he had planted weeks ago and were then blooming, and he walked her to the Cat Club. They listened to his little brother rap, it wasn't as terrible as Madeline expected, and she enjoyed the company. She only felt a little uncomfortable that her skin was several shades lighter than everyone else's in the club, but everyone Hunter introduced her to was friendly and welcoming. No one seemed to pay her skin tone any mind.

Afterwards they went out to eat, Hunter paid, even when Madeline insisted they split the bill. She didn't feel right, letting this man who worked two jobs pay for her when she was going to one of the country's most expensive universities without a penny of financial aid. "I would never in a million years let you pay," he once said to her later on. "I was raised to be a gentleman, and that means holding doors, paying and doing right by my woman." His woman, she quickly became. Her friends didn't understand it. When they were busy chasing the Wall Street type, she was going with Hunter to visit his friends' 'street art', which to another person's eye could look like graffiti. She went with him to underground poetry readings and ate the fried hush puppies Hunter's mom would make and he would bring to her.

Hunter wasn't educated like she was, but he was knowledgeable. He had grown up in Harlem, just blocks away from the university. He knew someone like him would never study there. Someone like him meaning the oldest of four boys being raised by a single mother in a two-bedroom apartment for which every month his mother fought for the rent. His mother was a cleaning lady, who trekked down to the Upper East Side daily, cleaning multiple apartments for people who lived in buildings with doormen and carpets out front. Her hands were always peeling from the cleaning materials, but it was honest work. Sometimes she'd come home with something one of her customers wanted to throw away—barely worn clothing (that Hunter and his brothers would never wear. Just think how badly they would get made fun of!), kitchen utensils which didn't match the apartments' décor, or even old computers or electronics that his mother would lug on the subway feeling like she had just won the lottery.

Hunter got his first job when he was 14. He started working for *Smith and Son's Landscaping*, cutting grass and pulling weeds wherever the company was hired. The company's owner, Bill Smith, took a liking to Hunter, as none of his actual sons were ever so dedicated, and soon taught him about planting trees, pruning bushes and turning a mess of greenery into something beautiful. Hunter used to work mornings before school and quickly became responsible for the shrubbery in front of some of the very same apartments his mother cleaned. When he graduated high school, he got a second job as a deliveryman. At first he worked for a pizza place down on the Upper East Side. But soon he was notified that customers didn't feel comfortable when a black man came to deliver their pizza. They preferred a white person come, especially when they had to open their doors and hand over money. So Hunter got a new job, delivering for *P's*

Diner, only above 120th street. In fact, he usually didn't deliver to the Columbia dorms because his boss understood that some of the privileged university students might take offense and stop ordering. He usually made deliveries only in the neighborhood, except on rare occasions when he was the only deliveryman available. He worked hard to help his mom pay rent, so she only needed to clean one or two apartments a day.

In his free time, he would read. He figured out how to use the New York Public Library to get any book he wanted. He loved Maya Angelou and Langston Hughes, but also read other classics from Mark Twain, George Orwell or Charles Dickens. He tried introducing his siblings to reading, but none were interested. One was busy dreaming about his rap career, while another didn't seem to be busy with anything at all. The youngest had gotten stuck in the crossfire between a gang fight and had been killed when he was 12.

Like Madeline, Hunter was also someone focused on his ambitions. He was also someone who believed he was going somewhere in life. But that somewhere was very different for Hunter, as was his path to success. Instead of reaching the top through private school, an expensive education, and associations with networking clubs meant to breed success, Hunter had to claw his way up through obstacles and his community who didn't understand him. They didn't understand why he read books by white authors. They didn't understand why he worked for a white man like Bill Smith. They didn't understand why he tried to follow a legal and political system that was built to suppress them. But Hunter understood things differently. Where he was going, he also needed to be a part of the system. The system that needed to be changed from the inside out.

Chapter 16

• — • ⟨◆⟩ • — •

The love story of Madeline and Hunter was thrilling as any young love is. The two of them fell hard and deep together, despite their differences. While Madeline was finishing her senior year at Columbia and figuring out what to do next, Hunter was working hard at his two jobs and volunteering at a local youth center to mentor young children. They welcomed each other into their different worlds.

Madeline brought him to her events for the College Republican National Club. Hunter hadn't been much interested in politics at the time, but he came to support Madeline and often found himself at the center of debates with Madeline and her friends. The college republicans enjoyed having Hunter there, he brought new perspectives, challenged them, and helped them finetune their debate talking points. He himself also discovered his own ability for oratory and often planned his own tactics for upcoming CRNC debates.

Hunter also brought Madeline to the local youth center, where she helped elementary school children with their homework and tried to instill in them dreams that they never could have come up with on their own. "Do your math homework, and you could become a doctor or an astronaut!" she would say to children who had never before been told that they could aspire to such professions. When kids called Hunter for help when they got in trouble, Madeline would sometimes come along, hugging the boys who moments before thought they were too old for mothering but soon realized they needed it. Madeline would never forget one time a 16-year-old girl had called Hunter and asked to speak with Madeline. She had been raped and found out she was pregnant. Not knowing who else to call, she figured the white lady would know what to do. Madeline took her to a Planned Parenthood for an abortion and then to a Tasti D-Lite for ice cream. Madeline had felt honored that the girl had trusted her enough to let her help.

They loved crossing over into each other's worlds, but even more than that, they loved being alone together. They could spend hours talking about their aspirations—Madeline was going to be a politician, the first female president if she dared to dream. She wanted to help women advance, with fair pay, control over their bodies, and less fear of sexual harassment when thriving in a man's world. In fact, she hated that it was a man's world and she hoped she could change that too. "You don't sound like a republican," Hunter would tell her. "Fiscally, I am," she'd respond and then she would talk about how she believed in smaller government and less involvement in people's lives. "Libertarianism," she called it.

Hunter also had dreams. He wanted to be a community organizer in Harlem and help turn around the neighborhood. He wanted it to be a place where everyone felt safe and 16-year-old girls didn't get raped on their way home from school because the boys were also busy doing productive things, having jobs and supporting their families.

Of course their relationship was more than just about dreams. When Hunter touched Madeline, she felt shock waves move through her body. Just his fingertips on the small of her back could make her tremble. When he kissed her, with his thick lips, she wanted to melt inside him. His arms, strong from hours of landscaping work six days a week, made her feel small and protected in a way no one else had. There was a fire between them that was hard to put out. Madeline wanted to always be touching him, whether holding his hand, brushing their knees or wrapped around each other in bed, it was never enough.

Unfortunately, their touch was not always a welcomed sight in public. While their peers said they accepted Madeline's and Hunter's relationship, their eyes said differently. When Hunter held Madeline's hand at university functions, eyes often drifted and stuck at their intertwined fingers instead of focusing on the couple's faces during conversations. At the community center, girls and women tsked their teeth when Hunter snuck a kiss on Madeline's cheek. The couple tried to ignore these instances. Other people didn't matter, they didn't understand their love. They were primitive in their beliefs and one day in the future, skin color and background wouldn't matter. People would see others for their brains, their personality, not their skin tone. It was only a matter of time.

When Madeline graduated, Hunter attended all the ceremonies and sat politely with Madeline's parents while she walked across the stage to receive her diploma. He took pictures of her and her parents and posed in pictures with Madeline in her teal cap and gown. When the weekend of festivities was over, Madeline's mother hugged Hunter and then pulled Madeline close and whispered in her ear, "It's time to grow up now, honey. You're entering the real world now." Madeline thanked her mother for the advice and said goodbye to her parents who drove back to their estate in upstate New York.

At that time, Madeline had already received a job offer from a top management consulting firm in New York. The offices were in Midtown, quite a trek from her apartment near Columbia. When her lease ended, she moved downtown into a three-bedroom apartment with two new friends she had met at events for the New York Young Republican National Federation. They were like her, young, ambitious and politically motivated to pave the way for women.

Hunter stayed living in Harlem with his mother and brothers. They needed him up there, about 100 blocks up from Madeline's new place. He couldn't move downtown, it was too far from his jobs and the community center where he worked. How could he change Harlem if he lived in Midtown? Even so, the couple made it work.

They spent hours on the Subway going back and forth, sometimes even meeting halfway on the Upper East Side, despite the looks they got from elderly couples walking their poodles passed their door manned apartments and French cafes. They still welcomed each other into their different worlds. Hunter sometimes came down to midtown to meet Madeline and her colleagues for happy hours where they spent $10 on fancy cocktails and called that a deal. Hunter would hold a single beer the entire evening and smile as Madeline's colleagues joked about the synergies they created for clients and complained about the limitations of analyzing data in Excel. On weekends Madeline traveled up to Harlem to visit the community center and listen to Hunter's brother's new rap tracks, while holding herself back from correcting his grammar. She tried to stay updated on the kids' lives, remembering to ask about their parents, siblings and the drama they were having with friends. She only occasionally confused the stories of two different kids, who would chalk her confusion up to "White girl" brain, which they believed made it harder for her to understand their world.

It worked, there was no reason it wouldn't for two people who were so in love. They tried to spend as many nights together as they could, even if for Hunter it meant getting up before dawn and commuting uptown for his early morning landscaping jobs. Madeline couldn't stay at his place, there was no room there in the bed he shared with two brothers. When Madeline slept alone, she missed him. She missed his strong arm wrapped around her body and cupping her breasts. She missed the rhythm of his breath, which masked the sounds from the street below. She missed the feeling of his naked body pressed against hers, and the sweat they generated together, even in her apartment with a working air conditioning unit.

For that first year after Madeline graduated, everything was perfect. Madeline got her first promotion to Senior Consultant and she became more active in the YRNF. Instead of just attending events, she became part of the committee that planned them. She became closer with the leadership of the New York chapter and was even invited to a few exclusive meetings with prominent republican leaders. During these meetings, Madeline was always outspoken and shone bright among her peers who were more likely than her to spend time listening rather than speaking out. Soon, the New York Chairman of the Republican National Committee, and elderly white-haired man who had weekly calls with the party's leadership, knew Madeline by name and often asked her opinions on specific policies and events that were important for the party. Madeline did well in the spotlight, so well, that she was invited into the inner circle of New York's Republican leaders. At the age of 23, she was sitting in lounges, drinking scotch and discussing line items in the federal budget with fat men in ties. They liked her ideas and began discussing her future in the party. She'd run for New York

Chairman of the YRNF next year, they decided. From there, she'd move on to run for office, in the state senate or the Federal House of Representatives. These were tough goals for a Republican in New York, a mostly democratic state, but Madeline was just what the country needed to see that Republicans weren't all just old white men.

Hunter was proud of Madeline as her future in the Republican Party began to take shape. In the meantime, he also became more interested in politics and started reading more about the platforms of the republicans and democrats. While he had previously always felt that there was truth in the things Madeline believed, he started to find himself leaning more toward the Democratic platform, more social services, universal healthcare, and liberty for all. Didn't Madeline believe in these things?

"Of course I do," she'd respond. "But I don't believe the federal government should be responsible for them. Why should I pay higher taxes because I work harder? I'm being punished for my hard work! Why do my earnings go to people who aren't even trying to get jobs? And if we agree that these people do need help, the government is completely inefficient in providing that help. Let's privatize social services. Privatize all healthcare. The government should do as little as possible and let corporations be in charge. Corporations live with balanced budgets and competition, making them much more efficient. Give them the power to help people in need."

Hunter didn't agree, but he kept his mouth shut. Maybe Madeline understood things he didn't. After all, she had a degree in political science from Columbia University. Not to mention, she'd already spent years studying political issues while Hunter was just starting to learn about these things himself for the very first time.

Sometime that second year after Madeline graduated, the New York Republican leadership invited her to a social event. At this event, they wouldn't be discussing legislation or policy, unless of course it came up organically, which it inevitably would! They'd just be mingling in front of an open bar with fancy hors d'oeuvres and enjoying the art at the gallery venue they had chosen for the event. In attendance would be everyone who was anyone in the New York Republican circle, and even some from outside of New York. There would be senators, governors, maybe even a Bush or two would make an appearance. Madeline was told to bring a date, after all, her colleagues had heard so much about her boyfriend—a self-made, intelligent, hard-working man who was able to proudly stand next to such a powerful woman without feeling intimated. He must really be something, Madeline's peers said, why wasn't he a member of the YRNF? Why hadn't they met him before? Madeline would shrug when asked those questions, Hunter hadn't been much interested in politics, other than to support her, she said, and besides he was busy working, and volunteering.

Did she mention he was also starting a new degree? She didn't mention it was a bachelor's degree at City College of New York and he had just registered for classes. She'd let her peers imagine what type of a degree her boyfriend was pursuing and at what institution.

She would bring him to that social event. He would do wonderfully speaking with the Republican leaders, just as he had with her friends in the College Republican National Club. Everyone would be intrigued by him, as people always were. Madeline was sure there would be nothing to worry about.

Chapter 17

Hunter looked great in the Brooks Brothers suit Madeline had bought for him. She had insisted on buying it as a gift, especially after everything he had done for her. Had he not paid for her when he took her out to dinner, even when she knew dinner cost him a full day of work? Had he not spent hours commuting to her Midtown apartment so he could be with her and support her when she felt stressed out about work? He was a great listener, taking time to ask questions about what upset Madeline instead of proposing solutions as most men tended to do. Madeline appreciated all his efforts and had taken him to choose a brand new suit that would be tailored perfectly for his body. Hunter hadn't been as enthusiastic about suit shopping, but once he saw himself in the mirror, wearing that jet-black jacket over a light blue shirt with a gray tie, he lightened up about the idea. He may have even liked how he looked in it, Madeline thought, noticing how his eyes traced his own outline in the mirror.

As he put on the suit in Madeline's bedroom, she couldn't help herself from watching him. She imagined herself helping him take if off at the end of the night, after he had impressed everyone she knew. She would pull loose the tie, carefully unbutton the shirt and ease him out of the fitted pants. She'd be turned on from watching him speak eloquently as he always did among her peers. She'd crave his attention after watching him nod knowingly while he listened to her peers before asking intelligent questions that often led to smiles and winks from stumped attendees.

Madeline came up behind him and wrapped her arms around his waist as he continued fiddling with the tie. It was already perfectly straight, as Hunter had spent hours perfecting how to tie the knot before this event. For her part, Madeline was wearing a light blue floor-length dress that she had bought specially for the occasion. It made her look sophisticated, maybe even a little older than 24, but also sexy in an intelligent sort of way.

The couple took a cab to the art gallery. After hailing one outside Madeline's apartment, Hunter hesitated by the passenger seat. "You sit in the back with me," Madeline said light-heartedly, knowing that Hunter had only been in a cab a handful of times in his life. He followed her in the backseat and they sat quietly holding hands until the cab pulled up to the venue. Outside there was a red carpet lining the sidewalk and crowds of people holding their tickets for the events while they slowly mingled toward the doors. Hunter insisted on paying for the cab and followed Madeline out where she was quickly recognized and greeted by an elderly man in a dark suit and red tie.

"Madeline! Dear!" He said, reaching out for her hand. "I want you to meet my wife, Cynthia. Cynthia, this is the little spark plug I was telling you about. She'll be running the White House in no time, mark my words."

Madeline laughed from the flattery as she squeezed the man's hand and then his wife's. "Let's first get through the chairman election and then we'll talk about the White House." Then she turned slightly to grab Hunter's arm. He was standing behind her, unsure what he was supposed to do. "This is Hunter," she introduced him to the couple. "Hunter, this is Bill Kensington, he runs the New York Republican Committee and his wife Cynthia." The couple greeted him politely and then excused themselves to move toward the door.

Madeline continued to introduce Hunter to everyone she greeted while they waited to get inside. Everyone hugged Madeline and gave Hunter their polite handshakes and soon enough the couple was inside the gallery. They were handed wine glasses and hors d'oeuvres and continued to mingle throughout the room. "Madeline, have you met Mitt Romney? He's the governor of Massachusetts. I think you two would really get along! Your politics are so similar!" Madeline had heard of the politician, he was a rising star republican who had won a race to lead one of the most democratic leaning states. Mitt was an inspiration for Madeline! Someone who proved that central republicans had a place in America and could easily win over votes from the other side. With approval from Hunter, Madeline allowed herself to be whisked away to meet Mitt and his wife and they surely did have a lot in common, both being in the management consulting world, and being Republicans who supported abortion rights, human and gay rights, limiting greenhouse gas emissions and certain tax reforms. She spent a good part of the evening speaking with Mitt and several members of his fan club who followed him around the gallery that evening.

From there, she was introduced to other prominent Republicans—both politicians and the (mostly) men behind the scenes that ran the party. She'd exchanged business cards with the national party leader who suggested they have drinks at the next convention and she spoke with Mitch McConnell, the Senate's Majority Whip, who offered her his mentorship should she ever run for office. A few other leaders promised their endorsements in her future run for chairman to lead the New York Young Republican National Federation, leaving Madeline sure her first election was already won.

When the evening ended, she was full of adrenaline, but her stomach was empty as there hadn't been time for her to browse the giant buffet that had lined two sides of the gallery and had been constantly refilled with new refreshments throughout the night. Even as the gallery emptied out, Madeline was still mingling, shaking hands and passing out the last of her business cards to new friends that she promised to have lunch with. She was one of the last people still in the gallery, along with the event organizers who she had thanked and complimented for the successful evening, and Hunter, who was standing by himself in the front corner of the room, holding a glass of wine and watching everybody leave. He had a pleasant smile plastered on his face, but to the other attendees he could have easily been invisible.

Madeline spotted him and immediately said her last goodbyes and hurried as fast as she could in her nude heels to reach him. When she did, she wrapped her arms around his neck and kissed him. He still had the glass of wine in his hand, which he held awkwardly as he rubbed Madeline's back with his free hand. His kiss was distracted, it wasn't like the kisses Madeline usually received in return when she kissed him. His lips were flaccid, yet stiff. His arms felt like he was hugging a whale instead of being tight around her. "I'm starving!" Madeline said when she pulled her lips from his. Let's stop somewhere on the way home. What do you feel like?"

"I'm not hungry," he responded. "I got enough of the buffet."

"Fine, so I'll just pick up something quick," Madeline responded, grabbing Hunter's wine glass and taking a sip before setting it down on a nearby table. She had been nursing one glass of the wine for the entire night, making sure she did not get drunk but still looked social and fun. She pulled Hunter's hand and led him out of the gallery toward a pizza place nearby. There were a few other party attendees at the pizza place, sitting together and already eating. They invited

Madeline to join them, offering extra slices and sliding on the benches to make room. Madeline looked at Hunter, before declining their offers and buying herself a slice of pizza to go.

With her pizza in hand, Madeline hailed a cab and led Hunter in while telling the driver her address. During the ride, Madeline devoured her pizza, wishing she had ordered a second slice, while reliving the evening for Hunter. She said things like "You wouldn't believe who I spoke to!" or "Guess what so-and-so said!" or "Did you see how many important people were there?" Hunter nodding politely, listening to her stories and chuckling when appropriate. This time Madeline paid for the cab, with no protests from Hunter, who followed her up to her apartment.

Madeline was exhausted. She pulled off her shoes and slipped out of her dress, without noticing Hunter gently taking off the suit that she had daydreamed about earlier. She brushed her teeth, wiped the makeup off her face and crept into her bed, waiting for Hunter to join her. He took a while, first getting himself a drink in the kitchen and showering off before he finally made it. All Madeline wanted to do was snuggle up against him and fall asleep. Her brain was exhausted as was her body from standing in her heels all evening. "Did you have fun?" she asked, her eyes already closed as she nuzzled up to his arm.

"Maddy," he said. She suddenly realized it was the first thing he had said since they left the gallery. "I can't be a part of your world."

"What do you mean? You're great. You did great," she responded, her eyes still closed and her head already drifting off to dreamland.

"Maddy, did you notice I was the only black person in the room?"

"I'm sure that's not true," she said, her head starting to drift back to being awake.

"It is true. Do you think that was a coincidence?"

"Nobody cares about skin color." Madeline opened her eyes and lifted her head slightly. "Nobody there was paying attention to that."

Hunter let out a huff. "I can't believe those people are your friends. That you want to be like them. They are all racist, self-centered, white supremacists!"

"What? Where did that come from? They are not, at all! You're used to meeting my friends. You know that's not true. You just have a chip on your shoulder and no matter what you'll be offended." It wasn't the first time Madeline and Hunter fought. They had the same fights as all other couples, from getting angry when someone was late—which happened with long commutes on the Subway—or when one of them said something that was misunderstood. They had even had a few fights that had touched on the issue of their skin color, but nothing so heated as this. Never had

Hunter thrown out the words racist or white supremacists.

"Those people want to continue suppressing us!" Hunter yelled. "All they care about is tax breaks for the wealthy, while reducing funding for programs that help people like me! They're against affirmative action, against funding Medicare, Medicaid and Food Stamp programs! All things that help more blacks than whites!"

"Hunter, that's not true, you don't understand their policies—"

"I don't understand? Why? Because I don't have a fancy degree? Because I couldn't pay to go to school?"

"Can you listen for a moment? They want to cut funding because the government doesn't run those programs efficiently, they could be privatized, there could be better programs—"

"I'm done listening," Hunter responded, sitting up in bed. "I've been listening all night. I think I've heard enough." He stood up and started putting on the clothes he had worn on his way over, before switching into the fancy Brooks Brothers suit—a ripped pair of jeans and polo shirt which he had once believed was expensive and classy.

"Hunter, stop, you're overreacting." Madeline sat up. "You're overreacting. Republicans are not racist. Abe Lincoln was a republican!"

"You all need to stop bringing him up every time someone mentions Republicans are racist. He freed slaves 150 years ago, that's not a free pass forever." Hunter gave one last look at Madeline and shook his head. "I just can't do this." Then he walked out of her bedroom, quietly closing the door behind him. Madeline stayed in bed even after she heard the click of the front door. She sat there thinking about what she should do. Should she go after him? Should she let him calm down? They'd resolve this fight in the morning. She'd invite him to some of the lunches she planned and he could see republicans weren't racist. Yes, that could resolve things, she thought to herself as she lay back down in bed. But this night, she was tired. Surely Hunter would call her in the morning realizing he overreacted. They'd kiss and make up like they always did and they'd figure out how to work through this issue.

The next day, Hunter didn't call. Madeline went to work, had lunch with a new friend she had made the night before and then went to happy hour with her colleagues. She kept her phone next to her, hoping it would ring, but it stayed silent. After happy hour, she said goodbye to her colleagues and walked home, thankful she had worn flats instead of heels.

Then the phone rang. Madeline reached into her purse with excitement that dwindled when she didn't recognize the number. "Hello?"

"Madeline! It's Bill, how are you?"

Bill Kensington who ran the New York Republican Committee, the first person she had introduced Hunter to while waiting outside the gallery the previous night.

"Bill, so great to hear from you. I'm wonderful, how are you? Did you enjoy last night?"

"You made quite an impression," he responded. "Dan from the National Committee called this morning to talk about you. He thinks you're gold. We have to start priming you for your future."

His words were everything Madeline would ever want to hear. The National Committee was behind her! With that sort of support, her dreams of changing the world—or at least the US—could be realized.

"Wow, that's great to hear."

"It is, Madeline, really, you are something special. But listen, life in the spotlight is not easy. You need to show the right image. You need to be more wholesome, more relatable, who you are seen with is extremely important. You need to be careful who you spend time with. Do you understand what I am saying?"

Madeline understood.

Chapter 18

It had been a long time since Madeline and Hunter had spoken when she called him that afternoon from her California Senate Office. Once the conversation had sunk in, she looked down at the papers in front of her and then Jane popped her head in the door.

"Madeline, it's time to go," Jane said. In an hour they would be on a flight to Washington DC for hearings and other important work in the capital. Madeline would even be spending the weekend in DC, attending a few state dinners and other events she couldn't miss. Then, Monday she would be flying to New York for lunch with the National Republican Committee Leadership to discuss her reelection. Lunch would be followed by an appearance at a YRNF event, dinner and a speech at an AIPAC event and one more late-night appearance at some other charity event that Jane had scribbled in her calendar. Then Tuesday, after her meeting with Hunter, she had a luncheon with the Daughters of the American Revolution, happy hour with a group of women from The WISH List, and then a few more appearances at charity events where she would give a few remarks. She had wanted to take the redeye home Tuesday evening, but Jane had said they wouldn't make it, so they'd stay an extra night at the Langham and fly back to California on Wednesday. Madeline felt guilty that she wouldn't see her children that weekend, but she promised Wednesday afternoon and evening, she'd be all there—no phone, no calls, no work.

Her time in DC seemed to tick by as slowly as possible. It was as though speeches in the senate had become slower, with everyone taking their time as they got out what they wanted to say. She met with a few colleagues to go over her SAVER Bill and each one seemed even more focused on the polite small talk that usually only took up a few short minutes at the beginning of conversations. This week, everyone seemed so interested in Brandon and the kids! What were they up to? How was CyTech doing? What did she think of CyTech's big new release? She had to mirror this feigned interest in her colleagues' spouses and children, listening to stories of missed school plays, crazy nannies, and some spousal gossip that she responded to, acting as though it were as important as the SAVER Bill she needed their support for. Some colleagues gave support. Some mentioned quid pro quo for bills they were working on and some requested a few changes in the bill. Jane sat in all the meetings taking notes to bring back to their legislative team to research and make recommendations to Madeline about what she could agree to.

At the end of each long day, she called Brandon, her heart pumping every time they were on the phone. She felt like she had been caught, as if she was in trouble. Brandon too seemed a little uneasy, but the two continued their conversations, as though everything were normal. He told her about their daily lives—how Noah's suspension was over, but he had started daily meetings with his student counselor. How Adam had decided he was going to build a nuclear power plant for the science fair—did Madeline know where he could get some uranium? How Brandon had taken them out for Chinese food on Sunday night and Noah's fortune cookie promised something big to look forward to. By the end of their nightly talks, Madeline would feel grounded. Reminded about the stability in her life that she so much appreciated, yet feared could tumble at any moment. But sometime between hanging up the phone and when she called the next night, her feet seemed to lift off the ground, she felt like she was hovering and she couldn't control forcing herself back down.

Monday she sat through a four-hour lunch with the National Committee, during which they discussed her reelection and what would be her next steps. Another six years in the senate and then she was ready for bigger things. Of course, she needed to accomplish a few things in those six years, getting onto some of the more sought-after committees and turning her name into one recognized in every household. What was her strategy there? The SAVER Bill was her big strategy, she reminded them. Voters loved it and they would never forget something so life changing. With her popularity, it would be easy to get onto the top Congressional Committees. The lunch ended with everyone confident that Madeline had nothing to worry about in her reelection. Although she couldn't help feel doubt when thinking about the one thing that could jeopardize her reelection. The unresolved blackmail case that could easily blow up on the brink of her campaign relaunch. It would ruin everything. There would be no reelection. No new committee appointments. Likely no SAVER bill. But she didn't say any of this to her colleagues. She continued through her appearances as though on autopilot, doing and saying the rights things, making everyone feel they had her full attention when in reality they had so very little of it.

Tuesday morning finally rolled around. Madeline told Jane she was taking the morning off. She was going to go for a run in Central Park, walk around Columbia and see her old neighborhood. She'd meet her back at the Langham long before they needed to leave for their DAR luncheon. Madeline did start the morning with a short run in the park. Then, after a shower, she had her car drop her at Columbia. She told the driver he could take time off and pick her back up in two hours, right at the university's entrance. Once he was out of sight, she left the university's gates and walked into Harlem toward Hunter's City Council Office. The office was nothing like her Senator office. Hers sat in a giant office building with a doorman and had multiple office rooms and conference rooms with teams of people huddled inside researching and brainstorming for her. Hunter's office looked like a remodeled convenience store. It stood right at the street with his name and title painted on the front window. Madeline pushed open the door, which rang a soft bell. Inside, Hunter was sitting at a large table in the middle of the office across from a woman and a young boy.

"I'll see what I can do," Hunter said to the woman who was rubbing the boy's shoulders. "Thanks so much for coming in." The woman and boy thanked Hunter and stood up. Hunter held out his hand, shaking the woman's and the young boy's, giving him the same respect he would to any adult. His guests then walked out of the office, averting their eyes so as not to meet Madeline's.

"JJ wants to get the basketball court up on 144th fixed," Hunter said. "His mom brought him in here to file an official complaint with the city." He held up a piece of lined paper that had been ripped out of a notebook and folded several times. He held the paper like it was an official document, or rather one written on parchment paper. Madeline could see the pride in his eyes, she could see the satisfaction he got from helping his constituents. It was the same pride she felt when she saw the impact of her work.

Hunter walked over to his desk and placed the paper in an envelope, which he stacked in one of the paper trays. Then he turned to Madeline. "Maddy, how can I help you? You want some coffee? I can make a fresh pot," he said, motioning to the far corner of his office where a little kitchenette with dull pink counters stood.

"No thank you."

"You sure? It'll just take a minute. I got some great coffee from this shop on 95th. I know 95th isn't technically my district, it starts at 96th, but it's close enough! And the shop sells amazing grinds. I'll brew a pot, once you smell it, you'll want some." Hunter walked to the kitchenette and dumped out the coffee machine in the trash. Then he added a new filter, filled it with the grinds and pressed the on bottom. With nothing else to do, he stood there with his hands on his hips facing Madeline. "So how's Brandon?"

"He's good, thank you," Madeline responded. "Can we sit? I need to talk to you about something." She felt awkward in front of him, her words felt jarring and coarse. It was hard to believe that once they were so close.

Hunter nodded and motioned to invite her to sit at the table in the middle of the room where JJ had filed his official complaint regarding the basketball court. Madeline took a seat, her back straight, legs crossed and hands folded in her lap. Hunter sat across from her, leaning back in the chair, pushing its two front legs up in the air.

"Are you moving back to New York? Setting up residency to run for office from here? I hear the governor race is pretty open for the next term. May be a good opportunity for you—"

"No," Madeline stopped him, but he continued.

"So what's the next step? Another senate term? There isn't much else to go from there, is there? Maybe a cabinet appointment? You'd be great as Secretary of State."

"Another senate term," she responded. "I'm launching my reelection campaign in a couple weeks."

"Great news," he said, tilting his head in approval. "So what can I do for you? I assume you aren't here for my endorsement."

Madeline took a deep breath. She had been rehearsing different scenarios in her head for the last few days, what she would say to him, how she would phrase it. What she expected from him in response. But no matter how many different ways it played out in her head, she still felt unready and unsure what to say. The words felt like bricks needing to be squeezed through a tiny hole.

"Hunter, someone is trying to blackmail me," she said, pausing for his reaction. He looked straight into her eyes, his head nodding slightly.

"What does it have to do with me?"

"They know." Until that moment, Madeline hadn't been able to admit it. Not to herself, not to anyone else that she had made a mistake. A huge mistake, one that could ruin everything that she had worked so hard to achieve. It was the kind of mistake that Madeline had promised herself she would never do. Until that moment, she had tried to erase that mistake from her memory. For a while, the mistake stayed like a stain that couldn't be removed, even with vigorous rubbing, but over time, the stain faded. The edges began to blend and Madeline was able to pretend it wasn't there. Maybe no one else would notice the stain, maybe no one was paying that close attention. But looking close enough, the stain was there. It was definitely there.

Chapter 19

Madeline was still working at the same consulting firm where she had started her career after college. But with 10 years under her belt, she was a partner at the firm, managing clients rather than spreadsheets, meeting CEOs instead of employees, and presenting findings instead of analyzing data. She was 31 and had just started planning her run for her first term in the senate. Winning a senate seat in California was a long shot, she knew, and that's why she was trying to keep her day job as long as possible. There was no question she was overextended—her job required a minimum of 60 hours a week, as did the initial campaign planning. That left her very little for Brandon and her two young children, who were both at a very pivotal point in their development— Noah was starting pre-k while Adam was just learning his first words.

As usual, Madeline believed she could handle it all—the lack of sleep, the stress, the guilt that she wasn't giving enough in each of the directions she was being pulled. She had to handle it all, to prove that she was who everyone thought she was—a successful woman, the kind that people knew would make it one day.

That particular week, she had been hoping to take a couple days off. A few of her projects at work had just been finished. The minimal staff who had started strategizing her senate run seemed adequate enough to handle things without her for a short time. She wanted to take the boys to the zoo, Noah had loved animals and it would be a great opportunity to teach Adam the sounds each one made. She made peace with her plan to take a break, she deserved it after all, she told herself when the guilt tried to creep in. But then she got a call from her firm's CEO.

"You're on the next flight to NYC," he said when she answered. She tried to tell him she had already blocked her calendar off, that she was taking a much-needed vacation, but the CEO wouldn't listen. Did she remember a project she had worked on when she was just a consultant in the New York Office? Back then, they were looking to improve efficiency in the procurement department at that banking company. Madeline had been in charge of interviewing employees, analyzing the data, and had proposed a plan that ended up saving the company almost a million that first year after the plan was implemented. Her firm was trying to win a new project at that banking company and the company's new CEO had worked with Madeline on that project years ago. He had asked about Madeline, whether she was still working at the firm. As the firm was competing with several other consulting firms to win this highly profitable project, they needed to send Madeline to meet with the CEO. Her rapport could make all the difference! It could ensure that they would win this project, which would be huge for the firm. Having this banking company on their recent client list would surely bring in other projects and lead to more revenues, which in turn, would find their way to Madeline's end of the year bonus. They needed her and she could not let them down.

And so she flew to New York, telling her campaign team to keep her updated and saying goodbye to Brandon who promised he would take the boys to the zoo on his own. Don't worry, he said, he'd send pictures and videos so she wouldn't feel like she missed out. The first thing she felt when she arrived in New York was relief. Yes, relief. It was like she was getting her much-needed vacation, a few days away from the business of her normal life. She had a few meetings planned with the banking company and her colleagues in the New York office, but aside from that, she had time for herself. She checked into the Langham, which was on the same street as the consulting firm's New York Office and then she switched on her running clothes and jogged over to Central Park. She did a quick loop around the park before buying a bottle of water from one of the street vendors. With the bottle, she walked around and took a seat near the Olmstead Flower Bed, where yellow and white tulips stood almost knee high. She sat watching the flowers as a gardener came by. The gardener started snipping a few dried leaves and added mulch at the base of the flowers. Madeline wasn't paying much attention until her eyes drifted to the back of the gardener's shirt, which said *Smith and Sons Landscaping*. From there, her eyes drifted to the gardener's head and a wave of familiarity rolled over her. It was like she had never left New York, like the last seven years hadn't happened.

"Hunter?" she said, still sitting on the bench. The gardener looked around and caught her eyes.

"Maddy? What are you doing here?"

"Admiring the flowers. Your handy-work?"

He nodded. Small talk commenced and the two easily slipped into conversation about how wonderful Central Park was in the summer. Was Madeline interested in seeing Shakespeare in the park? Attendance was free, but patrons had to come hours before to wait in line to get in. Working at the park, Hunter could get them in that evening if she were interested. This year they were doing Othello. Madeline agreed, thinking an evening out watching Shakespeare could be fun and a completely harmless activity. She and Hunter agreed to meet that evening, after she attended her meetings.

When the afternoon started to fade, Madeline turned down happy hour invitations from her colleagues and went to meet Hunter. He was already in their meeting spot, carrying a large bag over his shoulder. He led her past the long line of people waiting and into the grass seating area for the play. Then he opened his bag and lay out a blanket, on top of which, he spread out wine, cheese and a Tupperware full of hush puppies that his mom had made. They tasted exactly like how Madeline remembered them. Suddenly she was back in Harlem, at her apartment with a broken air conditioning and faulty lock. She was 22 and carelessly fun, the way she always believed she truly was until life came pounding down on her shoulders. They still had time before the play, but they quickly got to drinking the wine. Conversation flowed easily as they updated each other on their lives. Madeline told him about her husband and her boys, smiling as she described them to Hunter. But as she talked, she felt like she was describing a movie. Not her own life, for in her mind she was 22 and still lacking any real responsibilities in life. For his part, Hunter told Madeline about his wife, Rhonda. She was a TSA agent and they had a seven-year-old daughter. They'd been together almost since Madeline had left, and had gotten married after Rhonda found out she was pregnant. Hunter loved her, the pregnancy wasn't why they got married, he assured Madeline, it just got them to that milestone a little sooner than expected. Hunter also told her that he was now managing *Smith and Sons landscaping.* He was hoping to buy the business eventually from Bill Smith, who was still holding on hope that one of his sons would take on the business. Hunter was also still volunteering at the community center and had finished his bachelor's degree in citizenship and civic engagement. It was sort of like political science, he told her, but on a more local level. Madeline listened, her smile never leaving her face, but she didn't really hear what he was saying. She didn't absorb it, because how could she? Her mind had transgressed to the time that she and Hunter were still each other's.

175

When the play started, they had trouble staying quiet to watch the show. Others around hushed them and asked them to keep it down, but they couldn't help themselves. They had seven years to catch up on and it felt like they couldn't do it fast enough. Hunter had come prepared with multiple bottles of wine. They had finished three bottles by the end of the play, and had been so engrossed in conversation that the entire plot had eluded Madeline. Hunter offered her the last hush puppy, which she couldn't refuse. (Her 31-year-old would have because her waistline just wasn't the same anymore after two children.) Still talking, they folded up the blanket and Hunter walked her back to the hotel.

It should have ended there, with a hug and a sincere "Good to see you." But it didn't. Maybe it was the wine, or the feeling of relief that Madeline had since she had arrived in New York. Maybe it was that Hunter reminded her of a less complicated time, when she didn't think juggling would be so difficult. When Hunter leaned in to hug her, his fingers first brushed her back. A feeling ignited inside her, the same one she felt years ago whenever Hunter would touch her. It was a feeling she hadn't felt with Brandon, an electricity, a longing to be touched that she was sure had disappeared inside her. For the last seven years, she had convinced herself that she didn't need that sexual arousal, that her partnership with Brandon was so much more important than the physical. She had truly believed that the part inside of her that ached for touch had disappeared and no longer existed in the mature version of Madeline. But with the simple brush of Hunter's fingertips on her back, the ache woke inside her. She couldn't remember who kissed who first, but they kissed. Their lips interlocked and their arms wrapped around each other. Hunter followed her into the Langham, up the elevator and into her hotel room where he made her body convulse and move in ways she didn't know were still possible. He held her tight over night and in the morning kissed her before apologizing.

"This was a mistake," he said and Madeline agreed. She caught a glimpse of herself in the mirror and when her 31-year-old self looked back at her, everything sunk in. She felt sorry for poor Rhonda, alone at home with her daughter, not knowing why her husband hadn't come home the night before. She felt sorry that lack of control could ruin Hunter's marriage, which she had been so happy to hear about. He was such a good partner, she thought, and surely a wonderful dad. She had hoped she hadn't taken that opportunity away from him. Hunter put on his clothes and left the hotel.

Madeline stayed in bed. It was Saturday and she had nothing planned until Monday when she would have lunch with the banking company's CEO to finalize details of the project that she was pretty sure she had won for her firm. She tried to focus on that lunch, instead of the other thoughts that were swirling through her mind.

A mistake, a horrible mistake, she kept hearing in her head. She couldn't focus on it, otherwise she might tear herself apart. How could she have done that to Brandon? To her kids? How could she have done it to herself? Putting that stain on her reputation that she needed to keep clean for her future. At that moment she promised herself she wouldn't let one night ruin her life. No, instead, she resolved to be better. She'd be a better wife, a better mom, and she would win her upcoming senate race so she could help millions. This one night would be nothing in the long run, a blip in her otherwise faithful character.

The next time she saw Hunter was five years later. She was a rising star republican visiting New York to give a speech at The WISH List, the organization that supported women like herself in Congress. She gave the speech, wearing her red suit and perfect smile. Back at the Langham, she had gotten a drink at the bar by herself. She had seen Hunter walk in, wearing his short sleeved blue plaid shirt. He took a seat on the other side of the bar and looked at her. By this time, Madeline was already in the spotlight. People were already calling her the future of the country, the change people were looking for. Her every move was watched, to be an example for her supporters and a possible misstep for her opponents. She would never make a mistake again.

She saw Hunter at the bar and she gave a quick raise of her glass to him. He looked at her questioningly, as though asking to move closer, but she shook her head. Across the bar was close enough. She paid her tab and left the bar, feeling both proud of herself and guilty.

Chapter 20

"What do you mean, 'they know'?" Hunter asked her, standing up to get two mugs of coffee from the small kitchenette in his city council office.

"Someone knows about us and is using it to blackmail me," she responded.

"Us?" he questioned as though he didn't know exactly what she was talking about.

"The night we saw Othello," she reminded him. "Someone wants money or they promise to go to the media with proof that I cheated."

Hunter returned to the table and placed a mug in front of Madeline before sitting back down on his side. He nodded thoughtfully. "Madeline, that was years ago, who cares?"

"It's unethical."

"It was before you were a senator," he said. "What, is the ethics committee going to investigate you?"

"This will jeopardize my reelection. Voters don't want to vote for a cheater. And yes, instead of working to pass bills, I'll be fighting the democrats and journalists who will want to take me down."

"Can't they find the guy who's blackmailing you and stop it?"

Madeline sighed and explained to Hunter that time was running out and the FBI was failing at their job.

"What does Brandon have to say about it?" Hunter asked when she finished talking.

"He doesn't suspect anything."

"Uh huh," Hunter responded as though unconvinced. "What do you want from me?"

"I just wanted you to know," she said. "I don't know how much they know. If it gets out, if it gets to the media, your name could get out too. And if Rhonda or your daughter see it, it could be a problem for you too. Or I don't know about city council politics, but it could also hurt you here. I just don't know."

"Rhonda and I aren't together anymore," he responded. "We're on the process for the divorce. She has custody of our daughter, who hates me already anyway."

"Why?"

"Nasty divorce," he responded, waving his hands. "No need to get into it. How can I help?"

"Well, if it gets out, you can support me, say it's not true. People will want to talk to you, to know how we know each other. Just say good things about me."

"I only have good things to say about you," he said. "Everything wasn't your fault."

The word *everything* held so much weight between them. There was so much that had been left unsaid since the time they broke up. Even the

181

night of Othello they never spoke about how things had ended between them. There really was no ending, if Madeline looked back on it. It wasn't like a book whose pages ran out and everything was settled before the last word. Rather, it was like the last chapter was ripped out and she was left not knowing what happened after Hunter left her apartment that night. They hadn't spoken, neither had reached out to the other, both too stubborn to be the one to initiate anything. Madeline had waited. After a few days, she was angry. A week, she was annoyed. Two weeks, she was single.

Madeline nodded. "We were young," she commented. It seemed like the only logical explanation for *everything*.

"Yup," he responded. "What do you think of the coffee?" He motioned to her untouched mug in front of her. Madeline smiled and lifted the mug to take a sip. It was...coffee, completely average in every way.

"It's delicious," she said with a big smile.

"So, tell me what else is going on," Hunter said. "As long as you're here. How's life? It's been a while."

Madeline looked at her watch. She still had about 30 minutes until she had to leave to meet her driver who would be picking her up outside Columbia's campus to take her to her DAR luncheon. She had planned to spend any extra time she had wandering around the old library where she used to study, but talking to Hunter seemed like a viable alternative, even with the average coffee that she would have happily replaced from one of the stands on campus. The rhythm of conversation began, Madeline began telling Hunter about the boys, how Noah had been suspended for bullying, when it turned out he was being bullied. Hunter commiserated, telling her about his daughter Felicia who was in the middle of hitting phase that had started a couple years ago and they hadn't figured out how to end it. Madeline talked about the SAVER Bill she was working on and Hunter responded that he had heard about it on the news.

"It's a very long term solution," he commented. "If it lasts long enough, it may have an effect on our grandchildren's generation, but we need a more immediate solution." She asked if he had any ideas and he promised he would think about it. She wanted to ask about Rhonda, about the divorce he mentioned, but she figured it was better not to bring it up. Time was running out anyway and she needed to wrap things up.

Madeline finished her mug of coffee and stood up. "It's been wonderful catching up, but I have to go," she said. She lifted her hand to shake Hunter's, but her move felt unnatural and foreign. She had never shaken Hunter's hand. He came around from the table and grasped her hand in both of his. The touch of his fingers sent electricity through her, travelling from her hand, up her arm and down her torso where the electricity sparked. She gently pulled her hand away. "It was good to see you," she said.

"And you," he responded. "Enjoy the rest of your trip in New York and I hope everything turns out OK. Keep me posted."

She nodded and then left his office, walking as fast as she could back to Columbia to meet the driver. She didn't want him seeing her walking from Harlem. She wanted him to see her coming out of the university, as though that had been where she had spent her time. To her dismay, the driver was already waiting for her when she arrived. Damn him for always being early, she thought. She got in the car and sat quietly as they returned to the Langham to pick up Jane. Then they headed to lunch at the DAR where Madeline shook hands, smiled and listened to all the women's concerns. From there, she attended a happy hour event with women from The WISH List and commiserated with all of them about how difficult it was being a woman. Then she was whisked away between several charity events where she shook more hands, gave speeches about how important each charity was, swapping in their different names, and when the day and night were almost over, Madeline and Jane sat quietly as a car took them back to the Langham.

When the car dropped them off, Madeline and Jane went inside past the hotel bar where Madeline noticed a dark figure sitting with a beer in front of him. Their eyes caught quickly, but Madeline shifted hers away, careful not to let them stick. Madeline and Jane continued to the elevator, still conducting small talk about the day they just finished. Jane was commenting on the

184

shrimp cocktail at the last charity event when the doors of the elevator were about to close. A hand stopped them and they swung back open, letting Hunter walk in. He was in the same suit he was wearing earlier in the day, although the shirt was a little wrinkled and the tie had been loosened. He pressed the button for the top floor and stood quietly facing the doors, letting them close in front of him. Silence held the elevator as it traveled up, first stopping on Jane's floor. When the doors opened, Jane hesitated before getting out. She looked at Madeline for direction with fear in her eyes. "Goodnight Jane," Madeline said, freeing her from the elevator. Her chief of staff looked weary as she left her boss alone in the elevator with an African American man. No one wants to admit they are racist, but Jane's hesitation showed just how deeply racism was rooted inside everyone.

When the doors shut and the elevator began to move again, Hunter turned around. "Why did you come see me?" he asked.

"To tell you," she responded as the doors opened to her floor. "I have to go." She pushed past him out of the elevator but he followed her out. "What are you doing? Why are you here?"

"I'm doing what I should have done years ago," he said. "I should never have let you get away with everything. I should have made you answer me. Now tell me, why did you come see me? You didn't need to fly to New York to tell me that someone is blackmailing you."

"I didn't fly here to tell you," she responded as he followed her toward her room. "I was here anyway and I didn't want to talk about it on the phone. My phone could be bugged!"

"You didn't want to see me?" he asked when Madeline stopped in front of her room's door.

She stood in front of him, their faces just inches apart. It was close enough for her to feel his heat, to get caught in the electricity that radiated from him. "No," she responded. "It was purely out of consideration. I have to go. Good night." She turned around to open her door, just as Hunter grabbed her wrist and turned her back around. He pushed his lips on hers, pushing her back into the still closed door. His lips were heavy on hers, forcing hers slightly open to lock into his. She fought herself from getting caught in his kiss and found the strength to push him back. "Please, Hunter, I can't."

"Don't tell me you don't miss me," he said, pressing his forehead to hers. "That's why you came to see me. There's still something there. I miss you. I've missed you every day." He turned his head to kiss her cheeks as she stood pinned against the door.

"Hunter, please," she said. She wanted to tell him to stop, she wanted to tell him to leave her alone, but her body felt like it was giving in. Her body had missed him, even if her brain had tried to shut that feeling out.

"Maddy," he said airily, his lips moving from her cheeks down to her neck. With one hand he took the room key from her and slipped it into the door, opening it behind her while still kissing her. He gently pushed her inside and continued kissing her neck, her chest and her cheeks. He was still pushing her backwards toward the bed when the hotel room's phone rang. The ring immediately snapped Madeline awake and she regained composure, pushing Hunter back far enough to put inches of distance between them.

"Just let it go," Hunter pleaded, but for Madeline that was impossible. An unanswered phone could lead to more than just voicemails. Her job was to be available, as a senator, a mother, or whatever else she needed to be. She could not let the call go unanswered. She stepped back from Hunter to grab the phone and picked it up as Hunter sat down patiently on the king-size bed.

"Madeline? Turn on your TV!" Jane screamed through the line. "I can't believe this. It's totally out of left field! We were definitely not prepared for this, I can't believe I missed it. I'm so sorry, I feel like I failed." Jane continued to ramble through the line as Madeline looked for the remote. "Should I come up? We can talk about this. I'll get the team on it, right away."

Madeline saw the remote on the other side of the bed and motioned to Hunter to grab it. He tossed it to her and she pressed the red button, immediately searching through the channels for the news. What she saw made her heart pound. "Jane, I'll call you back."

Chapter 21

"Madeline Thomas is not who you think she is," said the man on the TV. The man was wearing a blue suit and tie and standing in front of a wooden podium with a sign on front: *Austin for Senate.* Behind him stood a crowd of indistinguishable faces all carrying the same blue and red sign. It took Madeline a moment to recognize the man, he looked so different out of his uniform and with his face clean shaven. It was Officer Austin, head of the Fraternal Order of Police, who Madeline had met with weeks ago regarding the SAVER Bill. Madeline remembered how hostile he had been during that meeting. How he had even stood her up during their originally planned meeting when her office building received a bomb threat.

"Madeline Thomas is part of the system she pretends to be fighting against. She's been a part of it for twenty years, planning and conniving with the system's leaders and then turning around and lying to the voters about how she isn't in their pockets. I'm so sick and tired of her lying, which is why I decided to run for her senate seat," Officer Austin said on TV. Behind him the crowd roared. "I know I'm not well known and I am definitely the underdog here, but I think that if you really want truth and change, you'll vote for me. I've been a police officer for the last forty years, serving and protecting my country by interacting with the people. Unlike Madeline Thomas, I don't sit in some fancy office and pretend I know what's best. I'm on the ground level, talking to constituents every day. I'm the guy that comes to your house when you need help, and the guy who stops criminals from hurting you." Again the crowd roared behind him.

"For the last ten years, I've been leading the Fraternal Order of Police, working hard to improve our forces so that the police who are protecting your streets have the best opportunities and are best situated to take care of you. And I want to tell you a story. In the last ten years, Madeline Thomas never talked to us. She never cared about how hard we work to keep you safe. But suddenly, she decided she needs my help. She invited me to her office, and of course, I went, because my job is to respond to every call. She wanted to know how we can *align* our interests and how she could *convince* me to support her." The officer made quotations with his hands and exaggerated the words *align* and *convince* to emphasis that they had a somewhat different meaning when Madeline had said them. He looked back at the crowd behind him, which was now booing in response to what the officer had said about her. "Yeah, that's right," the officer continued speaking. "And that's just the beginning of the stories I can tell you about Madeline. If you knew what I knew, you wouldn't want her representing you in Washington. You wouldn't even want her mowing your lawn. So I'm here to restore integrity for California. The same integrity that I've had in my longstanding career, I'll bring to Washington and continue looking out for you just as I've done my whole life. Austin for Senate!"

The crowd behind him again roared, this time even louder than before. Officer Austin turned around and started shaking hands as the picture faded to a news anchor who started reporting on the announcement.

Madeline turned around to Hunter, who was sitting on the hotel bed, his back leaning against the wooden headboard. He didn't look troubled by what they watched on TV. To Madeline, he looked rather bored, maybe annoyed even. He didn't look like he understood what Madeline believed she understood.

"Well?" She said to him.

"Looks like you have a big fight coming up to keep your seat," he responded as he stood up. "I guess I should go."

"That's all you have to say?" Madeline wasn't sure what she wanted him to say, but that was definitely not it. Maybe he could have said that she would win, or that she shouldn't worry. Or he could have said the one thing that Madeline had on her mind right then.

"I shouldn't have come up here," he said. "Have a good night, Maddy." He left the hotel room, leaving behind a hurricane of anger that began swirling around Madeline. She was angry at Hunter for what he did and what he didn't do, she was angry at herself for the same reasons and for not seeing Officer Austin as such a threat. She wasn't angry at Officer Austin though. No, for him, she felt spite, malice, disgust even.

At a time like this, there was only one person Madeline could count on, one person she needed to speak with who she knew would be thinking the same thing she was. Things had been strange with Brandon for the last few days. The uneasiness in their talks, and her feeling of being caught wrapped around her. She picked up her cell phone and called him. "Hey," he answered. "It's late. I was starting to wonder what happened to you."

"We had a lot of events this evening," she responded automatically. "Have you been watching the news?"

"I saw," he responded. "Officer Austin for Senate. It's got a nice ring to it."

"Do you think...?" Madeline asked without really asking. The truth was that the FBI had already investigated Officer Austin. He was on top of her list of adversaries, people who disagreed with her beliefs and spoke openly about it in the news. The FBI had investigated him after he didn't show up to their first meeting the day of the bomb threat. They investigated further after she did meet with him in her office. The only conclusion the FBI developed was that no further investigation was needed. But, Madeline now began thinking, Officer Austin was a police officer after all. He had all sorts of resources at his fingertips. Maybe he even had connections at the FBI protecting him.

Madeline started to feel something she had never felt before. A small tick that came from outside her, making her feel like she was being watched. She turned around and scanned the hotel room, which appeared empty, save for the feeling of paranoia that was growing larger, like a weed taking over the room.

"I don't know, Madeline. Your guess is as good as mine," Brandon responded. "No, your guess is probably better than mine." Madeline thought she heard a tinge of hostility in Brandon's voice. It was so small, she couldn't be sure it was there, but something—maybe the paranoia—was making her feel attacked by Brandon.

"What does that mean?"

"Nothing, just that something isn't adding up here," Brandon responded. "Come home, we'll talk about it. No use trying to solve everything over the phone like this."

Madeline said good night and hung up. A moment later her phone rang again. She hesitated to answer, afraid of what news it could bring, but she knew she could not let it go. When she lifted the receiver, Jane immediately started talking. "I think we should try to schedule a debate with Austin. You would obviously win and it would be great television. I know it isn't standard in Senate races, but why not? I'm trying to reach his campaign team. My friend who works in Sacramento is checking at the State House who filed Austin's candidacy. I'll contact them immediately..."

"Jane, I am going to hang up now," Madeline said. "Talk to our staff and tomorrow we'll go over the next steps." When she placed the receiver back down, she felt suddenly alone. She wished Hunter hadn't left, but she knew his presence only made her more isolated.

She washed her face, scrubbing the grease and makeup off her skin. Clean, she didn't look so fierce. She didn't look like the force of nature she felt like when all made up. So she closed her eyes and lay down in bed. She wouldn't sleep, but with the covers pulled up around her neck she could let herself crack open. A tear escaped her eye and she let more follow. Sometimes no matter how strong a woman is, she still just needs to cry.

Chapter 22

Madeline arrived home the next day after her early morning flight. She looked senatorial as always in her skirt suit and perfectly made-up face as her car dropped her off in front of her driveway. She thanked the driver and walked into the house, noticing that Brandon's car was in the driveway. Inside, Brandon was sitting on the couch with his computer on his lap and headphones on his head. His socked feet were up on the coffee table and his glasses reflected the screen. "NO! How many times do we have to go over this?" He yelled into the headphones. "These bugs are unacceptable at this stage. I shouldn't be hearing about these things. The product team should be taking care of them before bringing it to the CEO. Please fix and get back to me." Brandon looked up to see Madeline in the doorway with her small carryon luggage. He immediately straightened up and pulled his headphones off his head.

"What are you doing here?" She asked. His presence made it seem like something was wrong. He should be at the office, going through his normal routine. He never waited for her at home when she came back from a trip. There was no need.

"I wanted to see you," he replied. "I thought we could get the kids together from school. They have a lot of questions."

Madeline nodded and took her suitcase upstairs to unpack. She switched out of her suit and put on jeans and a blouse, making herself look more like a mom than a senator. She needed the afternoon off. Jane would handle the staff and update her in the evening. While it may seem contrary to take time off when things were becoming so heated with her campaign, it was actually the smart thing for Madeline to do. Time off gave her time to think. It gave her staff time to rethink before they gave her any rash recommendations. It was a move that had served her well through other stressful times in her career—when she had seen negative press against her for the first time, when she had been forced to support something her constituents would not understand. Time off always gave the right answers. Madeline hoped this time it would too.

When she walked back downstairs, Brandon was no longer sitting on the couch. The smell of coffee led her to the kitchen where he was pouring himself a mug. She grabbed her own mug and prepared a cup. The two stood quietly in the kitchen, the only sounds the slurping of coffee. Madeline averted her eyes. She felt full of things she should say, but none that she would allow to be released from her lips. They continued to stand together, quietly, in the kitchen, drinking their coffee. Then, with a thud, Brandon placed his mug in the sink. "I have to get back to work," he said and he left the kitchen and Madeline with her coffee that was no longer warm.

When the clock ticked towards when the boys' school let out, Brandon and Madeline silently made their way into Brandon's car. They always took his car when they drove as a family. It was an unspoken rule for no particular reason other than Brandon preferred to drive. Madeline's car had less mileage, was cleaner, maybe it was even a little roomier, but as a family, they traveled in Brandon's car. As they drove to the school, Madeline felt like Dorothy, waking up in the land of Oz. Something was different about the neighborhood, the streets they drove through. It took her a moment to notice what it was. At first, all she saw was a small square on someone's lawn. They drove past it before she could see what it was. There wasn't another square for a few more minutes, but this time, Madeline's eyes caught it before they drove past. *Austin for Senate.* There were already signs in people's front lawns. Not many, but enough to make Madeline wonder where her signs were. She quickly pulled out her phone and texted Jane. *Need to move up the campaign relaunch. Already behind.*

They arrived at the school right behind Mrs. Albertson, whose car's rear window had already been painted advertising Madeline's adversary. Madeline watched as Mrs. Albertson parked and got out of her car, wearing a blue t-shirt with *Austin for Senate* on it and giant red sparkly earrings that looked more like party favors than jewelry. Madeline let out a sigh before she and Brandon shared a look. The couple got out of their car and walked towards the school entrance where other parents were already waiting. A few kids had drizzled out, but the bell had yet to ring.

"Madeline!" Mrs. Albertson said. "I guess you heard the news." Madeline acknowledged her politely. "I'm volunteering with the campaign. It's great for teaching our children about civic duty. We'll be canvassing on the weekends." Mrs. Albertson had a smug smile on her face and nodded her head vigorously. The bell rang and students began swarming out like bees from their hive in desperate search for honey. Brandon squeezed Madeline's shoulder as they searched for their sons.

Soon Adam arrived and moments later Noah. The couple turned to their car, Brandon with the boys' backpacks on his shoulders.

"May the best man win!" Madeline heard Mrs. Albertson call from behind her.

"Or woman," She retorted, catching Mrs. Albertson's eyes for just a moment before they pulled away from the crowd. With the boys buckled in the car, the Thomas family began the drive home.

"Mom, are you going to need to find a job?" Adam asked from the backseat. Madeline turned back, catching Brandon's eyes for a moment before she did.

"I already have a job, sweetie," she assured him, still facing backward. She recognized the concern in her son's eyes. So young, but with such compassion for others. The kind of child who would make sure others had a cookie before he ate his own, who last year had asked to give away a few of his birthday presents to kids who had fewer toys than he did.

"Jamie said you're about to lose your job," Noah said. He was looking out the window, his tone bored and matter-of-fact.

"Jamie is wrong," Madeline responded. She was still facing back at her boys, even though the craning made her neck ache. "Everything is going to be fine." She sincerely hoped.

"Who wants to stop for ice cream?" Brandon suggested.

"Me!" Adam shouted. Noah still sat quietly looking out the window, but Madeline turned back forward. She faced forward just in time to see another *Austin for Senate* sign in somebody's lawn.

"How can you be so sure?" Noah said. "Jamie said in a few weeks no one will even think you have a chance."

"You believe Jamie over your mother?" Madeline peeked back again at Noah who shrugged as though pretending not to care.

"Why aren't you two working today? Molly usually gets us." Noah continued to speak in his monotone voice. Brandon pulled the car into a parking lot in front of a small strip mall with an ice cream shop.

"We wanted to spend the afternoon together," Brandon responded.

"Because something bad is happening? Like mom losing her job?"

"I'm not losing my job."

"Are you getting divorced then? Matt said his parents took him to get ice cream when they told him they were getting divorced."

"We're not getting divorced," Brandon said as he put the car in park. "It's just ice cream." As the family got out of the car and walked toward the ice cream shop, Madeline had the strange feeling of being watched. Not by anyone in particular, but like she was in a fishbowl. As a public figure, she often felt this way, but something was different. She felt as though she were a mouse running through a maze as scientists nodded and analyzed her every move, wondering when she would mess up.

Over ice cream Madeline listened to Adam talk about a cricket he had found during recess. He wanted to keep it and had brought it into his classroom by hiding it under his shirt. He them snuck it into his lunch box, but sadly, the poor cricket had died by lunch time. But Adam had given him a proper burial under the flowers near the school's administration building. Noah ate his ice cream silently, only speaking to make fun of his little brother's story.

To Madeline, this time, sitting with her family, thinking about the poor cricket's downfall, rather than her own, was a needed respite from what she had been going through. It reminded her that even with everything that was going on, she could still find joy. There was still meaning and love in her life even when they seemed missing from other parts.

After ice cream, the family headed home and back to their own lives—Brandon to his laptop and headphones on the couch, Adam to the yard with a basketball and a hoop, and Noah to his room with his video games. Madeline watched her family scatter, before going to her own spot, the kitchen table, where she would call Jane and discuss with her their response to Austin's campaign launch. Surely the team had been working hard to come up with a plan. How she could beat him, how they needed to change her strategy. She had full confidence that her team's brainpower could outsmart any other campaign staff's. She was ready to go over plans with Jane, but it just wouldn't happen that afternoon.

Instead, the doorbell rang. Madeline stood up to answer it, meeting Brandon at the front door. The couple opened the door to a UPS deliveryman who handed them a cardboard envelope. The deliveryman, who drove this route often but rarely stopped at the Thomas residence, smiled politely and greeted the couple a good day, not knowing the chaos he was handing them in that flat brown envelope.

Brandon followed Madeline into the kitchen to watch her open it, but when Madeline saw what was inside, she wished he hadn't. She wished he would never see what was inside.

Chapter 23

For their honeymoon Madeline and Brandon had flown to Italy for a week. Their apartment was full of boxes from their registry—china sets, silverware, crystal bowls, enough serving utensils for the couple to host dinner parties every night for a week without washing a thing. Madeline had already finished handwriting more than 200 thank you cards that she had personalized for each guest (*Salad tongs have always reminded me of you! It was lovely dancing together at the wedding! You looked stunning in your gown! You'll have to tell me your secret!*) and had dropped them off at the post office on their way to the airport.

They had their trip fully planned out—which hotels they would stay at, restaurants they had already reserved tables at, a cooking class where they would learn to make tortellini, tours of the Vatican, the Colosseum, a day trip to Pompeii, a walking tour of Rome. Days would be busy, so busy that by the evenings, Madeline was sure they would be exhausted. They would likely go straight to sleep without participating in the usual honeymoon activities in bed. Their honeymoon would be more cultured, it would enrich their knowledge of history and culinary skills. Of course, they would have sex a few times—how could they not? Madeline assumed that sex would happen on the first and fifth day of their trip: the first because it would be obligatory and the fifth because they were attending a wine tasting workshop that had promised to be romantic and aphrodisiacal. It just wouldn't be right if they didn't imbibe in intercourse afterwards.

On the way to Italy, they had a two-day stopover in New York. It would be their first trip to New York together. During their relationship, Madeline had flown across country a few times by herself—once for a YRNF event that she had spoken at, another time for a friend's wedding, and another time on her way to visit her family upstate. Brandon had offered to join her on these trips, but since none were more than a weekend long, Madeline had suggested he didn't trouble himself. The jetlag, missed work, it wasn't worth it. Besides, Madeline would have more fun without needing to babysit him, she teased. After all, he wouldn't know anyone at the wedding she was going to. The YRNF event would surely be boring, it wasn't like the events the California chapter hosted. Each time Brandon obliged and kissed Madeline goodbye after driving her to the airport.

Madeline had enjoyed her short weekends away in New York. She met up with old friends and glowed as she told them stories of California sunshine. She recognized the jealousy in their eyes as they listened to her talk about Brandon and how wonderful life was with him. Talking had even convinced her how perfect Brandon and their life together was. During her trips, she had never contacted Hunter, nor did any of her friends bring him up. It was like he had never existed.

Madeline was excited for her first trip to New York with Brandon. She had promised to show him around Columbia and her old neighborhood. They would also spend time in Central Park and attend happy hour with her old friends. She was an excellent tour guide and Brandon was an even better tourist. Brandon had listened intently as she weaved through the university's campus, telling stories of her memories. The quad where she would often read and once a bird pooped right on her book. The library cubicle she had fallen asleep in more than once. The statue she had once climbed and given a speech from during a rally for young republicans. She also showed him her old apartment, noticing that the small patch of dirt out front had been covered in grass. And she bought him a popsicle at the corner market where she had taken the kids from her downstairs neighbor.

Afterwards, they took the Subway down to Midtown to get drinks at a bar Madeline used to visit at least once a week. Her friends came, all hugging her and Brandon. Some had also just gotten back after being in California for their wedding. The ones who hadn't, had never met Brandon before. One drink turned into two, which turned into four. Madeline and Brandon had both eased up on their rule of sipping one drink for an entire night. After all, this occasion was purely for fun—there was no need for professionality, no chance of running into people they needed to impress at that small dive.

"You've changed so much," one of her friends—who hadn't attended her wedding—casually mentioned. This was a friend who had known Hunter well when Madeline and he were together. A friend who had respected their relationship and treated Hunter as an equal. This friend didn't mean much by the statement, didn't mean to send Madeline's head spiraling while trying to discern the statement's meaning, but that was what happened. Was this friend accusing Madeline of something? Had she changed for the worse? For the better? Madeline just raised her almost empty glass to cheer her friend while shouting "To change!" as loud as she could. Her friend giggled, meeting her cheers and slurping down the rest of her happy hour drink.

After a few more rounds, Brandon and Madeline stumbled out of the bar and into a taxi back to their hotel. With his arm around her, Brandon nuzzled her neck and began a conversation that most couples would have had before their wedding.

"Your friends must really miss you," he said, kissing her collarbone as the cab inched forward in evening rush hour.

"I miss them too," she said, enjoying the kisses, but with ample hesitation of what they would bring later.

"You have a lot of good friends," he continued and Madeline agreed. "Didn't you ever date any of them?" Madeline had many male friends. An occupational hazard of working in consulting and being active in the Republican Party.

"No! Of course not!" Madeline giggled. "Who did you think I would have dated? Gabe? He's a full head shorter than I am! Mark and his obsession with Star Wars?"

"What about Dan?" Brandon asked, bringing up another of her friends from the happy hour.

"Dan has been basically married since high school!" Madeline laughed and shook her head at the absurdity of her dating one of her friends.

"So you didn't date anyone when you lived in New York?" Brandon asked, his digging turned from playful to more serious.

"Of course I dated!" Madeline responded, but quickly caught herself. "But no one serious. I wasn't looking for a relationship. You know how New York is, everyone is so career-focused."

Brandon had to agree. Everyone in New York seemed more focused on getting ahead than getting a family. Hell, most of Madeline's friends (besides Dan) were single, married to their business suits and the corporate ladder.

"Let's get pizza," Madeline suggested and Brandon's eyes lit up. He would love a slice of New York pizza, what the city was famous for. He was sure Madeline knew the best spot, as any local should. Madeline wasn't sure why she didn't want to tell Brandon about Hunter. She had never kept anything else from him. She had told him everything else about herself and her life, but something in her wanted to keep Hunter to herself. Was it embarrassment? Was it fear of what Brandon would think? Was it because she hadn't truly let Hunter go? She was too drunk to know, so she brushed the thoughts aside and returned to the conversation about what made New York pizza so special and where to find the best pie in the city.

For the rest of their short trip in New York, Madeline felt haunted by Hunter. She was afraid they might run into him; New York sometimes felt like the smallest city on the planet. They had even run into a few people Madeline had known—someone she used to casually jog with in the park, the ex-boyfriend of her friend's old roommate, but not Hunter.

She was relieved when they got on the flight to Italy. It would be the perfect honeymoon they had planned out so diligently. The kind that would be perfectly captured through pictures of them kissing as they tossed coins into the Trevi fountain or gorging over handmade pasta and aged red wine. The week in Italy went exactly as expected, even the trains they took between cities all seemed to run as close to on-time as possible. Madeline didn't even think about Hunter once in the entire trip. She was too busy asking the tour guide questions about the acoustics at the Colosseum, or staring at their map to ensure they didn't get lost.

On their flight back to LA, they stopped over in London with only an hour window between flights. The couple returned home looking refreshed and as in love as any newlyweds could be. They were now officially the power couple each of them had dreamed of being a part of. The world was in front of them and they were ready to help each other up to the top.

Chapter 24

"Were you attacked?" Brandon asked with the picture in his hands. After Madeline had opened the envelope, she had clutched it to her chest, hoping to bury it inside. Her grip only made Brandon more determined to see the contents of the envelope and he stood in front of her beckoning her to hand it over. She had no choice. She couldn't refuse to show him—how would that end up? Yet showing him seemed like just as terrible of an option. If only she could make the picture disappear by holding it tighter to her chest, but eventually, she handed the picture over with her eyes down in shame.

Brandon studied the image, his face not knowing how to respond. To him it was like finding out your spouse was a mermaid before you met her, something so impossible that there must be some other explanation.

The image showed a white woman up against a door with a black man pressed up against her. The picture was taken from far away, through a window, but the image was unmistakable. It was an embrace—or an attack—and the woman was most definitely Madeline. Her profile was clearly visible, as was her perfectly styled hair. Seeing the picture made Madeline's chest warm as though she were still experiencing the moment the image had captured. The photo had clearly been taken the previous night when Hunter had followed her to her hotel room. Madeline knew this by the suit she was wearing.

Who took this picture? Was all Madeline could think. She was sure she wasn't followed. Her team had done a security sweep of the Langham before she checked in and had monitored the hotel closely. How could anyone have seen her and Hunter together? Had someone been waiting in the nearby building? Watching for when she would come back? Could they have known she wouldn't be alone?

"Do you want to tell me what this is?" Brandon continued, as though inviting Madeline to give a reasonable explanation. "Where was Jane? Security? Were you....were you *raped*?" Brandon whispered the last word as though saying it out loud would make it true.

Now, Madeline was in a tight position. She had kept Hunter a secret for the last thirteen years. She reasoned to herself that he just never came up, but that was because she never brought him up. It wasn't until this moment that her omission felt like a lie. When her omission had no consequences, it didn't seem like a betrayal. Why should Brandon care that she had been in love before? But now, with her previous love being accused of rape by her husband, her omission felt sinful.

Madeline looked at Brandon, her eyes begging for understanding, for a sign of how she should approach this situation. Should she tell Brandon everything? Should she tell him half of the story?

Should she continue to feign innocence? Her mind quickly began turning, reviewing her options and the possible consequences for each one: she could lose her family. She could end her career. She could...

"Madeline, whatever happened, you could use this to your advantage," Brandon said. He placed his hand on her cheek and looked at her lovingly. Madeline knew what he was thinking, it had crossed her mind as well, but she wasn't sure she could do that. "I'll support you if you want to come out with this."

While Brandon had left the political atmosphere for his company, his mind still worked like a politician, which meant trying to turn around a situation to gain sympathy (i.e., votes) from the public. Did you once smoke pot? You're a friendly person voters can relate to. Did you fail a few classes in high school? You're an inspiration for all those struggling in school. Were you raped? You can give strength to other women who are afraid to come forward.

Madeline knew that Brandon was thinking this. She could release this photo. Set up a press conference and give a speech about being sexually harassed at her hotel by a black man. This would lead to outrage in her constituency and wide support for the poor young mother who couldn't even do her job without being attacked. It would give fuel for her SAVER Bill, which would be spoken about in context of how black criminals are treated. Should she do this, her blackmailer would be beaten. He couldn't release the previous photos to the media—people would see them as more proof of her harassment. No one would believe she was unfaithful. Her campaign relaunch would be stronger than ever, as women would rally behind her—now a champion for harassment survivors everywhere. This was a sound political strategy. Madeline knew Jane would give her this same recommendation and she knew Brandon would stand behind her and hold her hand as she told the world of her assault.

But could she do that? To Brandon? Even if Brandon didn't believe her, he would stand by her. He knew their success relied on them being a united couple. His company benefited from the publicity of his wife's career. It would only benefit more as she climbed up the ladder. And his family—longtime supporters of the Republican Party—also benefitted. He had cousins in office. A nasty divorce would only make his family angry. Could she do it to Hunter? Surely he would be hunted by the press, the police, the angry public. If the police found him, his encounter with them would give Madeline much to talk about in promoting her SAVER Bill—how she still had compassion for her assailant and wished he be treated fairly. He would be ruined. No one would listen to his protests, his explanations. No one would believe a black man from Harlem over a beautiful white female from a wealthy Californian suburb.

As Madeline began to see it, either her life or Hunter's would be ruined. But there had to be another way. She always believed that if you don't like your options, create a new one. That was what she would do now, she decided. She wasn't sure if this new option would work. If it would avoid her ruin, but it was worth a shot. This option began with her telling Brandon—not everything—and ended with resolving the blackmail case one way or another.

"I wasn't attacked," Madeline said to Brandon, who didn't understand what his wife was about to tell him. "Let's sit down." He complied and sat across from Madeline at their square kitchen table and folded his hands in his lap and Madeline began her story. Because that's what it was: a story.

"The man in this picture is named Hunter," she started. "We were involved when I studied at Columbia. He is also a politician, a city councilman in New York." Up until then, Madeline was truthful as she was trying to decide what to say next. Then the truth started to bend off a tangent. "The blackmail is also against him. Someone wants to use him to ruin my career. When I was in New York this week, we met to talk. But nothing happened. He walked me to my hotel room and we hugged, but nothing happened." Madeline rationalized to herself that she wasn't lying, nothing had happened the night before with Hunter even though they were so close.

Brandon narrowed his eyes at her, a look showing that he was deciding how much he should believe, how much of a chump he was going to be.

He loved Madeline, he truly saw her as the love of his life, and it didn't hurt that his love helped him succeed.

"OK," was what he said. He stood up from the table. "I have to get back to work. There's a meeting in the office I need to get to." Madeline nodded and he left the kitchen, grabbing his laptop from the living room and walking out the front door. Madeline sat quietly trying to examine whether her husband believed her or if she had lost him. She didn't have much time to think quietly, as soon her phone rang.

"Hope you got home all right," Jane started as soon as Madeline answered the phone. "Sorry to bother you, I know you wanted some family time when you got home, but I have Officer Austin on the other line. He says he wants to talk to you about a picture. I told him you were busy and that we didn't get any pictures at the office, but he said he thought you'd want to talk to him."

Chapter 25

Madeline had never been to the offices at the Fraternal Order of Police. The headquarters were near the local police station, a small two-story building with a training center for policemen in the first floor and halls and offices on the second. In the hallway were headshots of the organization's members, smiling men in their uniforms and badges. Followed by Jane, Madeline walked down the hall toward Officer Austin's office and knocked on the open door.

"Yup," he answered, looking up from a file he was reading on his desk. "I didn't know running for office included so much paperwork."

"It's important to have a good team for that," she smiled, hoping to find some common ground. He motioned her to come in and she sat across from him. Jane stood in the doorway texting away on her phone.

"I'm not sure you want her in for this," Officer Austin motioned to Jane. She took the not-so-subtle hint and stepped outside, promising to be available if needed. She closed the door behind her.

"I understand you want to speak about a photo of me," Madeline said.

"Yes, let's cut to the chase, neither of us want to spend time chatting about the weather," Officer Austin said. He opened a drawer of his desk and pulled out the photo that Madeline had received that day: she and Hunter embracing outside her hotel room. Then, he pulled out a second picture: Madeline walking in the Langham, with Hunter walking on the sidewalk. He then paused as Madeline looked at the pictures. "The third picture I'd rather not pull out. It's not decent."

"You want me to drop out of the race." Madeline stated. "Is that what this has been about?"

"Well, of course that would make my campaign a lot easier," he began. "But these aren't from me. I received these pictures today in the mail with a letter. The letter said I was free to use them however I wanted."

Madeline looked at Officer Austin in front of her, unsure if she should believe him.

"I do have a good team," he said. "And it was my campaign manager who opened this envelope. He suggested we go public with it. Tomorrow morning, before your reelection campaign launches. That way you wouldn't even have a chance to start running. You'd be buried in this. The press loves a scandal and they would love watching your marriage crumble. It would be sensational—Madeline Thomas the perfect candidate, the perfect woman, is not so perfect. Not to mention the congressional ethics committee could have a field day. Do you have any enemies there? They'd probably investigate you to see if you used public funds for your extracurricular activities, or if you were using your sexuality to gain favors from someone—not sure who, but I'm sure it wouldn't be long before the press found out who this man was. Of course your SAVER Bill would also go down the toilet, people would think you were biased, working with the black community against the police. It might get you black votes, but your white supporters would be gone."

"So should I start preparing my response?" Madeline replied calmly. "Write a concession speech about why I won't run for reelection?"

"Maybe also start calling divorce lawyers," Officer Austin said with a smile and a wink. "Talk to all the good ones first so your husband can't hire them."

The pair sat quietly facing each other for several moments, both in deep thought of their next words. Madeline knew she wouldn't speak first. She would let Officer Austin continue, which he did after the pause started to drag on.

"But I am not going to do that," he said. "I'm going to squash your campaign fair and square. You can deal with your marital problems on your own time." He pulled an envelope out of the desk drawer. "The third picture is in here. You can take them. I won't be using them in my campaign, but I thought you should know that someone has them and is willing to use them."

Madeline was still. She looked at the pictures and envelope in front of her, but hesitated to take them. "So you're not blackmailing me?"

"Blackmailing you? I am an officer of the law, ma'am," he said. "I uphold the law and arrest those who don't. I wish I could give you more information about who sent these or why they want me to destroy your campaign, but I don't have any."

Madeline nodded and grabbed the pictures from the officer's desk. She thanked the officer and wished him good luck on his campaign as she let herself out of the office, into the hall where Jane was waiting, still texting away on her cell phone.

"So, what do we need to do to keep his mouth shut?" Jane asked when she saw Madeline. Madeline shook her head and the two of them got in their separate cars to drive to the office where Madeline's team was working hard on her reelection campaign launch.

Since finding out about Officer Austin's campaign, they had completely replanned their strategy. They scheduled a new event for the following evening with donors, supporters, community leaders and colleagues where she would officially announce her campaign. The previously planned event—still a week away—would stay and serve as a 'thank you' to her supporters who had helped her thus far while also motivating them to keep the momentum up.

In the next 24 hours her team needed to send out a press release and contact all the local and national reporters to ensure their coverage. They also needed to convince important donors and supports to be available for appearances at her event last minute.

Madeline also had to review her new speech that painted her as a professional, someone with a proven track record of making good on her promises—this would juxtapose her with Officer Austin who was inexperienced in politics. The speech wouldn't mention his name (a rookie mistake Austin had made by mentioning hers) because any mention gave him recognition and recognition—both for good or bad reasons—led to votes. Her speech would focus on the change she had started and her vision for the future.

Later that evening, after her staff had notified the press of her reelection launch and newspapers were starting to print articles leading up to it, Madeline sat in bed reviewing her speech. Brandon was already asleep next to her. They hadn't spoken since he saw the picture earlier. By the time Madeline had come home he was already in bed. Madeline took that as a good sign, at least he was still in their bed.

Between gazing over at him and at the papers in front of her, she found herself reading and rereading the same lines over and over. She told herself to concentrate, stay focused, but she couldn't, she kept checking her phone, reading the headlines with her name in them: *Thomas to announce reelection campaign, Thomas to run again, Thomas/Austin battle to heat up.* She usually didn't read the news on her phone (she'd wait for the morning Binder) unless something big was happening. The news on her reelection was not big enough to warrant her attention, drawing it away from what needed it more, but she was looking for something else. She was looking for the scandal to break. Surely her blackmailer had seen the recent headlines, that she had moved up her campaign launch. Did that mean the deadline for her to pay had also moved up? She would keep refreshing her newsfeeds until she would know.

She kept scrolling until she saw the headline. Her speech would need to be rewritten.

Chapter 26

Black male killed by Police

16-year-old Jay Flynn was shot and killed by an on-duty police officer Wednesday evening in Harlem. Flynn was on his way home from school when approached by the police officer who asked to see his I.D., according to Flynn's friend Damon John who was walking with him. Flynn questioned the officer why he was stopped and when he opened his jacket to take out his wallet the police fired his gun, John said.

"We are very sorry for the loss of Jay Flynn and are investigating the incident," said Harlem Chief of Police Martin Sanders in a statement. According to the statement, one shot was fired at the ground as a warning shot. The bullet ricocheted and shards hit Flynn in the chest and face.

Flynn and John were both rushed to the hospital in an ambulance. Flynn was pronounced dead in the ambulance. John was treated in the hospital and sustained minor wounds on his right arm and shoulder.

The police statement says that warning shots are only fired if suspects resist and show signs of violence toward the officer. Chief Sanders said the ricochet was an unfortunate occurrence and that the officer had not intended to injure the suspect.

The officer, whose name has not been released, placed the call for backup and the ambulance after the bullet was fired. Chief Sanders said the officer will be on leave until the incident is investigated.

When Madeline finished reading the story, she silently closed her phone and slipped out of bed. There was work to be done, a response to be drafted and she needed her full team working on it overnight. If only her SAVER Bill had been implemented already, she thought, this was exactly the kind of incident she believed her bill could avoid. If only that officer wasn't so afraid of African Americans and that young boy wasn't so skeptical of the officer's intentions.

By the time Madeline made it downstairs to her kitchen table, Jane had already texted her three different versions of the news story she had just read. Madeline called her chief of staff, who sounded wide awake even though it was already after 11:00 PM. Jane said all the team members were on the way to the office and would figure out everything before their upcoming event the following night.

Madeline too would head into the office, she said. She couldn't do much from home anyway. She quietly slipped back upstairs to get dressed and then jumped into her car to drive. As she drove her cell phone rang and who it was didn't surprise her at all.

"I guess you saw the news," Madeline said instead of *hello* when she answered.

"Saw the news? I just spent the entire evening in the hospital with Damon. He and Jay used to go to the community center when they were younger. Before they got involved with, you know, different activities," Hunter responded.

"So are you calling to tell me that my SAVER Bill is still a waste?" Madeline asked. As she spoke, she heard her phone beep notifying her of another call on the line. It was one of her colleagues in the senate who supported her bill. While her head told her to hang up on Hunter—she needed to answer that call—she wanted to hear what he had to say.

"Actually no," he responded. "I think I can help you. I saw your reelection campaign launch is tomorrow and I'm actually about to step on a redeye to California. Rhonda's there with the kids and we have a court hearing tomorrow morning. Bitch sued me for divorce across the country to screw me over. Anyway, I thought if you want, I could give a talk about your bill at your event."

Madeline's phone kept beeping. Jane was calling again. Another senator who opposed her bill. Madeline should be answering these calls. "Sure," she said quickly.

"Great, I think my perspective could be really useful for your campaign, seeing as this shooting was in my district and, well, I'm black. I guess if I help you win you won't forget me forever," Hunter said.

"Hunter, I have to go," Madeline responded. "Send a speech to Jane, my chief of staff, and she'll set everything up." Hunter seemed like he was about to keep talking but Madeline quickly hung up the phone.

"Madeline Thomas," she answered the next call that came through. It was another senator who had been on the fence about outwardly supporting her bill. But this incident seemed to change his mind. When she arrived at the office, Jane was waiting for her in the parking lot. She had drafted a statement for the press, as journalists had been calling to get Madeline's response to the incident. As they walked to the elevator, Madeline read the statement and gave Jane a couple comments before giving her approval. Jane also proposed she personally speak with the *New York Times* journalist who called, after all, that paper had been friendly to her, despite her being a republican. Madeline agreed and was handed a phone with the journalist on the line when she entered her office. She answered a few questions, plugged her talking points about the SAVER Bill and why her reelection was now so much more important.

"This must hit you close to heart," the journalist said after asking all the usual things that Madeline had expected.

"These events always hit close to heart," Madeline responded to the unusual statement. "Every incident like this is heart wrenching and avoidable."

"Yes, but this one specifically for you," the journalist continued. "I hear you knew Jay Flynn's mom."

"What? Keisha Flynn?" Madeline knew the name from the news. "I can't say I knew her."

"She used to go to a community center up in Harlem," the journalist said. "Where you volunteered when you were at Columbia. She said you took her friend to get an abortion."

"Oh," Madeline responded.

"Let me ask you, Mrs. Thomas, how come you never talk about your experience volunteering in Harlem? Especially when the bill you are championing significantly affects the population you volunteered with? It seems like your experience volunteering would make you a much more reputable source for this bill. But it's never come up in your campaigning."

Madeline thought for a minute on how to respond. She didn't like when journalists approached her with unexpected questions. Jane's job was to ensure that didn't happen. "Well, as you see, I dealt with some sensitive situations while there. To protect people's privacy, I don't really discuss what I did there."

"Apparently you were one of the only caucasians to volunteer there," the journalist continued. "What brought you there?"

"I lived in Harlem," she responded. "When I studied at Columbia. I thought I could be helpful. Do you have any more questions about my bill?" Madeline rushed the journalist off the phone and called Jane into her office.

"Everyone needs to be on their toes," Madeline said in a slightly raised voice. "Things are going to come up and we need to be ready for everything."

"Of course, we're always on our toes," Jane responded, unsure why she felt like she was being reprimanded. But she knew her boss was under a lot of stress and she got back to work, telling herself she would do better.

Madeline was unsettled by the mention of her volunteering at the community center. She had never mentioned it for the same reason she had never mentioned Hunter—it was something she kept safe, locked away in a box where she contained her old life. She couldn't pull out one part of her old life without pulling out the rest, everything was connected like a chain of linked circles. Her old life didn't mix with her new life. Hunter, the community center, the abortion she helped that girl with, they needed to stay in that box.

Madeline tried to remember Keisha, but the name didn't ring a bell. She remembered the girl she helped with the abortion. She was a young, timid girl who seemed like she was trying hard to fit in where she knew she didn't. What was her name? The years seemed to have erased that specific detail. Madeline didn't remember the girl's friends either, but she recalled other girls who used to hang out at the community center, all of them with their beautiful braids and fatal nails. She was surprised any of them would remember her after so many years.

Trying to put the comment aside, Madeline got back to work with her team. By morning they had rewritten her speech for the event, developed a new strategy for the SAVER Bill and perfected her response to the incident. She hadn't spoken to any more journalists. When they called, Madeline said to give out their prepared press release and email any other specific question. No one emailed questions about the community center.

When the sun was already up, and the first light of the morning had faded into daytime, Madeline decided to go home. She would take a quick shower, change her clothes and be back in the office until the evening's event.

Chapter 27

Rhonda was waiting outside her apartment at dawn. She was waiting for the white lady— Madeline she would try to remember to call her— to come pick her up and take her to take care of her problem. She was early because she hadn't slept the night before and once she saw that dawn was approaching she pulled herself out of bed and snuck out, careful not to wake up her brothers and sisters.

She had only told two people about her problem: her best friend Keisha and the white lady. "Congrats, bitch!" Keisha had said in response. "Do I get to throw you a baby shower or something? Get yourself some hopping new clothes to go over your belly? What'd the baby daddy say? He's good for it, right?"

Rhonda had feigned excitement with her best friend and the two of them fantasized about raising the baby girl—they hoped for a girl— together. They would dress her up, paint her nails, it would be fun, like having a doll, as neither of them had had a doll before. Keisha promised they would do everything together, they could both be mommies. All the meanwhile, Rhonda felt scared. It was fun pretending with Keisha, but Keisha couldn't understand. After all, she wasn't the one throwing up after first period at school. Nor was she the one who would destroy her vagina by pushing a baby through it. What would happen after that? She wasn't sure she trusted that Keisha's enthusiasm would last. And where would they live? Rhonda lived with her parents and two younger siblings in a one-bedroom apartment. Her mother, who was only 18 years older than her, had told her plenty of times that she would kill her if she got pregnant before getting married. Rhonda believed her mother was capable of following through with this threat, but even if not, she was sure her mother wouldn't let her raise the baby at home. Keisha, on the other hand, lived with her three older brothers. Her parents were gone—she didn't know where—and Rhonda wasn't sure there was room for a crib there either.

The baby daddy? Well, she didn't think he was good for it, as Keisha suggested. He was just 13 himself and—at the expense of Rhonda—was recently initiated into the Cobras, the most exclusive and scariest gang in Harlem. Rhonda hoped she wouldn't see him again and she wasn't sure she'd be able to ask him for help even if she did.

Unsure of her options, Rhonda had called the one person she thought might have an answer. After all, this person was older, white, and in college—Rhonda was sure she'd know what to do. Rhonda didn't know the white lady very well, but she liked and trusted Hunter. He'd been hanging out at the community center for a while and recently started bringing around his new friend. The next afternoon, Rhonda pulled the white lady aside and explained her situation. She expected the white lady to offer her money or teach her what to do with a baby—because white people both had money and knew things—but neither of those options came out of her mouth. Instead, the white lady surprised her by giving her another option: abortion.

Rhonda hadn't thought about that before; it wasn't something that her peers did. She had peers raising babies, peers who gave babies to aunts or grandparents to raise, but none had aborted. She didn't even know if that was even legal and if it was, where it could be done. The white lady assured her it would be OK and she would help her. Rhonda just nodded and followed along when the white lady told her when her appointment would be.

Madeline showed up right on time to pick up Rhonda in a taxi and take her downtown to a clinic where no one from their neighborhood would accidentally see them. Rhonda was afraid of many things and that was a big one—what if people knew she had an abortion? What would they say about her? What would the baby daddy say if he heard she killed his baby? Rhonda quietly got in the taxi as is sped downtown through neighborhoods Rhonda had never seen before. She hadn't seen red carpets in front of doorways, or apartment buildings with gold trim out front. She hadn't seen doormen or artisanal bakeries that advertised specialty dog treats.

Madeline held her hand during the car ride and Rhonda kept her eyes glued to the window. When they arrived, Madeline led her into the building and helped her fill out the paperwork. She sat with her in the operating room as she put on the hospital robe and held out her arm for the nurse to check her vitals. No one asked questions about why a young white woman was with a younger black girl at the clinic. No one looked at them judgmentally, nor did they give her a pitied eye. And this also bothered Rhonda. Why didn't they judge her? Why didn't they scold her or pity her or nod knowing that she was another cliché of her kind? Why did they just accept her and continue with their work?

Madeline hugged her before the anesthesia was delivered and promised to be there when she woke up. To Rhonda is felt like just a blink before she opened her eyes in a different room, with Madeline sitting beside her.

Madeline was reading a textbook and taking notes on a notebook when she saw that Rhonda woke up. She quickly put away her schoolwork and stood by the young girl's side. "How are you feeling?" she asked.

Rhonda felt hallow and numb. Like these white people who operated on her had stolen a vital organ of hers. "Is everything OK?" she asked, but she knew the white lady would lie.

"Everything went perfectly," Madeline responded. "We just need to wait until you feel good enough to get up and then we can go back home." Madeline handed her a juice box and poked the straw through the little hole for her. "You need to drink some sugar."

Rhonda took the juice box, feeling like a child who needed someone to take care of her. But she wasn't a child. A child wouldn't be able to bring a baby into the world. Wouldn't be able to have sex even. Rhonda felt suffocated and angry. Why had she let this white woman do this to her? Why had she listened to her? Why had she let these people kill her baby?

"You can probably go back to school tomorrow if you feel better," Madeline said. "But you don't have to, if you don't want to."

Rhonda nodded, finishing her juice. "I want to go home."

Madeline nodded and retrieved a nurse to organize Rhonda's release. Once they left, Madeline suggested they stop for a Tasti D-Lite. Rhonda had never had the famous soft serve ice cream before, and she truthfully didn't want it then, but how could she say no? She sat quietly and ate her dessert even though it made her feel sick. Then they took another silent taxi ride back uptown, past the fancy buildings and dog walkers leading poodles with bows in their hair.

"Drop me off here," Rhonda said when they were a few blocks from her apartment.

"But you shouldn't walk too much, let me help you into your bed," Madeline responded, but Rhonda refused. "Everything is going to be OK." Madeline rubbed her shoulder. The gesture reminded Rhonda of something she saw a mother do in a TV show she had seen once. It made her feel warm and even more hateful inside.

"You wouldn't understand," Rhonda said as she pulled away. "Everything is easy for you."

"You're right," Madeline responded. "But that's why I am here to help you. To make things easier for you. Call me if you need anything. I'm always here for you."

Rhonda nodded, but she would never call. She would never ask another white person for help. That afternoon she told Keisha about the operation.

"Those damn white people don't want us to reproduce," she said, shaking her head. Rhonda nodded in agreement. When she went back to the community center, she avoided Madeline. What did Hunter see in her? Shouldn't he be with someone like them? Were they not good enough for him? She started to flirt with him when Madeline wasn't around.

It only took five years, but eventually Rhonda got Hunter in bed. It was the second time she had gotten pregnant, but this time she would keep it.

Madeline had never told anyone about Rhonda's operation, not even Hunter. She felt proud of herself that Rhonda trusted her and that she was able to help the poor girl. She had high hopes for her. Maybe she would turn her life around and escape the trap that Harlem seemed to be for so many people. She had thought about it often right after the operation. At the community center she wanted to hug her and ask how she was doing, but she felt that Rhonda had a barrier around her. She sensed that Rhonda didn't want a hug, nor did she want to be questioned about her wellbeing, and Madeline respected that. Once Madeline moved downtown, she didn't see Rhonda at the community center anymore. She thought about her less and less until eventually she didn't even remember the girl's name. The girl's scared face and the way she shivered when Madeline touched her would stay in Madeline's memory a little longer, but even those things had faded over the years. Eventually the experience was filed away in Madeline's memory and she never thought it would come up again.

Chapter 28

When Madeline stepped into her kitchen, Brandon was filling a thermos with coffee. He had his laptop bag slung over his shoulder and was dressed for work. He nodded to acknowledge Madeline's entrance, but didn't make eye contact.

"Saw the news," he said as he closed his thermos and studied the cup with his eyes. Madeline nodded to him and eyed the empty coffee pot on the counter. "Would have made you some, but didn't know whether to expect you." He brushed by without giving her a kiss on the cheek as Madeline would have expected him to do.

"You're coming tonight?" she said, her tone more of a statement than a question, but she was still afraid of the answer.

"I don't have a choice," he said. "Don't worry, I'll be a good husband." He let himself out the door and Madeline heard his car start.

The boys were already at school and Molly was out, so Madeline had the house to herself. She started another pot of coffee and headed upstairs to take a shower. She set her phone down outside the shower so she could see the screen in case of an emergency—and so many things could be considered an emergency at that time that it seemed almost criminal to get in the shower. She had just put the conditioner in her hair when her phone startled her. She quickly wiped her face and looked through the shower's glass doors at her vibrating phone on the counter. Brandon. She stuck out her hand and dried it on the towel before answering the phone and putting it on speaker.

"Madeline?..." It was hard for Madeline to hear what Brandon said next with the water still pounding on her shoulders. She heard the words hospital, school, and...Noah? Madeline shut off the water immediately. She begged Brandon to repeat what he said.

"Noah was in another fight at school," Brandon said. "He's at the hospital. I'm on the way. I suggest you get on your way as well." While Madeline implored him for more information, he had none. He'd update her from the hospital after seeing Noah.

Madeline finished her shower and completed her face routine as quickly as she could, smothering on all the anti-wrinkle, anti-shine creams that she was required to use, especially on big days like today. She slipped into one her senator-suits, even though she knew she would need to focus on being Madeline the mother while Noah was in the hospital. It was just the worst possible day for Noah to get injured. The day of her campaign launch, the day after Jay Flynn was shot in Harlem, her full attention was needed to be Madeline the Senator.

She called Jane from the car, telling her she wouldn't make it back into the office that day, but would arrive at the event venue a few hours early to prepare. "Anything I should know in the meantime?" She asked as an aside.

"Madeline, I know you are busy, but you are a political genius!" Jane stated. "How did you get Hunter Williams to come speak at the event? It's perfect with everything going on and he sent over a great speech. Why didn't you tell me you were inviting him?"

"It was sort of a last-minute thing," Madeline responded. "Email me the speech so I can read it." She'd skim it on her cell phone from the hospital when she had a few minutes. Jane agreed and hung up just as Madeline parked her car. As she walked towards the entrance, her phone rang again.

"Where are you?" Brandon asked.

"I just parked," she responded. He gave her directions to their room and said a doctor was on the way to give them updates. It took her a few minutes to find the right ward and room, but when she did, the doctor was talking to Brandon above Noah who was lying in the bed with a swollen face and his eyes closed. Madeline leapt to her son and put her hands on his shoulders.

"Noah, what happened?" She looked at her son, but he appeared to be sleeping.

"Do you have any more questions for me?" the doctor asked. It appeared that he and Brandon had already had an extensive conversation that Madeline had missed. She could see the doctor was eager to leave, surely he had other patients, but he stood with patience that only doctors have when dealing with life or death situations.

"What happened?" Madeline turned to the doctor, who made eye contact with Brandon.

"I'll explain," Brandon said, thanking and excusing the doctor from their room. "Noah was climbing on one of the awnings at school. Apparently he and Jamie got in a fight on top of the awning and he fell down."

"Jamie pushed him?" Madeline was sure that other boy was to blame.

"Noah says he fell," Brandon responded. "It's hard for him to talk. It seems like he took a few punches to the face before falling down. He broke his cheekbone and a few ribs. He's on pain medication now, so he's pretty out of it. We need to just let him sleep."

Madeline nodded and sat down on the side of the hospital bed. She held her son's hand and watched him breathe. She felt like an outsider in the room, like she was intruding in an intimate family moment. But this was her family, even when she wore her senator clothing, she was still Madeline the mother. It was a costume she could never take off.

Brandon was sitting in one of the chairs in the room. She could feel him looking at her, but they said nothing. The clock ticked. Noah sighed. Machines beeped. Madeline and Brandon were silent. When her back started to ache from sitting on the edge of the bed, she moved to the other metal chair in the room and pulled out her cellphone. She had messages from Jane, Hunter's speech to read, a few other notifications.

"You're working?" Brandon asked. To Madeline it sounded like an accusation.

"He's sleeping," she motioned to her son with her cellphone. Madeline wished she could have left Madeline the senator at home, but it was one of those days she couldn't. Mothers are required to juggle hundreds of balls. The balls aren't just motherhood and career, but every little thing that each of those entail. In one hand, Madeline juggled Noah's problems at school, giving Adam the love and inspiration he required, finding time for family dinners. On the other hand, there was her career; the SAVER Bill, her reelection, her constituents. Then the blackmail was thrown into the loop and Madeline had to keep juggling, hoping no balls would fall. But balls will fall. No one can juggle everything. And no matter what falls, women will be judged for it. They will be judged for not handling everything. For not juggling even more balls. At this moment, Madeline knew she would have to drop the ball for Noah. She could be judged for holding onto her career balls above her family, but sometimes these things must be done. Brandon was there, he could catch this ball and be there for Noah when she couldn't. She would trade this ball for a sheet of guilt that she would struggle and fail to get out from.

She sat quietly in the chair and worked while Brandon sat with his hands in his lap looking at his son. When nurses came in, he spoke with them. Madeline looked up occasionally, but she was focused on her phone. When the morning turned to afternoon and Jane began pestering Madeline to get to the event, Madeline knew she had no choice.

She had to attend her reelection campaign launch event. She wanted to tell Brandon that it was important for him to come as well, but she knew she couldn't. That would make her also drop another ball on her marriage and it seemed like her marriage didn't have many balls left.

She would have to attend the event alone, hoping there weren't too many questions about the absence of her husband. Unfortunately, the absence of a spouse didn't look good for politicians. It suggested marital problems, which made people uncomfortable. Why should they entrust the country to someone who couldn't protect their own marriage? Madeline would have to be even stronger that evening to overcome Brandon's absence.

This was a big night for Madeline. For so many reasons. In the car, she tried to take a few deep breaths. She wanted to be able to enjoy the evening. After all, this event was part of her dream. She felt like she was being punished for wanting something for herself, wanting to pursue something that took away from her family. For a moment, she wondered if it was worth it. But the moment quickly passed.

Chapter 29

Three hours early was considered late for Madeline to arrive for her event. She needed to change her clothes, have her hair and makeup professionally done. She needed to rehearse her speech from the podium, reading it from the teleprompter and practice walking on and off the stage. She needed to learn the choreography for the evening, where she should stand during different parts of the events, how to get from place to place, how to mingle and make everything look perfectly natural and unchoreographed. Jane also needed to go through all the VIP attendees with Madeline and give her talking points for each one—Madeline would need to remember to ask about people's spouses, children, businesses, it was important for people to feel she had a personal interest in them and remembered everything they told her in previous meetings. With so little time to prepare, Jane went through the VIP list while Madeline's hair and makeup were being done, screaming over the hair dryer and accepting that Madeline couldn't respond while her lips were being painted.

When the event was about to start, Madeline looked nothing less than presidential. There were no bags under eyes even though she hadn't slept the previous night, and no wrinkles on her face. The gray in her hair had been painted over and she was glowing. She pinned an American flag on the lapel of her brand new, pressed navy-blue suit and was ready to go.

The room was starting to fill up and waiters waltzed through, passing out hors d'oeuvres and drinks to Madeline's many supporters. Jane stood with Madeline in the dressing room, for their last few minutes of quiet.

"This is it," Jane stated the obvious and smiled admiringly at her boss.

It was it, thought Madeline. It was a pivotal moment in her career—for the good or the bad. Even with everything going on, Madeline had continued to check her phone to see if news of her infidelity had made the press, but at least up until then, it hadn't. Her blackmailer had either let it go, or not upped the deadline to her new event. Journalists were already posting live from the events, showing pictures of the décor, and posting sound bites from attendees. Things were going smoothly as planned.

Jane led Madeline into the room to the first spot in her choreographed movements for the evening. She stood near Jason Bittley, the CEO of a major manufacturing company in her district, and asked about his wife. *How was she feeling? If there was anything else she could do while she continued her treatment, please let them know!* Jason responded positively, telling Madeline that his wife's chemotherapy was going well and they were likely on the last round. A full recovery was expected. Madeline voiced her happiness and Jane took notes.

She then swanned to her next spot for the evening. Where Laura McDermott was mingling with other heads of local think tanks. Laura ran a think tank that supported Republican Libertarians and had created a significant amount of content that swirled the web prior to Madeline's previous victory. *How was her son doing at Stanford? Had he chosen a major?* He was loving it! He'd be majoring in International Relations and minoring in French. Laura didn't understand the minor, but apparently her son found the language interesting, quotes and emphasis around the last word. *How lucky our children are that they get to study what interests them instead of studying in sole preparation for a career!*

Jane continued to lead Madeline around the room while taking notes of all her personal conversations. There was no talk of the campaign, nor of any of Madeline's political agendas. No one mentioned her opponent, Officer Austin, nor did they discuss her upcoming speech. From the conversation alone, it would seem as though Madeline was at a friendly dinner party, with only close friends who didn't all have their own agendas for attending this bountiful evening. But this is the political dance that one must dance in order to win. Pretend that everything is friendly and perfect, when in truth one misplaced word could tear it all down.

She shook hands with journalists, smiled for pictures, and deferred all questions to Jane. She could see even the press enjoying the evening, how could they not? With all the free food and alcohol that everyone knew reporters loved.

Madeline felt elated from the evening's ballet. She enjoyed the mingling, the handshaking, the smiles of assurance that she shared with supporters. It gave her confidence that she was doing the right thing, that she could win with the troves of support she had behind her.

When the time came, Jane led Madeline back to the dressing room to have her hair and makeup touched up before her upcoming speech. With adrenaline running high, Madeline and Jane smiled and even joked with one another about their excitement during the evening. Jane showed her some of the pictures that had already been published from the event and Madeline herself was surprised by how bright and sophisticated she looked.

With her face reapplied and her hair freshly sprayed, she went to the waiting room behind the stage where the speakers for the evening assembled. Aside from Hunter, there was the leader of the California chapter of Republican National Committee, Mark Waldo, who would introduce her, as well as California governor Timothy Boyd who had flown specially to spend an entire half hour at her event. Madeline thanked her guests and introduced them to Hunter.

"You must be busy these days!" Boyd exclaimed when hearing he was the city councilman for Harlem.

"A democrat speaking for Madeline?" Waldo said while pursing his lips in approval. "Are you sure you don't want to switch sides?"

Hunter used his charm to connect with these older white men, who weren't used to speaking with men like Hunter. They all voiced their praises for Madeline and the older men returned to their staff to finalize their preparations.

"How are you feeling?" Hunter asked Madeline when they were alone in the waiting room.

"Good," she said and she meant it. She wasn't nervous about public speaking, in fact, she loved public speaking. She found it empowering, especially when speaking about a cause she cared about, such as her reelection. At the moment, she was glad Brandon couldn't come with her. She couldn't imagine having this conversation with her husband by her side. "Jane really loved the speech you wrote."

"Glad to hear it," he said. "What did you think about it?"

"It could be a bit more refined," she said with a wink. "But it gets your point across. I liked it."

"Well, as it turns out, I Actually wrote a second that I am thinking about giving instead tonight."

"Oh? Get it to Jane if you want it on the teleprompter."

"I don't need a teleprompter for this." Hunter's eyes narrowed and suddenly Madeline didn't feel as light and high as she had all evening.

"I want to help you, Maddy. I want to help you win, but only if you will help me."

Chapter 30

"You're on in five," Jane said to Hunter as she brushed by him. She continued on to talk to Mark Waldo and give him his last handshake before he left the wings to step onto the podium to introduce the night's speeches.

"I want to tell you a story about an enthusiastic Columbia student I met almost twenty years ago..." he started saying to a roaring crowd.

Madeline knew exactly what he was going to say—he was going to talk about her idealism, her hard work, and how she was the future of this country. She didn't need to listen. She turned her attention to Hunter and pursed her lips in a smile. "I'm not sure what you mean," she responded to him. "You probably need to speak with a New York Senator about whatever you're looking for." Madeline was used to being asked for favors by city officials. They were always lobbying her for funding in their districts—new freeways that needed to be built, agricultural lands that needed to be reapportioned. Senators often stuck footnotes into bills that appropriated funds for pet projects in their states. It was something Madeline hated doing, but it had to be done. After all, all the other senators did it—why shouldn't she? Especially when she was representing one of the most populated states.

"This isn't about politics," he said quietly, leaning toward her. "I gave you a deadline. Tick tock, according to Jane, there is just under five minutes left."

Suddenly Madeline woke up. Her ears, like antennas, caught the signal Hunter was sending and everything made sense. It was Hunter. From the beginning. How could she have been so blind?

"You want a million dollars or you're going to ruin my career?"

"I knew you were smart," he responded, pulling a folded up piece of paper out of his jacket pocket. "You see, this here is my second speech. It talks about how we met: you were a privileged Columbia student, slumming it with me. Dating me made you feel so good about yourself that you could pretend you weren't racist and you're still pretending. But you are racists. Once I served my purpose, you dumped me to get ahead."

"I didn't dump you—"

"Let me finish telling you about my speech! Then, years later, when you're busy living your white privileged life in California you come back to me and make love to me. And you act like you really loved me, but then you go back to your white privileged life because you can. And because you chose privilege over love.

"Everyone thinks that Madeline is the perfect woman—beautiful, an amazing mom, wife, politician—but it's all a lie. She's a racist and an adulterer and I have the proof. Once I'm finished talking, all the newspapers in the country will receive proof of Madeline's indiscretions. See the pictures and then decide if this is the person you want to represent you. The person pretending she wants to fix race issues in America, when she is part of the problem. The person lying to you about her perfect marriage."

Madeline held her jaw closed as she listened to Hunter speak. "How did you take those pictures? And Why?"

"It was pretty easy. I took the picture of you in bed because I wanted to remember the moment. You didn't even notice when I snapped the camera. The other picture was handed to me."

"Other pictures," Madeline said, but she didn't wait for Hunter to acknowledge her correction. "Is this revenge?" she asked. "Because you think I dumped you? Or that I used you?"

"I guess. You're so privileged that you think you did nothing wrong."

"So why do you want the money? If it's revenge, isn't destroying my career good enough for you?"

"Well, I need the money now. You can't imagine what it costs to get divorced, especially when it's cross country in California. But I guess maybe you'll find out soon enough, or you won't because you white privilege people don't do that. You're like the Clintons, you stay together because it's good for your careers."

"You realize that blackmailing me is illegal. That I have an FBI team investigating this. That one phone call to them and you would go to jail. Another expense trial for you."

"That was a risk I was willing to take. Because, you see, I know you. If you take me down, I'm taking you down with me. Tell the FBI it was me, and I'll release everything to the press. I'd go to jail, and you'd be ruined. You'd just go home to your fake marriage—another kind of jail. You wouldn't do that to yourself. So you see Maddy, we're in this together. I go down, you go down."

Madeline's thoughts swirled in her head. She had loved Hunter so much, truly loved him, and a part of her still held those feelings for him. She had never believed that race was an issue in their relationship—but was there a chance he was right? That she was so privileged that she could believe that race wasn't an issue? Would news of her infidelity be even worse because it was with an African American? If she could overcome infidelity—there was a slim chance—she could never overcome racism. There was no rectifying that accusation in politics. She'd never make it to the White House. Her heart started to pound, she could feel beads of sweat collecting around her made up face, but she tried to keep her face straight.

"Two minutes!" Jane yelled.

"And if I pay, how do I know you won't come back in a year and do this again?"

"You'd have to trust me. I'll give you all the copies I have of the photographs. And I'll give you my word." Madeline wanted to believe she could

249

still trust him. Her heart did, her heart always trusted him, that he would always cherish her the way he once had. "What's it going to be, Maddy?"

Madeline looked to the stage where Mark Waldo was finishing his introduction. "Now, things have been difficult in this country lately, especially in the last 24 hours. And Madeline has made it her mission to fix these problems. Tonight, I am happy to introduce one of her long time supporters who proves that Madeline is what this country needs. I'm happy to introduce, Hunter Williams, a democratic city councilman from Harlem, the very district in turmoil right now. Once you see him, you'll know that if he believes in Madeline Thomas, so should you."

"Hunter, are you ready?" Jane stepped toward Hunter, ready to push him onto the stage.

Her mind had already made a decision, no matter what she believed she needed to do. She knew that she would deal with the consequences later. She would figure out how to pick up the pieces, no matter where they fell. It was what she did. She had no other choice. She nodded to Hunter.

"I need to hear you say it," he said.

"I'll pay," she whispered to him. "Please."

Hunter ripped up the paper he had pulled out of his pocket earlier and dropped the pieces to the ground. "It's the right decision, Maddy. You'll go far. I'll have a lot of faith in you, really, I do." He squeezed her hand and then turned toward the stage where Mark Waldo was waiting for his handshake. He shook the man's hand and clasped the podium with his large, knuckled hands.

"This country is in need of a revolution," he began. "There are lots of people proposing how to do this, but very few are looking at the big picture, like Madeline Thomas does. As you probably all know, yesterday an African American young boy was gunned down in my city district. I know you don't want to talk about that tonight, and I understand that. I also don't want to talk about it. I don't ever want to need to talk about these things happening, which is why I am supporting Madeline Thomas."

The crowd roared and Madeline closed her eyes. She tried to take in a few deep breaths to calm herself before she would be stepping out and giving her own speech. "Oh my gosh! Can we get makeup back in here?" Jane said. "You are sweating! Are you nervous? You don't usually get this nervous."

"I'm fine," she responded as the makeup artists leapt at her and started dabbing her face with powder.

"He's really something," Jane said, motioning to Hunter out on the stage. He was something, Madeline thought. His posture, his broad shoulders under his perfectly trimmed suit, he gave off an air of confidence, of assurance that Madeline had loved all those years ago when she used to bring him with her to events in college. She had been so proud of him then, when he spoke eloquently with her peers. He still had that same charm, she thought, watching him leaning over the podium. He had magic in him. "Where did you say you found him?"

"We we're friends at Columbia," Madeline responded.

"Oh, he studied with you?"

"Sort of," Madeline nodded as Hunter was about to finish his speech.

"Now, I know you didn't come here to see me," Hunter said with a huge smile on his face. "I'm definitely not the beautiful face you expected, so without further ado, I want to introduce my friend Madeline Thomas!"

The crowd roared as Madeline walked onto the stage waving her hand at the crowd. Her other hand felt empty. Usually at these events Brandon would accompany her. He would hold her hand and mirror her wave to the crowd in front of them. She clenched her empty fist all the way to the podium.

"Don't disappoint me, or them," Hunter whispered in her ear as they shook hands. She shone her wide smile and thanked him in the microphone for coming. Then she turned to the crowd.

Chapter 31

"Amazing job!" Jane clapped when Madeline entered back into the wings. "You are on fire! I video chatted with Brandon so he could see you. He gave a thumbs up. Brilliant!"

Madeline was handed a glass of water and her makeup artist again attacked her with a brush as Jane continued talking. "Now, we need to get a photo with Joe Gracias from the local ROTC and I also promised Judith Mandelbaum of the Jewish Republicans' movement that she could have a few moments."

"Where is Hunter?" she asked, noticing he was no longer in the wings.

"Oh, he left, but he said to give you this." Jane handed Madeline a card from a local Holiday Inn with his room number written on it. "Now, Madeline, maybe you should have him come to the office tomorrow for a meeting, I can have a car get him from the hotel if you want."

"That's all right," Madeline responded. She took the card and put it in her lapel pocket. She could feel Jane's curious stare on her. Madeline had never met anyone at their hotel. She could meet in offices, in restaurants, lounges, but not hotel rooms. Jane gave a short grumble, but got back to business. Jane gave Madeline background about the people she had to meet and what she should say to them. She smiled big for photos, both planned and unplanned, and shook hands until her knuckles hurt.

When the event was coming to a close and there weren't many more hands to shake, Madeline pulled Jane aside. "I need you to find a Rhonda Williams," she said to her chief of staff. "Tonight."

"Williams? As in Hunter Williams? I don't understand..."

"Jane, this must be kept secret. It's his ex-wife, I don't want him to know I'm looking for her. Surely the staff can find her easily." Jane hesitated while nodding slowly. "Great, then I want you to notify me as soon as you have an address. No matter the time. Shall we keep going?" Madeline turned from Jane and continued to greet the event's last parting attendees.

It was an odd request from Madeline. Jane knew anyone could be easily located. They had directories, connections with local governments, it wouldn't be a problem to find Rhonda. The question was why. Madeline had always been very professional with Jane. She had never so much as asked her for coffee, let alone ask her to find someone for an undisclosed reason. She wouldn't ask though, she would never ask about Hunter's hotel room, or why Madeline needed to find his wife in private. But she would complete the task discretely. She placed a call to one of her connections who promised her the information as soon as possible.

When the event ended, Madeline shared a bottle of champagne with her staff and congratulated them all on a job well done. But the real work was just beginning, she told them. Now they had to focus on running the campaign and beating Officer Austin. There would be no rest until Election Day.

Madeline took a car back home. When she arrived, she could see the light on in her and Brandon's bedroom, but the rest of the house was dark. Not even the outside lights were on, like they weren't expecting anyone. Madeline bade goodnight to her driver and walked to her door in the dim shine from the streetlamps. She pulled off her shoes, silently placed them in the closet and tiptoed upstairs to the master bedroom.

When she opened the door, she saw Brandon lying in bed with his laptop open. His eyes were glued to the screen and he had his headphones over his ears. She stood silently for a moment, feeling like she was disturbing him, like she was entering his private space instead of their shared bedroom.

"Hey," she finally said. He gave a "hey" back without looking up from the screen. "How's Noah?" she asked. Jane had updated her earlier that he had been released from the hospital.

"He's fine," Brandon responded, his eyes still on the screen. "The doctors thought he should stay overnight, but he refused. Said he couldn't sleep in that bed, even though he had been sleeping all afternoon. But the doctors agreed he could go home and gave us a prescription for pain medication. We'll go in tomorrow so they can check him."

"I'm glad he is OK," she said. She slipped out of her suit and walked toward Brandon wearing just her bra and underwear. Madeline had hardly ever walked around their room in her undergarments, maybe it had happened a handful of times at the beginning of their relationship when she was still trying to find her passion for her husband. But she was doing it now, because she felt like she should. In fact, the event had oddly reminded her that she and Brandon hadn't had sex in a couple weeks and that was at least a week too long. It was true their sex wasn't full of passion or fireworks or anything that could be used to describe sex in romance novels or movies, but if their sex life was one thing, it was consistent. And that, thought Madeline, was probably a lot better than most people at their stage in life. She sat down on his side of the bed and slowly started to push the top of his laptop down.

"Madeline, what are you doing?" Brandon stopped her from closing his computer. "I need to get through these reports tonight."

"I'm sure they can wait," she said, leaning forward toward him.

"No, Madeline, they can't. I'm tired. I didn't work all day today, which means I'm way behind. I just want to finish this and go to sleep." Madeline wasn't sure what the thing she was feeling was called. Could it be rejection? She had never been rejected in any aspect of her life, most certainly not in her marriage with Brandon. She had expected Brandon to be delighted to see her coming to him in her underwear, to accept her with open arms and tell her how perfect she was and how much he loved her. It was what she needed after an evening with her supporters—just one more person to love and cherish her.

"Did I do something wrong?" She asked without leaving her spot on the edge of the bed.

"I don't know, Madeline, did you?" Brandon himself now closed his laptop and looked at Madeline. "Do you want to tell me anything?"

"Well, I missed you at the event tonight," she said. "It felt weird without you by my side."

"I'm sorry about that," he said sarcastically.

"No, I know, you had to be with Noah." She felt like she was tripping over her words, like she didn't know what to say. If only she could have prepared a speech for this. "I'm just saying I missed you. Do you ever miss me?"

"What was that guy doing at the event?" Brandon responded. Madeline remembered that Jane had showed Brandon the speeches from the event and she wondered if he had seen Hunter's as well.

"City councilman Hunter Williams?" She clarified.

"Oh come on, Madeline, he's your ex-boyfriend for Christ sake. And maybe even more than that."

"He was speaking because of the shooting in his district! It's relevant for the SAVER Bill." Madeline tried to snuggle down next to her husband. "You should have seen me tonight. I was wonderful." She leaned over to kiss his neck.

"So convenient that your ex-boyfriend came to help you win the election." Brandon ignored Madeline's nibbles on his collarbone. "I really can't do this tonight."

Rejected, Madeline stood up from the bed as Brandon opened his laptop and continued to read on the screen. She covered herself with a bathrobe, feeling self-conscious of her body in a way she wasn't used to. On her nightstand her phone lit up and Madeline jumped to see who it was. The top notification was a text message from Jane: *Found Rhonda.* Then next texts that came in included a phone number and an address. Then: *Should I come get you?*

No. Thank you. See you tomorrow. Madeline responded. She stood up and walked to her closet, thinking of what to wear. What does one wear to meet the ex-wife of your ex-boyfriend who is blackmailing you? A suit seemed too formal. Jeans, too casual. She slipped into black slacks and headed out the bedroom door.

"Where are you going now?" Brandon asked, this time with his attention on her. She could see how it looked. Hunter in town, she slipping out late at night.

"I have an errand to run," she responded. "Just trust me."

"Uh huh." Brandon's eyes focused back down on his laptop.

Chapter 32

The truth was that Rhonda had thought often about Madeline over the years. She was a constant shadow in her marriage. Not because Hunter had brought her there, but because Rhonda did. She often found herself comparing herself to Madeline—she would never be as skinny, have hair as soft and straight, skin as bright and smooth. But while she feared her looks were way behind Madeline's, she was sure she could have been just as smart had she been given the same opportunities. But alas, she was born and raised in Harlem without a trust fund to pay for college, let alone someone who even spoke to her about higher education.

She often wondered what Hunter had seen in her, how he could be with her after being with someone like Madeline. If he would have stayed with her had she not gotten pregnant. She had asked him that a million times and each time he promised her the answer was yes, baby or no baby, they would have gotten married. Maybe not as quickly. Rhonda was sure if she had asked him a million and one times, the answer could have been different. Because why would he tie himself to someone like Rhonda? When he had already tasted a life of privilege?

These questions, Rhonda's doubt, sprayed every fight the couple had had over their relationship. If Hunter came home late—was he cheating with somebody better than her? If he didn't hold her hand in public—was it because he was embarrassed about her? When he once took her to dinner in Manhattan—was it because he was too good for Harlem?

Objectively, Rhonda knew that she was the one comparing herself to Madeline. Whether or not Hunter thought about her, he never brought her up, never once mentioned her name. Rhonda wasn't even sure if Hunter knew that Madeline had helped her those years ago. But still, Rhonda felt Madeline's presence in every aspect of her marriage, and she was afraid that one day Madeline would come back and ruin it for her. And she did, even if she hadn't known it.

Rhonda and Hunter were married for 13 years when she filed for divorce. They were a full thirteen years. In that time Rhonda had also gotten her GED, and somewhere in the middle of their marriage, after her daughter needed less attention, she had gotten certified as a TSA agent and gotten a job at LaGuardia airport. When she received her certification, it was the first time she had been proud of herself. She had accomplished something and this proved that she was just as smart and as capable as Madeline. She hoped Hunter was proud of her, that she could finally be someone worthy of being with him.

But the years rolled on. Rhonda worked hard and took her job seriously. Hunter also worked hard. When he purchased the landscaping company, Rhonda was proud to call her husband a businessman. She was even pleasantly surprised that Hunter owned a fancy Brooks Brothers suit that he wore to meet with the lawyers who finalized the purchase. He did look professional in that thing. But when he decided to run for city council, well, that was a different story.

Rhonda had secretly followed what Madeline had been up to. It wasn't hard since she had been involved in a very public career and had married a very public family that loved displaying their announcements in newspapers. Rhonda herself had celebrated when Madeline Clark became Madeline Thomas, after all, she was sure families like the Thomas' didn't believe in divorce, probably thought it was some mythical being like the tooth fairy or Santa Claus. She was sure people like the Thomases would never step in Harlem and that Madeline would never come in contact with Hunter again. Her fears of losing everything to Madeline were swept under the rug like dust that wouldn't disappear, but could be temporary hidden under a delicately woven accessory.

When Hunter announced that he would run for city council, it was like a gust of wind scattered the dust out from under the rug and all over the living room. All over the house, in fact. Why was Hunter going into politics? She railed at his decision, calling it selfish, even when Hunter tried to explain that his motives were about helping the neighborhood, the kids at the community center, where Hunter still volunteered. This was his chance to make a difference. But Rhonda wasn't having it. In her mind, all politicians were in an elite club where they all knew each other and met together to laugh at the common-folk they served. The last thing Rhonda wanted was Hunter and Madeline in the same club, where they could stand around together in their fancy suits and laugh at people like her.

But Hunter ran for city council anyway, even without Rhonda's support. He thought she'd come around once he saw all the good things he was doing. He hadn't really understood her resistance. This was the first big crack in their marriage. From then on, Rhonda questioned everything he did. City council meeting? She had to know exactly who was there. Why were all the meetings all the way down in Manhattan's financial district? Wasn't that prejudice against councilmembers from Harlem? Anytime he was invited for a local event—a new store opening, a recital for a dance academy—Rhonda went with him. Not because she was supportive, but because she had to see who else was there.

She could see how much he loved his position. He came home with a gleam in his eyes, his heart pounding from adrenaline. He'd beam when telling her about obtaining funding to fix a few potholes that had caused problems on Fredrick Douglass Boulevard, or when he helped a local storeowner gain a liquor license. Couldn't she see he was helping people?

After his first year in office, Hunter started coming home later and later. Meetings ran late, events kept him into the night, he needed to schmooze with his colleagues. He became friendly with local developers and landlords and sometimes they did a favor or two for each other. That's how city politics works. That's how things were done. Hunter was helping people. Everyone was benefitting.

After his second year in office, Rhonda had had enough. She didn't like that he often came home smelling like expensive cigars or that he had a watch collection that was worth more than their apartment. He seemed like he was getting too close to being the kind of person Madeline would have wanted and that crossed a line for Rhonda. She began snooping in his office, going to the storefront late at night after Hunter had already locked up and left. She'd searched through his desk, and all the files on it with city ordinances, notes in his scribbly handwriting, and memos he wrote. She'd searched and searched until she found exactly what she needed to end it with him.

She knew she'd been right not to trust him. And then she had proof. Proof so good, that she knew she could get whatever she wanted from Hunter. If he refused, well, jail would be like a spa holiday in comparison to where he could end up. She took her proof and their daughter and bought a one-way ticket to California. She'd never been on a plane before. Hell, she'd only left the state of New York once when Hunter took her on a vacation to the Jersey Shore. But she had heard great things about California. It was a place where dreams came true and she wanted to be there. She knew, of course, that Madeline lived there, but that was definitely not why Rhonda chose California. Definitely not, she told herself. But being able to vote against her wouldn't hurt.

That night she had watched Madeline's reelection campaign launch speech live. She saw Hunter give his endorsement and whisper something in her ear. It made Rhonda livid. So livid that she couldn't sleep that night. Which was why she was awake when Madeline parked in front of her house.

Chapter 33

It was a quiet neighborhood where cars slept at night before being woken up to commute in the morning. Rows of one-story houses with grass and shrubbery lined the street that was lit up by the tall overhead lamps. Madeline had never been in that neighborhood before. It was just a stone's throw away from her own—where houses had at least two stories, balconies, and lawns that were manicured as fashionably as the women who lived there. If these houses were described in a real estate ad, they would have been called quaint, comfy, and homey. Madeline slowed her car as she searched the houses for numbers... 1214...1220...1226...1232.

She parked right in front, noticing the porch light was on like someone had been expecting her. Before walking inside, she sat in her car and reviewed what she wanted to say to Rhonda. She had a few options, and she would decide the best once she came face to face with the woman. She knew Hunter wanted money to pay for his divorce. Madeline could try to convince Rhonda that an expensive divorce made everyone (except the lawyers) lose. Or she could try to see if Rhonda knew of her situation with Hunter. Was it possible she was behind it? If not, could she help Madeline end it?

Madeline was sitting in the car when a figure opened the front door of the house and peered through. When Madeline saw the figure, she knew her time was up and she stepped out of the car. As she approached the door she noticed the figure had a gun held in her hand facing the floor. The sight made her heart skip, but she pretended not to notice.

"Rhonda Williams?" Madeline asked quietly, as though afraid to wake the neighborhood up.

"Madeline?" Rhonda said in surprise. She had never expected to see Madeline close up again. "Hunter ain't here."

"I came to talk to you," Madeline responded. When she was in front of the door, she smiled brightly at the shadowed face in front of her. The porch light was not enough for her to make out Rhonda's large brown eyes and thin lips that may have triggered something in her memory. "You know who I am?"

Rhonda scoffed. It almost felt like a joke, being asked that question. Of course she knew. Not only was Madeline's face all over the news, but she had been a constant figure in all of Rhonda's dreams and nightmares. But Rhonda also knew how to play it cool. "You're that senator lady. But I ain't voting for you."

Madeline smiled. "Could I come inside?" Madeline said it more like a command than a question. The right tone could get you almost anything and Madeline needed to sit down with Rhonda. Rhonda opened the door and invited Madeline into her living room.

"But shh, my daughter is asleep." Rhonda led her to a blush red couch that had a knitted blanket draped over the back. It sat in front of an oversized TV and a coffee table covered in teen magazine and toy motorcycles. "I would have cleaned up if I knew I'd have company." She said, unconvincingly, while shuffling the magazines into a pile.

"I understand, I have two boys. They leave their stuff everywhere." Of course Madeline didn't mention that she had a fulltime nanny or a biweekly cleaning lady. There had never been toys left out at Madeline's house.

The house was still dark with only one lamp on in the corner, making it difficult for Madeline to get a good look at Hunter's wife. She wasn't sure how to read her yet. She seemed younger, tired, like she wasn't impressed with anything.

"How did you and Hunter meet?" she asked while Rhonda walked into the kitchen to grab two cups of water. Maybe the small talk would give Madeline a few more moments to decide what to say.

Rhonda scoffed. "Oh you don't remember?" She placed the waters on the coffee table in front of them and then turned on the lights in the living room. The flash made Madeline's pupils narrow and an image flash through her mind. She saw girls at the community center dancing around an old boombox, stepping to the beat and moving their bodies in ways Madeline never could.

"At the community center?" Madeline answered. "You used to go there."

"Mmhmm."

"How nice," Madeline responded into the silence. "Well, I should explain why I am here."

"You don't remember me, do you?" Rhonda cut her off with a big smile on her face. She sat on a chair next to the couch and shook her head side to side with her eyebrows raised. "You don't remember me at all."

Madeline had always tried hard to remember people. It was an important skill for a politician. And at this moment she was more than embarrassed by Rhonda's statement.

"To you, I was just another little black girl. One of your projects," Rhonda said, the smile still big on her face.

"I'm sorry Rhonda." But then it all came back to her. The look on Rhonda's face when she picked her up that morning. The sweat from her palm as she held her hand tight in the taxi. The way she quivered when she signed the forms at the clinic. How she looked disgusted as she ate her Tasti D-lite. Rhonda, with her long braids, red nails, had grown up. "Rhonda..." Madeline repeated. "I remember. I remember, everything."

This realization was quite a shock to Madeline. She had pictured Hunter's wife a million times, but she had never pictured the young girl from that day. The young girl who needed help. Who had seemed so lost. Who Madeline had helped. In her mind, Hunter's wife was nothing like that girl. She was a tough, strict mother, TSA agent with a scowl and bone to pick.

This changed things for Madeline. She wasn't exactly sure how, but the conversations she had played out in her head before coming in seemed completely irrelevant.

"Well, what do you want anyway?" Rhonda asked. She was picking at her nails, which were still long and perfectly manicured, but in a color much less flashy than what Madeline had remembered. "I told you, Hunter ain't here. And if he did come here, I'd kick him out all over again."

This was the opening Madeline had been looking for. "What happened?" The moment she said it though, she thought it was a mistake. Was she bringing up something that would turn Rhonda against her? "Was it...because of me?"

"Because of you?" Rhonda laughed harder than she would have allowed anyone else to laugh while her daughter was asleep. She clapped her hands hard and shook her head, before almost reprimanding herself for the loud noises. Her head glanced toward the hall where her daughter's bedroom was and then she looked back at Madeline. She continued speaking in a whisper. "Girl, not everything is about you." Although in her mind Rhonda was nodding hard. "You see that's the problem with people like you. You think that the world revolves around you. That you are the catalyst that causes everything to happen."

The truth was that Rhonda had no idea that Hunter had strayed. She may have accused him of cheating hundreds of times, but in her mind, she never believed it was a real possibility. Not Hunter. He was a gentleman, if she had ever met one. He wasn't like other guys she knew in Harlem. Hunter may have been a lot of things, but Rhonda did not think that a cheater was one of them.

Instead, she blamed Madeline for the invisible influence she had over her husband. She was sure it was Madeline who inspired his political career, who taught him how to find loopholes to jump through, who gave him the courage to do what he did. Surely that all came from his previous relationship with her.

"You're right," Madeline said. "How selfish of me. Do you want to tell me what happened?"

Rhonda shook her head, but began talking anyway. "Well, maybe you are right. Maybe it was because of you." She leaned back and crossed her arms in front of her chest. "But I don't need to tell you nothing."

"Right. I'm sorry for prying." Madeline sat quietly and sipped the glass of water Rhonda had put down for her. The two women sat in silence for a few moments before Rhonda spoke up.

"Why are you here?"

"Well I heard about your divorce, and maybe it is too intrusive, but I want to help."

"I don't need your help."

"Well Hunter does. He asked me for money to help pay for the divorce." Madeline bent the truth for Rhonda, still unsure of her involvement in the blackmail.

"He wants money for the divorce? Well that is a laugh, ain't it? Our divorce is the least expensive thing in his life right now. You think I'm paying a fancy lawyer? My lawyer's face is on a bus stop."

"So why did he ask me for money?"

"Well that's a story."

Chapter 34

Rhonda herself had discovered the truth about a year ago while searching through his office. She found a small figurine of a cobra in his desk drawer. Seeing the cobra shot her heart rate through the roof and made her hairline sweat. It was instantly recognizable—a symbol she had seen in many places throughout her life, including tattooed on the neck of the man that had raped her when she was 15. When she saw the figurine, she wasn't sure what to make of it. Why was it in Hunter's desk? She left the figurine where she found it, and did what every smart woman would do when suspicious of her husband. She placed a hidden camera behind a vent in a wall of his office. She placed it just so, so she had a clear view of the office and desk and, as long as the heat or air conditioner weren't on, she could hear pretty much everything that was said.

She began watching endless footage of her husband. She watched him sitting at his desk, typing on his computer. She watched him on the phone and meeting with constituents. A few times she even watched him taking a nap. On the city's dollar! She clucked her tongue at her lazy husband.

Most of the footage was uneventful. After several sleepless nights and a few warnings from her boss that she was taking too long of breaks at work, she almost stopped watching. But then, her husband received a visit from someone who looked rather different from his usual visitors. Most people who came to see him wore suits, or at least a collared shirt. This visitor wore black. Black pants, a black t-shirt. The only color was a green bandana tied around his wrist. Rhonda recognized the bandana. Everyone in Harlem knew what it meant. Only members of the Cobras could wear it. If you weren't a member and were brave enough to be seen with a green bandana, well, you could be sure you wouldn't have an arm to wear it on by the next day.

The man—if Rhonda could call him that—he looked like a young boy—placed a thick envelope in Hunter's hand. "Bumpy says thanks. You did good, H-man." The boy in the bandana left and Hunter moved a framed map of the city to show a safe behind it, where he put the envelop. Rhonda had no idea who Bumpy was, or why he was thanking Hunter. It even took her a few moments to understand who H-man was. But this was enough for her to keep watching.

Over the next few weeks, she watched different members of the Cobras come in and out of Hunter's office and hand him envelopes that he continued to store away in his safe. Rhonda even once snuck into the office to try to open the safe, but she knew the key was with Hunter and she really had no idea how to pick a lock. Watching her husband meet with members of the Cobras made her blood boil. Her rapist was a Cobra. All the Cobras were rapists—that was their initiation. It was a known fact in Harlem. What was her husband doing with them?

In the meantime, Hunter had started buying her more and more jewelry. Every week there would be a new box left for her on the table. One time it was earrings, another a gold bracelet. They were beautiful and Rhonda really wanted to wear them, but she couldn't. How could she wear something bought with money from her rapist? Hunter often asked her why she didn't wear them, he offered to exchange them, but Rhonda just lied and said she was saving them for special occasions.

This went on for a few months, long enough that Rhonda began being tempted enough to start wearing the jewelry. In fact, she had barely closed the clasp of a new necklace when Hunter came home early from work. "It is so beautiful," she said to him. He was sweaty and his face seemed to droop when she said it.

He gave a loud sigh. "I need it back. All of it."

"No, I promise I'll wear it! I'll wear it all! Here, I'll put those earrings on now," she responded, thinking he was punishing her for not wearing his gifts with pride.

"No!" he yelled. "Give it all back to me." He lunged for her jewelry box and scooped it under his arm. "The necklace too. Give it to me." Rhonda suddenly became very afraid of her husband. Her hands shook as she unfastened the shining necklace from around her neck and handed it to her husband who disappeared with the jewelry.

As soon as the front door clicked closed, Rhonda jumped for her cellphone to check the footage from her camera. She hadn't watched in a while, having gotten bored of seeing her husband rotate from sitting at his desk, to sitting at the table, to napping. It felt like a movie she had seen over and over and knew the lines by heart. She opened her phone and started watched footage from that day. She saw the usual movements in his office, visitors, phone calls, typing on the computer. Then the boy in the green bandana came in.

"Bumpy is not happy." The boy said. "Deadline is tonight. Got it?" In the video, Hunter nodded.

Rhonda didn't understand, so she started going back further in the footage. She found another meeting with the Cobra member.

"What the fuck, H-man?" the boy said. "Dreads got life. You said this was cake. Bumpy says he expects you to return everything. With interest."

"Bro, I can only do so much. I talked to the judge," Hunter reasoned.

"Bumpy doesn't care. You are no longer useful to the Cobras. And you know what happens to useless assets. How's Rhonda, by the way?" The boy disappeared without expecting an answer.

Rhonda had heard enough to have a vague understanding of what happened. She closed her phone and started packing. She wasn't safe there in their apartment. Hunter had betrayed her. She didn't want to be with him for another second.

She moved her daughter to California and filed for divorce. Luckily, her job could be transferred to any main city with an airport so she started working harder and taking on extra shifts to pay rent for a small house in a nice neighborhood where her daughter would never even meet a gang member. Occasionally, she would spy on Hunter, just so she would know what was happening. From her spying she learned that Hunter didn't meet his deadline to pay back the money with interest. She learned that Hunter promised double if they gave him a month. She knew that month was coming up. How Hunter was planning on coming up with the money, Rhonda had no idea until Madeline had come to her home that night.

Chapter 35

Rhonda sat with her arms folded and lips sealed. She didn't owe Madeline anything. She especially didn't need to tell her anything about what had happened between her and her husband. But then she had a thought. She hated her husband for what he did to her. For taking money from the gang that had stolen her innocence all those years ago. She hated him even more because he still seemed to have everything figured out, so much so that his perfect, beautiful, white ex-girlfriend was at Rhonda's home on his behalf.

She still wasn't sure why Madeline had come to see her, but she was starting to have an inkling. It made sense and she knew it all along. After all these years, after everything, she had been right about Hunter and Madeline—they weren't really over. They had never been really over and now that Hunter was getting divorced, he could go back to what he really wanted.

He never really wanted her, Rhonda believed. Yes he was mostly a good husband and a good father (aside from his betrayal!), but he had done it from an act of duty, not love. Had there been no pregnancy, Rhonda was sure she and Hunter wouldn't have lasted so long and instead he would have been back with Madeline even sooner.

And now that Rhonda filed for divorce, Hunter could have whatever he wanted. He could have Madeline and even her money to fix his problem with the Cobras. Well, Rhonda could not allow that. It wasn't fair. He shouldn't get what he wanted. And how convenient for her, Rhonda still had a chance to ruin it for him. With Madeline in her living room, she had the chance to ruin everything for Hunter, just like he had ruined everything for her.

"You remember what happened to me?" She said.

"Of course. You were so young." Madeline responded. Madeline, however, didn't know the whole story. How could she, being an outsider in Harlem?

"You know who did it to me?"

Madeline shook her head. Back then, Rhonda had refused to tell her anything more than that she had been raped and impregnated.

"Well, in Harlem, there is a gang called the Cobras. You don't mess with them and they run the neighborhood. If you see someone in a green bandana, you look down and you walk the other way." She paused to gauge Madeline's interest. "I was a victim of their initiation ritual."

Rhonda hadn't thought about that day for a very long time. In fact, she had tried not to think about it since the moment it was over, but she remembered every little detail, down to the dirt in the boy's fingernails.

The first time she saw Ray was the day before it happened. She was with her friends sitting on the bleachers at the basketball court on 140th when he walked by. He hooked his fingers on the outside of the fence and stared in at the boys shooting hoops and the girls watching. He stood like that for a while, nothing but his eyes moving from person to person. No one seemed to notice him there except Rhonda. She caught his eye one time and quickly looked back at the lighter her friend was flicking on for her to light her cigarette. A little later, she caught his staring right at her. It made her blush and she smiled at him. He was cute, she thought. With his almost buzzed hair and broad cheekbones, his baggy designer jeans, he looked like a 15-year-old's dream guy. She thought he might have winked at her, but she wasn't sure. After all, guys weren't usually interested in her. They liked girls like Keisha or her other friend Tatiana.

That evening, when the girls were ready to disperse from the basketball court, Ray came right up to Rhonda and introduced himself. He asked if he could walk her home. Rhonda wanted to say no, she liked walking home with her girlfriends and they still had so much to talk about. But Keisha and Tatiana oohed and aahed and gave approving looks to their friend. So Rhonda agreed. Anyway it was about time she started dating. She knew she was way behind her friends.

Ray was sweet. They talked about Tupac and their favorite songs. Ray told her about a movie he had just seen that Rhonda had to see. She took note in her head to watch it that evening so she could tell him next time she saw him. When they got to Rhonda's home, he asked for her number and she gave it to him. She asked him why she never saw him at school and he told her he went to a different one. Rhonda had heard of his school, she knew it was for kids who had been expelled and that excited her. He promised to call and said goodbye.

That evening Rhonda watched the movie he recommended and she prayed he would call so she could tell him. Her prayers were answered later that night. They talked on the phone for an hour about their friends and hobbies and then he asked if he could meet her again the next day. "Like a date?" she had asked him.

"Sure," he said. "Exactly." They made plans to meet after school. He'd come to the courts and they could go from there. Rhonda hadn't been able to sleep that night, she was so excited. In the morning she did her nails and put on her favorite outfit and went to school. The minute the bell rang, she ran to the courts and sure enough, Ray was there. He smiled when he saw her and handed her a Snickers bar. So thoughtful, she mused, remembering that she had told him her favorite candy the night before.

He said he wanted to show her something, so they started walking away from the courts. He led her up Adam Clayton Powell Boulevard until they got to the river. She had never been to this part of the river. The boardwalk wasn't completed and there was no one else around. How romantic, Rhonda thought, opening the Snickers bar. She offered him a bite and he said no thanks with a big smile on his face.

Before she understood what was happening her back was pressed up against the railing. The bar was hurting her back and if she looked to the side, she saw the river below. With one hand, Ray held her neck and with the other he tugged at her jeans. Her jeans that already had holes in all the right places tore easily as he pulled them down her legs. "Stop," she tried to say, but she wasn't sure if she said it out loud. Maybe she didn't and that's why he didn't stop.

It hurt and she dropped the Snickers bar into the river below. She was afraid she'd fall back if she fought him, so she just stood there with her eyes closed, the railing bar banging further into her back with every thrust. It was just a couple minutes and then it was over and Ray stood back. She opened her eyes to see him smile at her and then he yelled "Cobras unite!"

Suddenly, a group of boys wearing all black except for green bandanas tied around their right arms, appeared. They were clapping and cheering and patting Ray on the back. She watched as one of the boys tied a green bandana around Ray's arm and then sliced his palm open. The boy handed Ray the knife and he too sliced open his palm. The boys shook hands, mixing their blood, and then bottles of alcohol were passed around. No one looked at Rhonda. It was like she wasn't there. But she didn't move. She stood there, with her ripped jeans by her ankles, and watched the boys celebrate. It felt like hours when she finally had the courage to move. They boys were still celebrating and no one seemed to notice her pull up what was left of her pants and go.

She didn't tell anyone about it, not even Keisha. When her friend asked what happened with Ray, she just told them he was a scrub and they all nodded knowingly. So many guys were.

It wasn't until two months later that Rhonda took a pregnancy test. She had had her suspicions for a while, but couldn't face it. What were the chances? It only lasted a couple minutes, maybe even just one minute. There was no way...

She took the test in Keisha's bathroom and pretended to rejoice with her. Then, she went to Madeline, the only person she thought would know what to do.

Chapter 36

Rhonda didn't need to go into all the details with Madeline. But she gave her a brief explanation of what happened that day so Madeline would understand how evil the Cobras were. The Cobras were horrible people, all of them, and anyone who associated with them was just as guilty.

"And Hunter works for them," Rhonda concluded her story. "That's why I left him."

Madeline nodded without giving away any glimpse of how she felt. "I'm so sorry that all happened to you."

Rhonda felt satisfied, telling Madeline the truth. Now, if she were close to the decent person she pretended to be, she would never be with Hunter. She would never be with someone who worked with rapists.

"So you see, the money ain't for the divorce," Rhonda said. "So you giving him money doesn't free him from me." She tried to bait Madeline, wondering how she would respond. That woman didn't give anything away. "That's why you're here, right?"

"Well, that's not my business," Madeline responded. From this conversation, Madeline was sure Rhonda wasn't behind the blackmail. Had she been, she would have tried to convince Madeline to pay rather than spend her time bashing her husband. "But I believe I got what I came for." Madeline took another small sip of water from the cup in front of her and stood up. "It's late, I should be going."

Rhonda agreed. Indeed it was late, so late, that it was actually early morning. She wouldn't get much sleep before she needed to get up and get the kids to school before heading to court for a hearing in her divorce proceedings. She was tired of the divorce and didn't understand what took so long. She just needed alimony and child-support and was sure that Hunter could fund her lifestyle, even with just his salary from city council and his landscaping business.

She walked Madeline to the door, thinking about how strange it was to be face to face with the woman she had thought about so many times over the years. "Well, goodbye, now," she said, and Madeline thanked her for her time. Rhonda hoped this goodbye was for good—both in person and from her thoughts. She hoped that after this encounter, Madeline would no longer cast a shadow over the new life she was trying to create.

Madeline had no idea what influence she had had over Rhonda's life throughout the years. She was unaware of her constant presence and the deeper meaning of Rhonda's goodbye. To her, this encounter had a completely different purpose. She got into her car with a feeling of relief. This new information gave her something on Hunter, something she could use to get out of her situation with him. The question was how?

It was already after dawn when she arrived home. The lights in the kitchen were on and the smell of coffee wafted through the air. Molly was inside preparing breakfast for Adam who was already sitting at the kitchen table. "I couldn't sleep," he said to his mother when she kissed him on the cheek.

"Nightmares," Molly mouthed and Madeline understood. They always tried to keep Adam away from the TV when there was news on. He was sensitive and could have nightmares for a week when seeing something that triggered his young emotions. Madeline could only imagine the nightmares that could be triggered by him seeing his older brother's bruised face returning from the hospital. Madeline sat down to eat breakfast with her son and helped herself to the pancakes Molly stacked on the table.

Soon Brandon came down and filled his to-go mug with coffee. He greeted Molly and told her he'd be back late that evening. Madeline waited for her greeting, for her kiss on the cheek, but it didn't come. Brandon gave her a quick nod and was out the door.

Madeline stayed with Adam until it was time for Molly to take him to school. When he left she quickly glanced at the newspaper on the counter.

Hundreds show up for funeral of teen shot by cop

Cop taking leave of absence during investigation

Shooting victim had ties to local gang

Thomas reelection to focus on race/police violence

The main picture was of Jay Flynn standing in front of an old muscle car. His arms were folded in front of his chest, but Madeline thought she saw a flicker of green hidden in the folds. Below the last headline, there was a small picture of Madeline and Hunter shaking hands from the previous evening's event. She knew the picture looked good for her.

After her last sip of coffee she went upstairs to check on her other son. He appeared to be sleeping, but when Madeline stepped into his room, he opened his eyes. She took that as an invitation to come inside and she sat next to him in bed. He tried to sit up, but he winced as the pain from his broken rib shook through him.

"You did a good job last night," Noah whispered.

"You saw?"

"Dad was watching at the hospital. He thought I was sleeping. He's proud of you." Madeline blushed and thanked her son.

"Do you want to talk about what happened at school?" Noah shook his head. "Was it Jamie?"

"They keep saying you're going to lose."

"Well I might," she said. "That's part of running. But I'll do my best not to." Madeline's phone started ringing and she pulled it from her pocket to see who it was. Jane.

"Senator Band has agreed to endorse you!" Jane yelled into the phone. "This is big, I'm sure

Austin was hoping for the endorsement. Also I think I knew who was vetting you for a vice presidential run. Can you get down to the office? There's a lot to do after last night."

Madeline agreed and gave her son a gentle hug. He went back to sleep, something Madeline wished she had the time to do. It wasn't easy going for days without sleep. When she was younger, it seemed easy. She remembered pulling all-nighters to study in college, taking exams and then going out to celebrate afterwards. Now, looking back, she had no idea how she survived.

She quickly showered and changed her clothes before getting back into her car and driving to the office. On the drive, she received a call from Agent Murray, one of the FBI agents on the blackmail case.

"So we believe it was an empty threat," the agent said. "The deadline passed and there hasn't been anything in the news relating to the blackmail."

Madeline rolled her eyes, but then she had a thought. "There is a new lead that I'd like you to look into." All the information she had received from Rhonda had sparked new emotions and ideas in Madeline. Multiple problems could be solved if the FBI could just do their job. She spent the next few minutes telling the agent a story, carefully woven to ensure he could follow through and solve this issue. She thanked the agent for the team's hard work and hung up the phone. When she arrived at the office, she saw a text message from Hunter: *See you this evening at the hotel?*

Yes, she responded and slipped the phone back into her bag. She spent the day reviewing her campaign with her team. They discussed their conversations with supporters from the evening's event, news coverage, and what they proposed to do moving forward in the race against Officer Austin. Madeline tried hard to concentrate and give her input, but in truth, her mind was elsewhere. The lack of sleep mixed with the knowledge she had gained the previous night made it impossible for her mind to be where her body was. She just nodded along, thankful that she had a competent team taking care of her campaign.

When the second half of the day came around, Madeline was dizzy from the lack of sleep. Jane could see the dark circles under her boss' eyes and suggested she leave to get some rest. Madeline didn't protest, but she knew that there were things to do before she could rest.

She drove her car to Hunter's hotel. It wasn't the Langham, but it was a nice hotel. A large parking lot underneath, carpeted elevators with upbeat music in the background. She wondered if this was where Hunter always stayed when coming to California for his divorce court hearings. She took the elevator up to his floor and walked out into the hallway. A mirror across the way caught her off guard. The face looking back at her knew what she needed to do.

Chapter 37

Inside his hotel room, Hunter was sweating. He had the air conditioning turned on high, but it wasn't helping the dripping down his back. He had just gotten off the phone with Bumpy. It would be a complete understatement to say Bumpy wasn't happy. He was livid. Raged. Fuming. He didn't like showing up at Hunter's office to find it closed. Especially when Hunter owed him money.

Hunter would get the money for him. He had to, he didn't see any other choices. He thought he heard the elevator ding, but when he opened the door, the hall was empty. Where was she? It's funny how things spiral, Hunter thought to himself as he waited.

To be honest, Hunter wasn't sure how he got caught up in this mess. He had always been an idealist and moralist. He believed in hard work and taking care of himself and his family. Those things seem so easy when you're younger. There would be no reasons to stray.

One of his early goals was to be a man his children would be proud of. That's why he worked hard and bought the landscaping business. He thought he was doing a good job, providing and taking care of his family. But then, one day, a remark from Rhonda made him realize his failure. She was sitting in the kitchen holding a book that their daughter had brought home from the school library. Half the pages were ripped out and the other half had been drawn all over. "What's the point of going to school in Harlem, anyways," she said and Hunter nodded.

Maybe the easy solution would have been to move his family Downtown. Certainly they could afford to rent a small place in one of the neighborhoods where his business primmed the fauna. Maybe one of his clients would have given him a good deal. But Hunter loved Harlem and the easy road wasn't his normal route. So he decided that if he wouldn't switch neighborhoods, he would change the neighborhood. And that's when he decided to run for city council.

He could see Rhonda's disapproval. Sure, she would have liked to live somewhere else, but this was more important. City council also came with a good salary and he promised to himself that he would provide Rhonda and his children the life they deserved, even in Harlem. He'd have to work harder, but it would be worth it.

The election was easy. The previous city council member from Harlem was retiring and had helped Hunter. In fact, no one was even running against him, which made him feel a little like the win was undeserved. But no matter, he would prove himself in office.

His predecessor congratulated him and promised to help him get started at the beginning of his term. Hunter was thankful because he really had no idea what he was supposed to be doing on a daily basis. What did politicians do all day? He briefly thought about Madeline, how she would know the answer, but he wouldn't talk to her. The last time he saw her—a few years back when she was visiting New York—he made a dreadful mistake. He couldn't trust himself around her and he didn't want to betray his wife or family again.

His first year in office, his predecessor came almost every day to sit with him. He'd introduce Hunter with locals that Hunter needed to know and give him insights about dealing with other city council members. Hunter even brought him along to a few introduction meetings he had set up for himself. Everyone seemed to like his predecessor and he appeared to be pretty good at getting things done, so Hunter respected him. He wanted to emulate him and prove he was just as worthy.

And then one day a boy with a green bandana came into Hunter's office. Hunter recognized the bandana and stood up. He had a gun in the desk drawer, but truthfully, he was afraid to use it. He wanted to tell the Cobra to get out, but his predecessor stood and gave the boy a hung.

"Meet Handy," his predecessor said. "He's your liaison." Hunter wasn't sure what he meant, but he nodded and shook Handy's hand. Handy placed a big envelop on Hunter's desk, a "welcome present" he said and then he left.

"I'm not dealing with gangs," Hunter told his predecessor. "You have to give this back," he motioned to the envelope.

"You don't have a choice," the predecessor said. "You won't be able to get anything done without them. You want to represent Harlem? You represent all of Harlem. Not just the pretty parts. The Cobras are Harlem." Hunter politely asked his predecessor to leave. "You'll see," the predecessor said.

Handy came back the next week with another envelope. This time Hunter was alone and he told the boy that he wasn't interested. Handy laughed, said OK, and left. Hunter was surprised how easy it was and was proud of himself for sticking to his ground. That evening, when he locked up his office, he was attacked by two hooded boys. They weren't wearing their bandanas, but Hunter got the message.

The next few weeks he accepted the money from Handy. He'd decided to donate it to the community center and reasoned that what he was doing was good and that it would make a difference in the community. He started to wonder why they kept giving him cash, until one day a new boy showed up.

"Handy was arrested last night," the new boy said. "He needs to go home."

"But, I can't really do anything," Hunter reasoned. "I'm on the city council, I just deal with city ordinances and licenses and stuff."

The boy chuckled. "Well, I'm sure you'll figure something out."

Hunter called his predecessor who laughed when he took the call. "I was wondering when I'd hear from you." He explained to Hunter who to talk to, which police officers could be arm-twisted and which judges to look out for. When Handy was released, Hunter was actually proud of himself. Maybe this was part of helping the community. After all, there was a steady stream of funding going to the community center and he could keep an eye on Handy and try to mentor the young boy.

Things were going well. Hunter worked hard at his job. Favors for the Cobras started to come up often and Hunter figured out how to deal with them. He'd get members out of jail, ensure there would be no police stationed at specific locations at specific times, and would give them permits for big events they wanted to host. Guilt did pour through him, but he reasoned that he was helping his constituents. Right? He was more afraid of the Cobras than he was of the guilt.

Aside from his dealings with the Cobras, he became more active in the city council, proposing his own ideas for new ordinances and integrating Harlem with the rest of Manhattan. The other council members appreciated his enthusiasm, but none of Hunter's proposals ever passed a vote.

One evening, after a particularly grueling day when Hunter had argued with the council to approve the route of a new Hip Hop Parade through Harlem, Hunter came home to see Rhonda with her arms folded on the couch. She was watching TV and immediately let Hunter know how tired she was. "You don't appreciate how hard I work," she said. Hunter told her that he did appreciate it. He knew it was tough raising their daughter and working toward her certification as a TSA agent. "So prove it," Rhonda challenged him.

The next day Hunter bought Rhonda a pair of gold earrings. They were simple, nothing special, as Hunter's bank account barely allowed for impulse purchases. They had just bought their apartment and raising a child in Manhattan wasn't cheap, even if it was Harlem. Rhonda called the earrings "cute" and asked if any of his colleague's wives would be caught dead wearing anything so small.

Hunter was embarrassed because she was right. His colleagues—from districts in lower Manhattan—all wore Rolex watches, had diamond cufflinks. Maybe that's why they didn't approve Hunter's proposals. He needed to be more like them. So the next time he got an envelope from the Cobras he saved it. He kept saving them until he bought himself a Rolex and his wife a flashy new necklace. Rhonda was pleased with the gift and that night they made love more passionately than they had since becoming parents.

The next day, with his new watch, Hunter proposed a city ordinance to allow more food trucks to come to Harlem. The proposal passed without opposition and Hunter returned home, proud of his work. Rhonda's spirits were still up and things seemed to be going well for him. He told himself he'd donate the next envelope from the Cobras to the community center. But then, Rhonda made a comment about a new bag she wanted and how difficult things were and so Hunter bought her the bag with the envelope and reasoned it was necessary to keep his wife happy.

One day, he was feeling particularly down. Something terrible had happened. A kid had been killed in Harlem after being caught in the crossfire of a gang fight. Hunter felt responsible. After all, many of those gang members were on the street because of him. He could have saved that kid's life. On that day, he saw in the news that Madeline Thomas was in town speaking at a local event for the WISH List. He thought that maybe she would have advice for him. She'd been in politics much longer—did she know how to avoid corruption? Did she know how to get out of the mess he was in? He took a cab to the Langham downtown where he knew she'd be staying. He waited outside and when he saw her walking in, he followed. She went to the bar to get a drink and he did too. But when he saw her, he knew not to approach her. She treated him like a nobody. Worse than ignoring him, she gave him a look that made him feel worthless. That's when his feelings toward her turned to anger.

On his way home he stopped at a jeweler in Midtown and bought his wife a bracelet. At least she thought he was doing a good job. Hunter continued. He started feeling worse and worse about himself, for being weak against the Cobras, for pretending to be someone he wasn't with his colleagues in order to get ordinances passed, for being unable to please his wife without jewelry in hand.

He began thinking more and more about Madeline. How did she do it? Why did everything come easy to her? Why did he ever let her go? His thoughts about her oscillated between missing her and hating her for everything that she stood for.

When Dreads got arrested and Handy told Hunter he had to get him free, Hunter was already near the bottom. He half-heartedly talked to the judge and didn't follow through to see if Dreads got free. Why should he? He thought, Dreads was probably guilty. He deserved jail. But when Dreads got sentenced to life in prison, Hunter didn't realize there would be consequences.

At first, Handy asked Hunter to "fix the problem." Hunter said he didn't know how. Then he started receiving pictures of his daughter at school with red circles around her face. The threat scared him and he didn't know what to do. On one hand, he could go to the authorities, but on the other, he knew the authorities were also corrupted. He knew the Cobras had half the police in their pockets and they couldn't protect his family. Hunter knew he had to pay back the money, but he didn't know how.

Meanwhile, his wife left him. He wasn't sure why—maybe it was because he took all his gifts back, or maybe because he just wasn't man enough anymore—but he was happy she left for California. It put distance between the Cobras and his family. But flying to California for divorce proceedings got him thinking about something— or someone—else that was in California.

Why did Madeline have it so easy? Her life was so perfect, with her perfect family and career. He started to blame her for his situation—why hadn't she helped him when he came to her at the Langham? Why had she left him in the first place? His life could have been so different had she not ruined it for him. He wanted her to pay, and sometime when he actually was at rock bottom, he decided that she was the answer to his problems. She had money, she could fix things with the Cobras. And why shouldn't she? Didn't she owe Hunter something? After everything they had been through together? After all, he could ruin her career if he wanted to. Didn't she owe him something for not doing that?

When smart men are pushed into desperate situation, they can make mistakes. When fear clouds vision, they can fail to see all the options in front of them. Sometimes the only option they see is the one surrounded by the bright frame of anger. The option that in hindsight, would not have made any sense at all.

Chapter 38

Madeline didn't need to knock when she approached Hunter's hotel room. He had been waiting with his eye on the peephole for ages, alerted by every ding of the elevator or brush of a footstep on the hallway carpet. He opened the door for her before her fist could tap the door.

"Good afternoon," she greeted him with a friendly smile. Not the smile of the someone whose career or marriage hung on by a thread. She stepped into the room and sat down on an oversized square fake leather chair that was stiffer than it appeared. With her straight back and bag on her lap, she motioned for Hunter to take a seat. He did, sitting down on the edge of the perfectly made bed in front of Madeline.

"Where is the money?" he asked. He felt a little panicked. It had seemed too easy to get Madeline to agree. He knew her better. Had he thought about it more, he should have known Madeline would be empty handed.

"I saw Rhonda last night." Madeline ignored Hunter's question. "She seems like a lovely person."

Hunter scoffed. He didn't know that Rhonda knew of his situation with the Cobras, but he thought that no good could come of Madeline meeting his wife.

"She had a lot to say about you," Madeline continued speaking.

"What does that mean?"

"It means that I'm not giving you any money, but I'm taking care of your problem." Being a politician is all about taking care of problems. It's about solving inextricable situations in ways that please everyone. Or at least ensuring that everyone believes they are pleased for the time being. Future displeasure can always be fixed with future solutions.

"My divorce?" Although even as Hunter said it, he knew that was definitely not what Madeline was talking about.

"You can stop the pretense," Madeline responded. "With the Cobras. It's all settled. They won't be bothering you."

Hunter sat with his mouth dropped open. It was clear Madeline knew everything—even more than he knew—and that, like always, she had figured out a way to come out unscathed and on top.

"What did you do?" he asked, more curious than anything else.

"Tomorrow morning the FBI is going to show up here and ask you to come in."

"Maddy, please, I'm so sorry, I can't go to jail—"

"You are going to tell them that the Cobras have been following you for the last few years. When they saw you with me, they took it as an opportunity to take me down."

"Why will the FBI believe a gang in Harlem is trying to take you down?"

"Harlem is exactly the kind of place where my SAVER Bill is needed. There is always pushback to change. My SAVER Bill has been the subject of significant controversy. There is no end to the amount of angry phone calls and letters my office has received about it. Some even come all the way from New York. The evidence has already been handed to the FBI."

Relief, grateful, awe, Hunter felt multiple emotions pounding down on him as he continued to look astounded at Madeline. He wanted to ask more questions, to understand, but his lips were unable to form the words. Instead, he said two words that were extremely difficult to say. "Thank you."

"You're welcome," Madeline said without getting up. As Hunter should have known, there were no real favors in politics. Madeline fixing his problem was part of a bigger tit-for-tat that he would be sucked into and unable to break free for the rest of his life.

"Maddy—" Hunter began to speak. He felt foolish and he wanted to show Madeline that he really wasn't as pathetic as the whole story made him seem. He was about to say two other words that were very difficult to formulate, so difficult that he probably hadn't said them enough in his lifetime: *I'm sorry*. But before he could utter those words, Madeline continued to speak.

"But you're going to step down," she said.

"What?" Hunter's mouth could easily form that word. "I thought..."

"I value our political system in this country," Madeline said. "Corruption at every level is unacceptable to me and I see it as my job to weed it out. You cannot serve in a political position. You will vacate your city council seat immediately."

"Why?" Now anger fell down on him. He knew he had no choice, he would do what Madeline said, but maybe he could change her mind. "I'm helping people. This is the only way to help people. The person before me did it and the person after me will too."

"That's not going to be your problem anymore. You will step down."

Hunter shook his head, although he knew his protests were for naught. "Maddy, this is all I have. What am I supposed to do?"

"Well, I actually believe you will be very busy in the near future. Possibly in the far future as well, depending on how things go."

"I don't understand..."

"You made a really big mess," Madeline continued. "You're going to clean it up."

"How?"

"Well, there are two things you are going to do. You're going to start by ensuring I win my election."

"Me? How can I do that if I step down? Isn't it better that I'm a city council member to help you?"

"No, I need someone out of the spotlight who will help me. I need support and I think you have just the acumen required to get me that support."

"I don't understand."

"My SAVER Bill has two constituents: the police and minority communities. At the moment, neither support my bill or my reelection. The police are not going to support my reelection because of my opponent, which means I need the minority vote. That's your job."

"How will I do that?"

"You'll figure it out. I know you already know how to deal with the underserved community. There are places just like Harlem here and you will get them to support me out loud and in public. Once they are supporting me, it will make the police look awful for being against what I am proposing."

"OK," Hunter agreed as though he had a choice. He could do it, he believed. He was a politician, after all, and the skills needed to succeed in that could carry over: he was charming, able to influence people. He just needed to figure out the right people. "Maddy, I'm so sorry about all this." He stood from the bed to approach her. "It's just, I love—"

"Don't say it," she cut him off and stood up from the chair with her hands held up in front of her as a stop sign. "You and me, Hunter, were a very long time ago. That must never come up again, understood? I love my husband." She paused a moment. Previously, Madeline had said there were two things he needed to do. The first was a colossal task, something that from many angles seemed impossible, but Hunter would find the right angle where a sliver of possibility shone through. A second task, well Hunter was hoping it had a different magnitude. "You are going to convince Rhonda to forgive you and the two of you will have dinner with me and him."

Chapter 39

A month went by and Hunter hadn't heard from Madeline. As she said would happen, the FBI knocked on his hotel room door the following morning and he followed them to their offices. He told them exactly what he was supposed to. He told them exactly where to find the gang's leadership: where Bumpy and Handy lived, where the gang congregated. They asked how he knew so much about them and Hunter responded that they were his constituents. It was his job to know them, to fight for them, but his main duty was to his country and that's why he was coming forward now. When the FBI agents were satisfied, they let Hunter go and he flew back to New York.

He held a poorly attended press conference to announce his resignation—stating his failure to protect the poor Jay Flynn who was shot in his district recently. He said he wanted to focus his efforts on fighting the root of the problem. Being in city council made it difficult to do so, he said. He wanted to spend his time making a difference instead of fighting for permits and ordinances with the councilmembers from more affluent neighborhoods in New York. A reporter from *The Harlem Times* asked him specifically what he would do, and Hunter gave a vague answer about being more involved in the community. He didn't mention the community he meant was across the country.

A special election would be held to elect his replacement and Hunter convinced the manager of the local community center to run. The election would be unopposed and Hunter was sure his successor would do just fine.

Then, Hunter packed up his apartment, which was still full of teen magazines and clothes that Rhonda had left behind, and called a realtor to find renters. He packed up what he needed and donated the rest before getting on a flight back to California. With nowhere to go but a hotel, he showed up at Rhonda's doorstep. After throwing a few cups and a hairdryer at him, she agreed to let him stay on the couch until he found his own place. She consulted Keisha, who had been with her all these years, about what she should do. *He followed you to California? Punish him, but DON'T LET HIM GO!* Was her texted response. Rhonda and Keisha continued to text around the clock, which was how Rhonda learned that Ray "Bumpy" Johnson was among those picked up in a big gang sweep through Harlem. No one knew what caused the arrests—not even the local police. *Some federal shit* Keisha wrote, and Rhonda was satisfied that karma existed even if it took 15 years. She had suspicions that Hunter was behind it. Ultimately, it couldn't have been a coincidence that Ray was arrested right after Hunter stepped down. To her, it was proof that he loved her. She silently forgave him, but resolved to punish him for at least a few months so he would appreciate her more.

From his wife's couch, Hunter began his new job. There was no one telling him what to do, what hours to work, but he knew he had an unforgiving boss that he needed to please. He started shooting hoops at the basketball courts in rundown neighborhoods and attended church services with large gospel choirs. He started making friends and gaining respect from members of his new community.

He watched Madeline's reelection from afar. He read every headline from: *Polls show tight race for senate* to *Thomas' secret to a happy family*. He tried to contact Jane a few times, but she brushed him off, telling him the senator would speak to him when she needed to. It made Hunter wonder if she had forgotten about him and their arrangement, but the truth was that Madeline too was scrutinizing him from afar.

During that month, Madeline herself was very busy. She was flying coast to coast even more often as campaign events often brought her to California for the evening after senate votes in the morning. She couldn't let go of her main responsibilities as a lawmaker, even when appearances were required to gain more votes. She followed a strict schedule between speaking engagements, events, meetings with community leaders. Jane had even partitioned time for coffee with Brandon or pancakes with Adam. Even just a three-minute window would be useful—for family time and posing for the photo opportunities that proved Madeline could do it all.

Hunter saw all the photos, of Madeline with her husband by her side supporting her while she ran. He wondered what would happen, when he and Rhonda would have dinner with them and why this was one of Madeline conditions. Truth be told, he had hoped Madeline had forgotten about this condition. He was not looking forward to it one bit. Not meeting her husband, nor having her sit across from his wife. Why Madeline wanted this, he had no idea, he wracked his brain over that month wondering if it were some cruel joke, a way to further punish him, or for Madeline to gain some amusement. He wasn't even sure if Rhonda would agree to such a thing, she hadn't even allowed him to eat anything in the house for the first week of his stay. It wasn't until just recently that she invited him to eat with her and their daughter.

He had just convinced himself that Madeline had forgotten about her request when Jane had called him that day after his first month in California. He was sitting at the tutoring center at a local middle school when his phone rang. The ring annoyed him; his student, Damon, was just starting to understand the secret language of algebra that was splayed across the notebook and Hunter didn't want to be pulled away. But his thirst for knowledge about Madeline got the better of him.

"8:00 p.m. at La Quinta," Jane said. "Reservation under Thomas. Don't be late." Hunter nodded as though Jane could see him and put the phone away wondering how he would convince Rhonda. They had never spoken about Madeline, about the conversation the two women had or what part she had played in Hunter's move. Should he pretend the dinner was just the two of them? He wasn't sure he could survive the consequences at home when Rhonda found out otherwise. Should he pretend like it was just a friendly double date with an old acquaintance?

Hunter tried to get back to his tutoring session with Damon, but his mind had already packed up and left. He whizzed through Damon's homework and hurried home, hoping that Rhonda would be there. She had left early that morning for her shift at the airport. If she hadn't taken on a double, she would most likely be resting until their daughter came home from school.

To his luck, Hunter saw Rhonda's car outside when he pulled up to the house. He smiled to himself, feeling like the husband he wanted to be. He fantasized about walking in the door and saying "Honey, I'm home!" and kissing her on the cheek like they did in movies. But that was too cheesy for real life. In real life, he'd settle for "Hey, Rhonda," and hope she didn't give him a stink eye when he walked in. Inside, Rhonda was in her bedroom, a place Hunter had yet to walk inside. It was like a forbidden chamber and Hunter always felt he was about to get shocked if he approached. But this time, he gathered his courage and was ready for the shock. He knocked on the door.

"What?" Rhonda said from inside. He peered in, gazing on the room for the first time. It was plain, white walls, a white bed in the middle with a nightstand on one side. Rhonda was sitting up reading a magazine and gave Hunter a look he didn't quite understand. It wasn't disdain or anger at him for broaching her chambers, but it wasn't welcoming either. "Need something?"

"Let's have dinner tonight," Hunter began, deciding not to mention who dinner was with.

"Sure, there's a lasagna in the freezer."

"No, I mean, outside. Just us."

Rhonda put down the magazine. "Are you asking me on a date?" Her tone was judgmental and accusatory.

"Yes," he responded. Baby steps, he thought to himself. Get her to agree to one thing before the next. "Go out with me."

"I'll see if Marie can come." Rhonda pulled out her phone and called her neighbor. Marie, a retired woman with no family nearby, had been friendly to Rhonda when she moved in. She'd watched their daughter a few times for her, even though 13 might have been too old for a babysitter. Hunter stood in the doorway while Rhonda spoke to Marie, who agreed to come by. For a little while, Hunter would pretend that he hadn't omitted anything. That he and Rhonda really were just going out on a date, like any normal couple should.

She was impressed with the restaurant selection, knowing it wasn't an easy place to get a reservation. Looking at her closet, she discussed out loud her options for apparel and Hunter just nodded along, telling her that she would look beautiful no matter what she chose. It seemed like everything was how it should be. A couple with 13 years of marriage going out. The wife excited to dress up for once while secretly feeling sorry that she didn't have the body she used to. The husband reminding his wife that she was more beautiful as the years went on. Hunter even felt comfortable enough to put his toes into the bedroom. When he wasn't electrocuted for the offence, he walked in and sat on the bed while Rhonda got ready.

After their daughter came home, the lasagna was baked and ready to be served by Marie, Hunter led Rhonda out to the car. She even looped her arm through his as they walked down the driveway. In the car, they spoke like a normal couple. They talked about their daughter, how she made Rhonda crazy; their days. Rhonda talked about her job, watching all the people going off to destinations like Italy, Brazil, or Australia. Maybe when they retired, they'd go somewhere like that together. Hunter promised her they would just as he pulled into the restaurant parking lot. Before turning off the car, he turned to Rhonda.

"Did I mention that tonight is a double date?" Rhonda looked like she could kill him with her tiny purse.

Chapter 40

Madeline sat with Brandon's arm around her shoulders. Their fingers were interlocked and she could feel Brandon's thumb rubbing against her hand. She loved the feeling of his hand holding hers. It was strong, protective.

"How do you two do it?"

Madeline and Brandon glanced at each other and smiled like they were sharing a secret, before turning back to the reporter in front of them.

"Well—" "It's—" They both started to speak at the same time and that made them both chuckle. "Ladies first," Brandon said, kissing his wife's temple.

"It's a lot of work," Madeline said to the reporter. They were being interviewed for a segment that would run during one of the early morning talk shows about being a strong career-focused couple while raising a family. They were sitting in their living room, which had been professionally cleaned and organized and supplemented with fake sunlight for the shoot. "We're very lucky that we have help. I know not everyone has the opportunities that we do and for that we are so grateful. We try to outsource all the miniscule tasks around the house so we can focus on our family relationships. Time is so limited; the key is making the most of every minute; which means when you are with family, you are focused on family. There is no thinking about work when you are with the kids. If you ask your son how his day was, you listen and absorb every word."

"Brandon, you want to add something?"

"At the end of the day, it's really all about trust," Brandon said. "We're partners, we're a team and we work together so that we can succeed in the most important project of all, which is our family. We support each other, pick up slack when we need to, and most importantly, we don't judge each other when someone drops the ball. We know it happens, but as a team, it's each of our jobs to catch the ball when the other drops it. This is really the most important thing: instead of fighting about these things, we lift each other up."

"That's romantic," the reporter commented, looking at the filming camera for a moment. "It's easy for couples to be so focused on being a team that they forget they are also a couple. You two seem like you still have that romantic connection. Any tips for other parents?"

"It's about being present," Madeline said, patting Brandon's thigh. "Whether that means closing your phone for three minutes to have coffee together or making sure to check in on each other during the day to show your support. Every little thing counts. We are both constantly thinking about how to make the other one happy. Anything you can do to put a smile on the other's face, you do it. Like last week, for example, Brandon forgot his coffee at home." Madeline glanced at her husband. "Anyone who knows

Brandon, knows he always brings his dingy, old plastic mug to work, even though he can get fresh coffee there. Anyway, I saw that, so I had a fresh coffee—in a plastic mug, of course—delivered to his desk and waiting for him when he got there."

"That was really thoughtful," Brandon said with a big smile on his face. "It's little things like that."

"That's so nice to hear," the reporter said. "Now, we have just a minute left and we haven't even spoken about your upcoming election. I'm sure this puts an extra strain on your family life."

"Of course," Madeline responded. "But I'm so lucky I have Brandon who picks up any slack for me at home. He truly is the perfect husband." Madeline turned her head and her lips met Brandon's for a quick peck.

When the filming was finished, the reporter and film crew packed up their equipment and thanked the couple for their time. Madeline said she couldn't wait to see the segment and hoped they'd provided valuable advice for the show's viewers. She and Brandon continued to hold hands until the crew had driven away in their van.

"I have to go," Brandon said pulling away his hand and running to the stairs to change out of the collared shirt he wore specially for the interview. His happy face that had been on earlier seemed to have melted off and his tone became tired. Madeline watched him until he disappeared on the second floor. The last month had been difficult for her and it was anything but how it looked on camera.

Brandon attended all her campaign events and interviews, smiling and supportive. He did it because he still believed in her. Believed in what she stood for and where she was going. But at home? He barely looked at her, nor said a word other than what had to be said. The more he ignored her, the more she craved his attention. She reveled in the way he touched her in public, never wanting to leave the spotlight for their cold marriage at home. As the month went on, she began to realize more and more how lucky she was to be with Brandon and how badly she wanted their marriage to work, especially in private.

How could she fix things? Even after the Cobras were arrested for the blackmail and explanations were given, Brandon still held his suspicions. The pictures were no longer to be seen, but their images did not fade away.

Madeline was determined to fix things with Brandon and she had an idea that dinner with Hunter and Rhonda could fix things. Brandon would see that Hunter was happily married. That he and Madeline were just a long-ago memory. That Hunter was not a threat to their union. On the other hand, she was curious how Brandon would act at the dinner. Would he be the public Brandon? The loving supportive one? Or the private Brandon? Cold and suspicious? For someone with Madeline's aptitude for strategy, it may have been an amateur plan, but it was the only plan she had.

When Brandon returned down the stairs in his regular t-shirt, Madeline was waiting for him in the kitchen. She filled up his mug with coffee and handed it to him. "Thank you," he said. He was about to head out the door for work when Madeline stopped him.

"We have dinner plans tonight," she said.

"Fine," he responded. He was used to dinners with donors or influential community members.

"This isn't for the campaign." Brandon stopped and turned around with a questioning look. With his attention, Madeline continued. "It's for us. We're going to have dinner with Hunter and his wife."

"Madeline, I don't want to have dinner with your ex." The way he said ex made it sound like he didn't believe it.

"I'm asking you, as a favor. It's important to me." The magic words: *It's important to me.* Madeline and Brandon had an unspoken rule in their marriage. If someone invoked these magic words, the other complied. Brandon nodded and was out the door.

Madeline herself had a busy day before dinner—there was rarely a free moment when campaigning—but her mind was busy strategizing for the evening. This needed her full attention at the moment. This would be one of the biggest campaigns she needed to win.

Chapter 41

La Quinta was a quiet restaurant where even the waiters seemed to whisper so as not to be overheard. Clothed tables checkered the floor at distances that provided the limited privacy that diners could have in close proximity. It was the kind of place where hands were shook, deals were made, and alliances forged. In fact, just the previous night a billion-dollar business acquisition was negotiated over hot ramekins of crème brulée.

Madeline had been to the restaurant many times before. Her first experience was just after she moved to California. She and Brandon had been invited by the state's Republican National Committee chairman to discuss the future of the young couple. There Madeline's future was decided, and along with it, Brandon's. That was just the first of many dinners at La Quinta. Madeline's first run for office and Brandon's company's IPO were just a couple topics that had been discussed at the restaurant thereafter. But this particular evening was a first for Madeline and Brandon. It was the first time they came for a personal reason. The country's future or the state of CyTech's stock did not depend on this evening's conversation. Only the couple's marriage was at stake.

The car ride over was quiet aside from a few sprinkles of conversation about the boys.

Normally, silence between the couple would be broken with questions, *What else? Anything new? So?* But this evening the couple forwent the pleasantries and chose to sit quietly next to each other. When Brandon parked the car, he looked over at his wife.

"Madeline, tell me again why we are doing this."

There was just one reason why, Madeline thought. Because she couldn't see any other way to fix things with Brandon. Should he see Hunter with his wife, see that there was nothing between Madeline and him, maybe Brandon would come back to her and be the life partner she needed, both in public and in private. "So you can see," she said. The couple got out of the car and Madeline quickly grabbed Brandon's hand as they walked into the restaurant. He didn't pull away, which, to Madeline, was almost as telling as though he had forgiven her out loud.

Inside they were informed that Hunter and Rhonda were waiting for them. A smiling hostess navigated to their table, choosing a path that avoided passing occupied tables as much as possible. The couple was sitting next to each other in silence, Rhonda was focused on her nails while Hunter studied the menu in front of him. As the second couple approached, the first looked up. Hunter put on a smile and stood to greet them, while Rhonda put her fidgeting hands under the table.

318

"I hope you haven't been waiting long," Brandon said in his charming voice. "I'm Brandon, nice to finally meet you." He emphasized the word *finally* as though he had been waiting years for this moment and stuck out his hand to Hunter's ready for a firm shake.

"Hunter. Likewise," Hunter said as he accepted Brandon's hand in return. Madeline watched as the two men held their hands stiff in each other's for a long moment. When the handshake was over, the couples continued to greet each other—Hunter and Madeline gave a quick hand squeeze, as did Brandon and Rhonda. Madeline squeezed Rhonda's shoulders before taking her seat across from her. The four of them were such an odd combination for so many reasons. Not just because of everyone's relationship to Madeline, but also because of the stark differences between them all.

When the waiter came around, Brandon ordered a bottle of wine, insisting that it was one that everyone would love. "It comes from the vineyard next to my family's," Brandon said, initiating the first topic of conversation.

"Your family has a vineyard?" Rhonda questioned, immediately interested in hearing more. Brandon nodded and began explaining to her that his family had owned it for years. There hadn't been a Thomas working there for a few generations, but the family still owned it and spent weekends and holidays tasting the barreled wines before they were bottled and corked.

"In fact, that was Madeline's and my first official vacation," Brandon said, interlacing his fingers with his wife's. Madeline remembered that first trip to the vineyard. The couple had been there with Brandon's parents, a fact that at first disappointed Madeline, but it was during that weekend that she first fell in love with Brandon's family. "If you two ever want to visit, just let me know. I can arrange it for you," Brandon generously offered. He wasn't just saying it either, he would arrange it if asked. He had done it for plenty of friends before.

With the wine poured, Brandon led a toast. "To Madeline, for bringing us together." Madeline wasn't sure if it was meant to be sarcastic or vile, but she smiled and clinked her glass against her companions' and accepted the toast like a compliment.

The group ordered salads for starters and steak and fish for their entrees and the conversation throughout the meal was jovial and friendly. There weren't any lulls in conversation, nor awkward moments. Everyone seemed to be on their best behavior and even enjoying themselves. Even Rhonda had lightened up around the time Brandon chose a second bottle of wine and began telling stories of her work as a TSA agent and all the things people tried to smuggle through security. "Last week a woman came with a bird under her shirt!" Rhonda laughed. "A freaking parakeet! Can you believe it? Like what was she thinking? That we wouldn't catch it? What would she do on the plane? Just let it fly around?"

The group continued to get to know each other, but there was one topic that was not yet discussed: how everyone was connected to Madeline and how deep those connections were. But like a blistering sunburn, this topic could not be completely ignored. It was Brandon who finally brought it up when the waiter arrived with their chocolate soufflés and the aperitifs that went along with them.

"This is weird, right?" He started. "Hunter? You with me?" Hunter looked back and forth between the couple across from him unsure how to answer. He felt indebted to Madeline, obligated to answer in a way that would please here, but unsure what that affirmation should be. "You can agree," Brandon continued noticing Hunter's uncertainty.

"Yeah," he chuckled. "I guess so."

"I just don't get it," Brandon said, picking up a spoon and breaking open one of the soufflés. He stuffed the chocolate in his mouth. "Wow, this is good, you all need to try it. Madeline? You'll love it. Hunter, Rhonda, don't be shy."

"You know I can't resist chocolate," Madeline smiled and the three of them all helped themselves to a bite.

"That, I know," Brandon laughed to himself like he had just heard an inside joke. "That's why we're here, right?" It must have been the wine, they had gone through three bottles before the aperitifs, but Brandon's tone became sharp and combative in a way that Madeline had never heard it before. The table fell silent. The echo of the evening's banter, the camaraderie, all seemed to drop in an instant.

"Dude," Hunter began. "Let's not go there." It wasn't the first time Hunter had been compared to chocolate, and it certainly would not be the last. It was the kind of comment that people who staunchly insisted they were not racist would say thinking it was a genuine comparison. Instinctively, Hunter put his arm around his wife.

"You're right, I'm sorry for that," Brandon responded. "That didn't come out right. Too much wine." In truth, Brandon wasn't especially racist, no more than the average American who locks their car doors when driving through certain neighborhoods and would hesitate for just half a moment when noticing an interracial couple. "But how can we not talk about this?"

"Brandon," Madeline put her hand on her husband's shoulder. She knew it was too good to be true that all confrontation between the two men would be avoided. That was best case, also known as an unlikely, scenario. But the way the rest of the conversation would go would determine her future. She hoped he would take her clue.

"Rhonda? You don't think this is weird?" Brandon turned to her, making her feel slightly uncomfortable. She leaned into her husband.

"Yeah," she said. "It's freaking weird."

"Yeah, it must be freaking weird for you," Brandon continued. "Like, I know some of what's going on here, but not all. And you, well, I don't even know how much you know. Maybe you know less than me. Maybe you know more. I don't know."

"I'm not really sure what you mean," Rhonda responded. She took a second bite of the soufflé. "I'm just enjoying the dessert." She smiled, trying to keep a light tone. Rhonda didn't like confrontations or tense situations. They made her anxious, and sometimes she'd get attacks. If she had ever seen a psychologist, they might have said she had PTSD, but she had never been diagnosed. Truthfully, she was enjoying the evening. She had never been to such a nice restaurant and she liked feeling like she was mingling with the one percent. It gave her a taste of what she believed Hunter had given up when he and Madeline broke up.

"Hunter, you can be straight with me, dude," Brandon said quietly. In fact the whole conversation was so quiet, that from afar it would appear the group was still having a friendly conversation about a serious topic. "What's going on with you and Madeline?"

Hunter shook his head. Madeline's heart began to pound. Here it was. The turning point where things could go either way. "I'm working for her," Hunter said coolly. "To pass the SAVER Bill."

"And you're OK with that Rhonda?" Brandon said as though Hunter had just said something totally different.

"Sure," she said. "I mean, it's whatever."

"It's whatever," Brandon repeated, nodding his head. "That's a great endorsement. And you believe that's all it is? Working together?"

Rhonda looked at her husband and then at Madeline. She had accused her husband of cheating multiple times during fights and heated lack-of-sleep induced arguments, but she had never actually believed it was a true possibility. Not Hunter. Not the man who dated a woman like Madeline before her.

"Brandon," Hunter said before his wife could give an answer. "What are you trying to do here?" He rubbed his wife's shoulder with his arm that was already around her and grabbed her hand with his free one. He had just started to get back on Rhonda's good side and that was a place he really wanted to be.

"Just want to get to the truth. We all deserve that, don't we? Rhonda, don't you want the truth?"

She thought about it and the answer was that she wasn't sure. Was truth the most important thing? Honestly, she was happy to be back with Hunter. She had left him in a flurry of impulsive anger and her stubbornness had stopped her from going back. But she didn't like being alone. She liked Hunter back, even if he was just on the couch. She wasn't sure she could go through another breakup with Hunter. Her mental state was not strong enough. So, she thought again to herself, did she want to know the truth if it could ruin her marriage? Did she prefer to just assume that she had no reason to doubt Hunter?

"I'm going to go to the bathroom," she said. She stood up and left the table. After a moment of silence, Madeline too stood up.

"I'll check on her to see if she's OK." She shot Brandon a look. "You should cool down in the meantime." She followed Rhonda to the bathroom and waited by the sinks until a toilet flushed and Rhonda opened the stall door.

"I'm sorry about Brandon," she said as Rhonda washed her hands.

"No, it's cool," she responded intuitively even as her mind was telling her it was definitely not cool. "I can understand him."

"You know that me and Hunter are over and that there is nothing going on between us," Madeline said while placing her hand on Rhonda's shoulder. "He is a good man."

"I know," she responded while drying her hands. That seemed to be enough for Rhonda. She had no evidence of the otherwise, she had not seen the pictures from the blackmail, nor had she ever had any clues of Hunter's infidelity.

Madeline ached to get back to the table, afraid of what was being said in her absence. But as the women approached, the sight was strange and unexpected. Both men were leaning back, looking relaxed, smiling and sipping their aperitifs.

"Did we miss anything?" Madeline asked, wary of the answer. She sat back down in her seat.

"No, all's good," Brandon responded and even gave her hand a little squeeze. The couples finished their drinks over discussions of their children and everyone seemed to be in a good mood once again. The atmosphere pricked Madeline, who was unsure what this complete turnaround meant.

When the check came, Brandon insisted on paying and the couples walked out together to their cars. With hugs and kisses on the cheek, they said goodbye and parted.

"Did you enjoy the evening?" Madeline asked Brandon as they got in the car.

"I did." He rubbed her knee as he pulled the car out of the parking lot.

"What did you and Hunter talk about when Rhonda and I were in the bathroom?"

Brandon took his eyes from the road for a moment to give Madeline a grin. "He told me everything."

Chapter 42

When Madeline followed Rhonda to the bathroom, Brandon felt victorious. That was exactly what he wanted, a few minutes alone with Hunter. "All right," he said. "I'm surprised at you. You know I could have ratted you out when this whole thing started."

"But you wouldn't do that," Hunter responded, taking a sip of his drink. "That would have incriminated you as well."

The truth was that Brandon had had an inkling about his wife's infidelity for what felt like a very long time. Well, it was more than just an inkling, he felt that he had all the evidence, he just wanted a confession. It had started years ago when Madeline was in New York on a business trip. She didn't often take business trips—the consulting firm she worked at had offices in every major city, there was rarely a need to send someone to a new location—so this in and of itself was unusual and led Brandon to be on high alert for anything else that veered from the norm.

The couple had been texting throughout her first day in New York. She told him about her jog in Central Park (everything was in bloom!), the lunch she had with the CEO of the firm's potential client. She even told him she was going to see Othello in Central Park with an old friend (Brandon had assumed this old friend was female). But the texting stopped somewhere around the end of the workday and didn't commence again until the following morning. It was a Saturday morning and Brandon was alone with the kids. He got them up and dressed and took them to the zoo just like he had promised Madeline he would do. He took pictures in front of the giraffes, the zebras and kangaroos. He videoed Noah scratching his armpits and going ooh ooh ahh ahh in front of the gorillas. All the pictures, he sent to Madeline. She responded curtly, *cute! Fun! Miss you!* But the text messages had given him a funny feeling. They were shorter than what he was used to and too many exclamation points. Madeline was not an exclamation point over-user. He asked her what she was doing that Saturday in New York and she said she was getting a manicure and pedicure and just relaxing on her own for the weekend.

Brandon thought it must be the stress getting to Madeline. He had sensed that things had been difficult lately even though she would never let on. Being a mother and an ambitious career woman, not even mentioning her candidacy for the senate, would be tough on anyone. So Brandon did what good husbands do when their wives are juggling too much: he called her hotel and asked if he could schedule Madeline a massage in her room for the next morning.

"Would you like it to be a couple's massage?" the receptionist asked when scheduling the spa treatment.

"Oh, no, I'm not there with my wife," Brandon responded. The receptionist on the other side of the country went silent. "Hello? Everything all set?"

"Of course, sir," the receptionist responded. "We will have a masseuse in the room Sunday morning at 9:00 a.m." Brandon hung up the phone feeling proud of himself for doing something so nice and thoughtful for his wife. Surely she would appreciate it and it would help her relax before her busy day on Monday. Brandon didn't think twice about the awkward silence he received from the hotel receptionist.

Madeline was pleasantly surprised by the massage. It was so thoughtful that it made her feel extremely guilty about her transgression that weekend. She promised herself she would never ever betray Brandon again and that she would work harder to appreciate all the wonderful things about him. Her texting after that improved, making Brandon feel even better that his gesture did the trick and got Madeline back to her normal self. He was eager to see her when she returned. *Have a good flight! Wine awaits when you return*, he texted before her plane took off and she responded with a heart.

Her flight was delayed and Brandon was home with the bottle of wine he had brought from his family's vineyard. The boys were asleep and he had the wine aerating for Madeline's arrival when the house phone rang. They rarely got calls to the house, so Brandon answered unsure of who it could be.

"Mr. Thomas?"

"This is he."

"I'm happy to hear you had a good flight," the voice on the other side said. "This is Amanda from The Langham. It appears you left your jacket in the room during your stay this weekend. If you could provide an address, we will ship it to you."

This time Brandon was silent. "Mr. Thomas? A black leather Levi jacket? Do you recall?"

Brandon didn't have a black leather Levi jacket. He wore a blazer or peacoat, something that wouldn't look out of place in an office. "Oh, right," he responded and provided the address to his office so he could receive the coat without Madeline knowing. He thanked Amanda for the hotel's excellent service and continued waiting with the aerated wine until Madeline arrived. When she did, she was extra affectionate and the couple took the wine to their bedroom where they had—what Brandon believed was—passionate, explosive sex. He all but forgot about the jacket until it arrived on his desk a few days later.

At first he thought it was a gift. Had Madeline bought him a jacket in New York? But it wasn't new. It wasn't even in the kind of shape that could be considered vintage. The elbows were worn, there was a tear in the inside lining. There must have been a mistake—maybe the jacket belonged to the guest who previously stayed in Madeline's room? Or a guest from a different room altogether? Brandon searched the pockets and pulled out a small card. *Smith and Sons Landscaping.* There was no name on the card so Brandon Googled the business. It had a basic, amateur website, boasting about the company's services. He learned the company was based in Harlem and owned by Bill Smith—an elderly man who started the business mowing lawns when he was a teen. He also learned that Bill Smith had retired due to backpain caused by years of work as a landscaper and that the business was being run by Hunter Williams. The website had a picture of Hunter, a strong, smiling African American man standing in front of a perfectly trimmed rose bush. Brandon couldn't see what connection these people could have to Madeline, so he brushed any untoward thoughts aside and dropped the jacket off at a goodwill. At least he thought he had brushed his doubts aside. He did however keep the *Smith and Sons Landscaping* card in his desk. Something nagged at him when he least expected it. When he came home late and Madeline had to rush out for an emergency meeting or when her campaign events dragged on longer than expected.

Maybe he was paranoid, he told himself, Madeline was a good wife and a good mother. She was a good partner and all that should be enough for him. She hadn't traveled back to New York for a while after that. She had won her senate race and quit her consulting job. The only place she ever flew to was Washington DC and back. But then a few years later she was going back to New York for a speaking engagement. Brandon remembered his old doubts from her previous trip and felt he had the tools to do something. It didn't matter that his tools were designed more for destruction than building, he felt he had to use them. He used his years of programming and cyber security experience to spy on Madeline when she was away. It wasn't difficult to hack into the Langham's closed circuit security system, which had cameras showing the main entrance, the lobby, the elevator bay on every floor and a loading station out back. He couldn't access film from Madeline's previous trip to New York, but he could access real time footage during all of Madeline's future trips. He told himself he was doing it to prove his paranoia was unfounded, it was just a way for him to exercise his programming abilities which he didn't get to use much as CyTech's CEO once the company became big.

Whenever he knew Madeline would be coming and going from the hotel, he would watch her. Usually she was alone, but sometimes she was with Jane. Then, one time he saw Madeline arrive at the Langham wearing her beautiful red suit that made her look fearsome and sexy. He watched her approach and greet the doorman and then another figure caught his eye. The figure was hard to miss, dark skin, broad shoulders; Brandon had a feeling he had seen that man before. He still had the *Smith and Sons Landscaping* card in his desk and dug through his drawer, pushing away pens, paperclips and other slips of paper until he found it. He navigated to the company's website and saw that the company was now owned by Hunter Williams, who was pictured on the homepage wearing a short sleeved blue plaid shirt. Was it the same shirt Brandon saw on the man in front of the Langham? Was he being really paranoid now? He snapped an image from the Langham's security footage of Madeline and the man walking into the Langham and thought about what he should do.

He continued watching the security footage. He saw his wife and Hunter sitting at the hotel bar. Later he watched his wife go to the elevator bay alone and Hunter leave the hotel. There was no interaction between the two, but something inside him still itched. Was this all a big coincidence?

Brandon anonymously sent the image to the email on Smith and Sons Landscaping's website with the subject: *I'm on to you.* It was probably the most aggressive thing that Brandon had ever done. He wasn't sure what he expected to happen next, so he waited. Using his hacking abilities, he knew his email was opened and the attachment downloaded several times, but he never received a response. Maybe Hunter thought it was spam, maybe the image meant nothing to him. Brandon didn't know and he didn't follow up. He didn't think he would ever see the image again until it showed up on his kitchen table with the note requesting $1 million otherwise news of Madeline's infidelity would be released.

When he saw it, Brandon acted surprised—he was surprised, here his own image, which he thought was maybe nothing, was being used as proof that his wife cheated. He knew the image had to have come from Hunter—no one else but he had it—but Brandon decided to keep his mouth shut. He wanted to see what Madeline would do. Would she confess her infidelity? Or did she think that Brandon was just another dumb person she could play around with? He'd show her. He'd push her to confess or watch her being punished publicly as her career was ruined.

Brandon was ready the next time Madeline went to New York. He watched her at the Langham. Saw her and Hunter go up the elevator together and exit on Madeline's floor. He snapped a picture of them embracing in front of Madeline's door. This was what made him really angry. So angry that he wanted to watch Madeline squirm, so he had the picture sent to the house and pretended it was part of the blackmail.

He wasn't sure what to do next as Madeline had still kept her cool. He started to feel defeated by her, like maybe he was as dumb as she treated him to be. He felt betrayed, lonely, like a failure. Why couldn't he break her? After all these years, why didn't he know her well enough to get under her skin? And then Madeline asked him to have dinner with Hunter and Rhonda.

Chapter 43

"So where do we go from here?" Hunter asked Brandon as the two sat alone waiting for their wives in the bathroom.

"After everything, why hasn't Madeline just told me the truth?" Brandon asked this rhetorically, not expecting that his wife's ex-boyfriend from years ago might have an answer.

"You aren't playing on her level," Hunter said. "She feels safe with you, you aren't going to challenge her."

"I challenge her," Brandon defended himself. "Of course I challenge her, all the time." He wasn't sure he was really convinced himself. He remembered a time when he felt more in control. When he dictated their relationship. That time was real. What had changed?

"So what would she do if the tables were turned?"

"Put me in a corner. Force me to do what she wants. Make me think that what she wants is for the greater good."

"So that's what you need to do," Hunter responded and Brandon suddenly felt inspired by this man he was sure he was supposed to hate. The men were smiling, drinking their aperitifs when their wives arrived and that was when something switched inside Brandon. He grabbed his wife's hand and gave it a squeeze. He could beat her. He could control her. After all, he had done it once before.

The rest of the evening, he acted very lovingly. A hand on her knee, a fleeting grin, it would keep Madeline on her toes instead of letting her think she had everything all figured out. In the car, when she asked what he and Hunter had spoken about in her absence, he responded, "He told me everything." It may not have been exactly true, but figuratively, it was.

"And what's everything?" Madeline asked with a sarcastic tone as though she didn't believe it.

"Madeline, let's stop playing this game," he said. "I'm done with it." Madeline didn't respond. She knew that she couldn't win with anything she could say. Silence was her best option. When the couple arrived at home, Brandon hung up his keys and walked into the office—the room that neither of them spent time in unless they were looking for something they had long ago stuffed away for storage. When he came back out, he placed a card on the kitchen table in front of Madeline. The red and white business card was faded but instantly recognizable with its cursive lettering: *Smith and Sons Landscaping*. "Hunter left this in your hotel room seven years ago," Brandon confronted her. "It was in his jacket, which the hotel thought was mine and shipped here. I've known all along. I'm the one who took the photos of you with him at Langham. You think a bunch of kids from Harlem could have hacked into the hotel's security system to get the photos?"

Madeline looked at her husband. "Why didn't you say something?"

"Because I know you and I knew you would never admit it." Brandon paused. "Look, here we are, and you still won't admit it. I love you and that's why I've stayed all this time. We're good partners. But I can't stay with you lying to me anymore. I'm leaving." Without waiting for a response, Brandon left the kitchen and went up the stairs to their master bedroom. He was ready to pack a bag, stay in a hotel for a night or two and see what would happen.

Downstairs, Madeline stayed in the kitchen, the echoes of Brandon's words still hanging in the air. She felt caught, cornered, in a way she had never felt before. It tickled her, made her itch all over, made her squirm in her skin; a new sensation for her. The thought of Brandon leaving terrified her. On the surface level, this could greatly ruin her reelection campaign—nobody could win an election in the midst of a divorce. On the second level, she relied on Brandon. For support, partnership. At her core, she felt a primal connection to him. Like if he would leave, so would her source of energy. She couldn't lose that energy, it would end her.

She could hear his footsteps upstairs, the floorboards creaking in a familiar way that she realized she would miss. Should she go to him? Beg for forgiveness? Implore him to stay? Her core wanted to, but the shell she had built around her stopped her from moving. She waited.

Brandon came back downstairs wearing jeans and a t-shirt. A Stanford duffel bag was swung over his shoulder. He sighed when he saw her in the kitchen. With a nod, he went to the door, grabbing his keys from the hook.

"Wait!" Madeline said, shocking herself. "Wait a minute." She was ready to tell him everything. Anything to get him to stay.

"No," he said. "I'm done waiting. Let's figure this out like adults." He opened the front door and left, leaving Madeline in the dim light of the foyer. She listened as the car door clicked open and swung shut, the engine roared to life and the wheels rolled away. In the silence, she stood still.

Slowly, she went upstairs to the bedroom, navigating her house in the dark. Once in the master bedroom, which now seemed too big and empty, she turned on a light. Her eyes were drawn to the bed, where an envelope sat, neatly placed upon her pillow. Her core beckoned her to dive for it, to find out its contents, but her shell held her back. She should first brush her teeth, wash her face. Read it after a few moments of processing the evening's events. She followed her shell's advice and walked to her closet to change her clothes, but then her core took over and she found herself reaching for the envelope.

Her fingers ripped it open. Inside was a picture that Madeline had never seen before. It was a picture of her from years ago. She was standing on the grass outside Uris Hall, the business school at Columbia. The spot was instantly recognizable by the curl sculpture that marked the school's entrance. Next to her were a few other members of her college Republican club: there was Avery, who she had kept in touch with until she moved to California. Ryan, who had surprised everyone by becoming a democrat a few years after graduation, and Michelle, who Madeline hadn't seen since college. The students were standing together, laughing, each with a smile on their face. Madeline could see she was speaking in the picture, and everyone's eyes were on her. She had her bookbag slung over one shoulder and her arms were up in gesticulation— a habit she had gotten better at controlling over the years. (It was quite distracting to anyone watching her, her image consultants had said.) It was obvious the students didn't know they were being pictured. Madeline tried to remember the moment captured, but she couldn't exactly place it. There were so many similar memories she had on campus, standing around with her friends, debating politics, complaining about roommates or classes, making weekend plans. She wished she could go back and hear what she was saying when this picture was taken, surely it must have been interesting to have warranted being photographed. When the nostalgia of seeing herself at Columbia passed, the confusion set in. What was the meaning of this picture? Who took it? Why had Brandon left it on her pillow?

Luckily, Brandon had also left a note in his envelope. Madeline pulled the piece of notebook paper out and gently unfolded it to reveal Brandon's sharp handwriting.

Madeline,

Do you remember the first time we met? I'm not talking about the convention where we formally introduced ourselves and became a couple. Yes that is a beautiful and romantic story of our beginning but it is far from the truth. This picture is the day we met. We didn't exchange names, or phone numbers, but it was the day that the rest of your life was decided for you.

I was visiting New York that day to speak with a group of potential investors for my new startup. It's funny thinking of CyTech as a startup, but that is all it was back then. I walked into the auditorium at Columbia where the pitching event was held and I stood in front of the podium and told them about why CyTech would revolutionize the cyber world. They smiled and thanked me, but I knew they wouldn't invest. Why? Because I bombed the pitch. I mean, it was horrible. I was probably one of the best programmers and developers around, but I couldn't public speak for the life of me.

I stayed and watched the other startups pitch and when the event was over, I still stayed in the auditorium. I was alone, and it was nice to sit in the quiet, but then you came in. You walked in with your friends from the College Republican National Committee and started ordering everyone around the room. You saw me sitting in the room and you asked me if I had come for the mock election debate. I shook my head and you turned away and continued to explain to everyone their tasks to prepare for whatever this mock debate was you were planning. You had such presence in the room and everyone listened to you unquestioningly.

When you left the auditorium, I followed you outside and took this picture. It was then that I decided that I was going to marry you and you would be the presence in the world that I always wanted to be. It wasn't hard to find out more about you. From your t-shirt I knew you were in the College Republican National Committee and since my parents were active in the party, it just took a few questions and I had your name and everything else you had written on your admission forms. I had never shown interest in the Republican Party before, so my parents were excited when I started attending events and asking questions. They had always wanted me to be a politician, but I knew that I would never be good at that. So I put all the expectations and eyes on you. It was me who brought your name forward to the party's leadership. I told them to keep an eye on you, I told everyone that you were the star they needed to polish. And everyone listened to me because of my parent's money.

While you were basking in the attention and your stardom in the party, you didn't realize that you were being handed to me on a silver platter. Everyone knew I wanted to marry you and make *you the leader my parents had wanted me to be. They spoke to you about me, placing hints in your mind and ensuring that you were single and already primed to be with me by the time we met. Meeting you officially was just a formality. Everything had already been planned.*

Aristotle believed that we don't really have free will in the way we believe we do. All of our actions and choices are based on sequences of circumstances around us, including the environment, others' actions, and our own personality traits. Your every decision was determined by sequences of circumstances that I created for you. I recognized your love of the spotlight and I helped you get exactly what you needed so long as you continued making the decisions that I primed you to make.

You continued making all the right decisions, until one day you didn't. I forgave you, thinking maybe it was my mistake that I led you astray. But that wrong decision has come back to haunt us and it threatened everything I had planned.

What I want you to see, is that you would have been nothing without me. Had I not seen you that day at Columbia, you certainly wouldn't be a senator with eyes to the White House. Chances are your name wouldn't have even been known in the Republican Party.

Today, what you want and what I planned for you are one and the same. So I want you to understand that your success isn't possible without me in the background. You won't win your election without me by your side. You won't be vetted for Vice President and you definitely won't be nominated for president.

You took me for granted. Everything I did for you, everything I made you achieve. You could have confessed and begged for my forgiveness. And because you didn't, you lost everything. I'm done. I'm out.

Brandon

Madeline held the letter in her hands. She didn't remember anything about the day Brandon had first seen her, but everything seemed to make sense. All the comments people made to her about Brandon before she met him, how she was simply picked out to run for leadership in the New York Chapter of the Republican committee. She had always done what she had wanted, had achieved everything on her own accord, or had she? Had Brandon been a puppeteer for her all along?

For many women, this type of revelation might induce fear or anger. But Madeline took it differently. Maybe it was because she was primed to feel that way, or maybe it was because Brandon had finally shown that his own strategic planning rivaled Madeline's. Madeline was impressed. So impressed that it actually made her love him more, giving her another reason why she couldn't let him go.

Chapter 44

She knew where she would find him, but she decided to wait until morning. Surely Brandon would expect her to come running to him right away and beg for forgiveness, but she had other plans. She didn't think she needed forgiveness from him. Rather, she would go to him seeking something much more important for the long term of their relationship: compliance.

Because, you see, a marriage as successful as theirs isn't based solely on love or passion. It is about two equals meeting and forcing each other to achieve their goals. This is what Madeline needed to do now. In the morning, after kissing her boys goodbye and promising them that their dad would be home for dinner, Madeline drove to Brandon's office. It was still early, before other employees arrived and sure enough Brandon's car was parked in his designated spot. Madeline parked next to him and let herself into the office building and up the elevator to the top floor where Brandon's office was. She pictured him sleeping on the large plush couch he had there. That couch had once been in their living room before they replaced the furniture and Madeline had many memories of Brandon napping there.

Without knocking she entered his office and he was exactly where she had pictured him. Lying down on the couch, his head nuzzled in the cushions on one side. She sat at his desk quietly and waited for him to stir. It didn't take long before his eyes fluttered and he noticed her. A grin peeked on his face and he slowly sat up.

"You're too late," Brandon said, rubbing the stubble that had grown on his chin overnight. "It's over, Madeline."

"Actually, I don't believe it is," she responded. "It is far from over and we're going to finish what we started." She paused. While she usually liked to wait to hear what others had to say, this was a time that Madeline knew she would be doing most of the talking. She would be telling Brandon how it would be and why he had no choice but to follow her. "You think that you discovered me, that you made me, and maybe you're right. And if so, you need to live with what you made. I'm going to continue with the goals, I'm going to win my election and get into the White House and you are going to help and do what you are supposed to do."

"I'm not, Madeline," Brandon responded. "I'm done."

"You are, and I will tell you why," Madeline said. "Because you betrayed me as much as I betrayed you. Maybe I cheated, but you spied on me for years. My betrayal was wrong, but yours was illegal. Now there are two ways this can go right now. You can decide it's over and that we're getting a divorce. I'm sure both of our betrayals will be exposed in that situation. But only one of ours will have legal repercussions. Or the second option is that we continue focusing on our goals.

From your letter, I learned something new about you. You crave power. Without me, you will never be fulfilled again. You will never have any power."

Madeline sat quietly at her husband's desk as he absorbed what she said. She could see the wheels turning, his brain processing. His response was something Madeline never would have imagined. He stood up from the couch with his eyes focused on her. There was something feral in his look, something fearless and determined. Madeline held his gaze as he approached her in a way that he had never done before. Without looking away he walked around to the back of his desk where Madeline was still sitting. With one hand he grabbed the back of her neck, catching her hair in between his fingers. With gentle force, he pulled her up to standing. Madeline let herself be guided by him and starred into his eyes as he pulled her head toward his eye level. He challenged her to look away, to pull away, to give some symbol of her subservience, but she didn't budge, challenging him right back. The moment was so intense that it sparked something inside Madeline that caused her to inch forward and bite her husband's bottom lip. She bit down hard, causing him to start tightening the grip he had on the back of her neck. Before she could pull her lips away, Brandon caught them in his and pushed her down onto his desk. Madeline complied and braced herself with her hands as Brandon pushed up against her. She then bit his lips harder, signaling him to keep going. With his free hand, he fiddled with their clothing and fiercely pushed himself inside her. He thrust hard as she arched her back and let herself be taken over by Brandon.

Thirteen years of marriage and a year of dating before that and this was the first time they had sex outside of a bedroom. It was the first time Madeline had let herself feel dominated by her husband and it was the first time that she let herself go with him. When it was over, Brandon let go of her neck and stepped back from his desk.

She looked at him with new admiration as though she were seeing him for the very first time. Her skin still tingled from feeling him on top of her. She waited a moment before sitting up and fixing her skirt. Brandon had already tucked his shirt back into his pants and grabbed two bottles of water from the mini fridge in his office. "Now what?" he said as he handed her a bottle.

Madeline took the water and opened it for a sip. "Now, I'm going to go home, freshen up and get back to work," she responded. "And I'll see you at home this evening." Without waiting for his reaction, Madeline left his office and walked through the halls to the elevator. Employees were starting to arrive, setting bags down in their cubicles and starting the roar of the coffee machine.

Epilogue

The hotel suite was silent except for the voices on the television. Madeline was sitting on the bed with her back against the headboard and her feet crossed with her shoes still on. She had that feeling, the one where her heart pounded like she was about to get caught, even though there was no reason she should feel that way. She watched the television intently as the newscasters continued talking without saying anything of substance at all.

Next to her, Brandon lay down with his head on the pillow and his eyes closed. He was tired of listening. "Tell me when it is over," he said and curled his hands under his cheek. Jane and Hunter were also in the hotel suite, sitting on the chairs stationed around a small table under the window. Their eyes too were glued to the TV.

"Early predictions show you'll be two points ahead," Jane reiterated for the fifth time that night as though saying it again could make it come true. Madeline would have liked a bigger lead, winning by two points was not the victory she had hoped for. Now, in the hotel room, just minutes after the polls had closed, the team waited to hear if she would serve her second term in the senate.

The newscasters continued showing predictions and maps with Madeline's and Officer Austin's faces opposing each other on the screen. There were clips from their election night events, which had started hours before and were still going on, waiting for someone to be announced the victor.

Officer Austin's event was at the Fraternal Order of Police Headquarters, where uniformed officers were filmed drinking champagne from the early afternoon—when less than 20% of the population had cast their votes.

They deserved to celebrate, Madeline thought. It hadn't been an easy campaign and Officer Austin had performed better than anyone could have expected. He held rallies in neighborhoods that had previously supported Madeline and had been eloquent when interviewed by journalists who were tough on police. Madeline had tried to focus her campaign on the SAVER Bill, which weeks before the election had passed in the Senate. She had made a few compromises, added a few pork belly line items in the bill, but the overall integrity of the bill had remained intact. It was now awaiting a vote in the House of Representatives, where congress members were trying to stall a vote until after the election. She knew there were congress members against it, who would try to shred the act apart, but with Madeline's win, she was sure she could rally enough votes to get the bill onto the president's desk for signature.

Madeline rubbed her hands together noticing the small bruise around her wrist. It made her smile, remembering the evening before. Her arms pressed up above her head, squeezed so tight that she almost lost the feeling in her hands.

The Madeline here was not the same Madeline that had existed months ago. To outsiders it might appear that nothing had changed—she still had her presidential presence, her quick wit, and her guarded smile, but those in the room had sensed the change. They had all changed.

Jane turned a cheek when gray areas were entered, lines crossed, and personal lives interfered with work. Hunter became used to back door meetings and strong-arming negotiations for Madeline's support. His employment was as professional as anyone's could be when being paid a large amount with no official title or job description.

Brandon may have been the one who changed the most, but it was the least noticeable. He was still the supportive husband, the strategic thinking CEO, and perfect political partner. But now, he wasn't just the partner in public that Madeline needed him to be. The enlightenment of their power struggle had added new layers to their marriage, opening doors for them and helping them explore new ways to please each other. Madeline longed for him when she slept in her apartment in Washington DC. She dreamed of his touch, only to wake up covered in sweat. He made her feel submissive, unsure, in a way that she never felt in public. But it was what she needed and it thrilled her behind closed doors. She finally felt like they really were meant for each other.

The pictures, the blackmail, the adultery, it was never spoken of again and any remaining resentment or feelings about it had been blown away by the new dynamic. Hunter understood the dynamic. He too felt dominated by Brandon, afraid of his watchful eye and therefore focused more on his wife, who appreciated Hunter's new job. Rhonda called Hunter the get-it-done-guy and noticed that he too seemed more in control than he had ever been before.

The four of them continued sitting in silence watching the news as the anchors started to become confident enough to voice their own predictions. "It seems that Madeline Thomas will continue to serve California," one anchor said. "This is a landmark election for a republican senator in one of the most democratic states."

"This only shows her potential," another anchor commented. "If she can win California, we can be sure we'll be seeing more of her."

"The question is what's next for Madeline Thomas," said another. "If the Senate is just a stepping stone. If it is really possible for a woman to get into the White House."

Smiles broke onto Jane and Hunter's faces. Brandon started to look up from the pillow at the TV. But Madeline sat still. Jane flipped through the channels to see that other stations were also calling the election for Madeline. "A big win," one called it. "A very close call," another said.

Moments later Madeline's cell phone rang. Jane jumped to answer and handed the phone to her boss.

"Congratulations, Senator Thomas," the California governor said. "A very impressive win."

It was impressive. And it was only the beginning.

Did Madeline run for president? Did she get away with everything?

Go to my website www.avivagatauthor.com to get the FREE bonus chapter.

A note from the author

One of the themes that I thought a lot about while writing this book was the double standard for women. This double standard affects women in daily life, and even more so when women cross certain lines.

This double standard followed Madeline in parenthood – that she wasn't a good enough mother because she pursued her career; and it hurt her in that she could have been considered unfit for political office for cheating.

Unfortunately, men don't receive this same response. Men who work hard and don't raise their children are considered ambitious. And cheating is almost a given for male politicians in today's world.

On a lower level, I think many women, including myself, have felt this double standard pushing down on their shoulders, especially in the last year. When things become difficult for families, women are expected to take on more. Women put their ambitions aside for their families without question, because this is what is expected from them. That is how I have felt over the last year, which is why it took me so long to finish this book.

As COVID closed schools and kept people home, I was forced to put my own ambitions aside to take care of my family. Maybe forced isn't the right word, I did it on my own choosing. But was it really a choice?

It has been proven that in response to COVID, more women than men were forced to quit jobs or juggle careers and childcare. This has pushed so many women, including me, to the breaking point. We push ourselves too hard.

While I feel lucky to have had that time with my children, it was difficult and I often felt the unfairness of having to put my career on hold. I felt judged for wanting to pursue my career while my children suffered from the side effects of a global pandemic. Judge by whom? Mostly, by myself, which I realize is only because the double standard is so ingrained in my head. Did I judge my husband for working hard? Of course not.

This book is for all the ambitious women out there. The ones who break stereotypes and pursue their goals. The ones who maybe feel guilty for doing so, but are strong enough to not back down.

I salute you. I admire you. I am doing my best to be you.

Acknowledgments

This book may have one author, but there are many people who contributed to it. First of all, I want to thank my husband Ori who helped me come up with the idea for this story and participated in hours of brainstorming along the way. He is always supporting me and pushing me to dream bigger. I also want to thank him for being a wonderful husband and father.

I also want to thank my dad Nahum for reading the book and his unending support. Thanks also to my friends Naomi and Alisa for reading and giving feedback.

Thanks also goes to all the other hands that touched my book: Isabelle G, who did the final round of proofreading. Angela Stevens for designing the cover.

The biggest thank you goes to all my readers, especially those who leave me reviews on Amazon and Goodreads. Reviews (and recommendations!) are the best way to give back to an author you like. They help other readers decide whether to read a book and encourage writers to keep going.

Learn more about me by following me
on Instagram @aviva_writes
Facebook.com/avivagatauthor
or check out my website,
www.avivagatauthor.com

Printed in Great Britain
by Amazon

78308253R00203